"Do you know of
the Doom of Dahayart?"

When Adeh shook her head, Iskiir quickly continued. "It was destroyed. Less than a year ago. A handful of villagers survived, and few believed their tales. I know because I am one of them."

In his mind, he saw again the huge stones, jagged black monoliths that towered high as a temple. In close formation, they had flowed out of the wilderness, splintering trees, gutting houses, leaving no opening for escape.

"Rocks that move. Great black boulders...death!"

"Then we must go," Adeh said.

"Go, yes," Iskiir said desperately. "Go from this town in search of help. Before the circle closes. If there is still time...."

Also by M. Coleman Easton

Masters of Glass

Published by
POPULAR LIBRARY

ISKIIR

M. Coleman Easton

POPULAR LIBRARY

An Imprint of Warner Books, Inc.

A Warner Communications Company

Acknowledgments

I am grateful to Clare Bell for numerous readings and suggestions, and to Eva Cumming for her comments on the next-to-final draft.

M. C. E.

Chapter 1

The kip-beetle, in its cage of copper wires, would not keep still. Its burnished wings fluttered and its song trilled above the deep thrumming of the potters' wheels. Despite the distracting sounds, Iskiir continued to whisper his entreaties into the ear of the potter's daughter. Her father and uncle bent over their work while their scowling apprentice pumped a foot-treadle to keep the platters spinning. The treadle squeaked, the wheels rumbled, the kip-beetle sang, and Iskiir continued his fevered whispering.

The girl, named Adeh, was blessed with full lips and delicate white teeth. Her complexion was darker than the clay bricks of the shop wall, but not so dark as Iskiir's sun-baked skin. Her nose was gently curved, her neck thin and graceful, her fingers slender. And beneath her loose jubbah with its broad stripes of red and thin stripes of white, the young man sensed a soft and ripe body. That thought made him dizzy as he inhaled the scent of her braided hair.

To steady himself, Iskiir closed his eyes and slowed his

breathing. Even so, he strongly felt her presence. Something beyond the obvious was working here, he suspected, and the mystery served only to increase her attraction. "Come along to the caravans' market," he said softly, reopening his eyes. "I'll buy you something pretty. Why stay here when your chores are done?"

The girl's father glanced away for a moment from the tureen that was taking shape beneath his clay-smeared hands. *"Bolu,"* he said, pointing his hawk's-beak nose at Iskiir. *"Bald-and-lazy-one,* your master will be looking for you."

Iskiir stiffened at the epithet. Its frequent repetition by many mouths had not dulled the pain. Was it his fault that a fever had taken his hair, leaving his head bare as a patriarch's? By folk tradition he was viewed as dull and lazy because of his disfigurement. Yet young women, he had found, were often attracted by his appearance. This compensation only the gods could explain.

"Go now," the potter insisted. Not wanting to anger the man, Iskiir whispered a last suggestion to the daughter. Then he slipped away from the open-fronted shop to wait for her in a nearby street. Evidently Adeh's father had not taken a good look at him, Iskiir mused as he walked, for the potter hadn't noticed the lack of a guild badge on his indigo kaftan. It was true that nearly every young man of his age was long ago apprenticed. Iskiir was an exception, having arrived here to live with his cousin less than a year earlier. He had not yet found a master of any trade who cared to take on a *bolu*. Thus, though called on to assist his cousin with various errands, Iskiir was often free to explore the city. After a boyhood in the mountains, he found the bustling streets endlessly fascinating.

The young man stood in front of a row of tinkers' shops and waited for Adeh. He was a tall youth, thin of face, with a small tuft of dark beard beneath his chin. He was brown-eyed, wiry and well-muscled beneath the kaftan. The muscles had developed in his years of climbing hills and wrestling with goats. But he would no longer admit to anyone that he had once been called Iskiir the goat-boy. Now he was Iskiir Ketamlu

of the famed city Tajmengus. Even if it were possible, he would
never return to his former life.

Iskiir thought about his appearance briefly and hoped that
Adeh found it as pleasing as he found hers. He shuffled his
feet impatiently while he waited for her to arrive. Behind him,
the clinking of hammers was even more bothersome than the
sounds in the potter's shop. He looked about for a better place
to stand, but there was no getting away from the hammering.
On other days he had found the noises of craftsmen exciting,
but now his teeth were on edge. *What if she did not come?*

Watching in the direction of her approach, he saw only *daor*
wives, city women with shopping baskets, their heads cowled
against the afternoon sun, their black jubbahs sweeping the
ground as they passed. His pulse quickened when he saw a
bare-headed figure and a flash of red, but the girl was some
other *daor* daughter. Where was Adeh?

If she failed him, he thought uneasily, he would have to go
to the market alone to take care of his cousin's errand. The
dazzle of displays and the jabbering of the nomad traders would
help him forget about cold-eyed potters and their fickle daughters. For half a *meno* he could buy a few puffs on a hookah,
and then he would not even recall her name. Ah, but Adeh
was one he did not wish to forget.

"You're waiting for someone?"

The voice, coming unexpectedly from behind, startled Iskiir.
He reached, out of old habits, for the curved knife that he had
carried for years in his sash. Of course, by city law, he no
longer went armed. Clutching at empty cloth, he began to laugh
when he saw that Adeh had crept up on him from the opposite
direction.

"I had to take a different route than you did," she said with
a sly smile. "Father is not so stupid as you might suppose."

Iskiir continued to grin. He felt his pulse racing with excitement just from looking at her. "You would make a good
mountain girl," he said without thinking.

"And how would you know about mountain people?"

"Oh . . . I've done some traveling."

"Is that how you lost your hair?"

Suddenly Iskiir became solemn. He was not angry, as he had been with her father, because he sensed no malice in her question. But he had learned to turn such teasing to his advantage if he could maintain a serious tone. He bent slightly to confide his tale. "It was great Karkilik," he said, seeing in his mind the leonine figure that decorated every fire-temple. "We crossed paths in the Eastern Wastes. I was leaning over the pool at Wej oasis when he came down from a dune. What a sight! He was twenty paces behind me, but when he roared, his fire burnt off all the hairs of my head . . . and turned me as dark as I am."

"You saw Karkilik!" Adeh's face lit up. "He only shows himself to the worthy. You must be pleased with yourself."

"Pleased that he let me live. I claim no proof of my virtue."

"No virtue?" Her voice rose, then broke into laughter. "Appeasers' beards!"

Iskiir shrugged. "Enough talk of *my* adventures." He smiled and beckoned for her to follow him. "Come along if you want one of your own." He turned toward the northern districts, and they began to make their way along the level streets. The thoroughfare narrowed, and Adeh dropped behind to let people pass in the opposite direction. Fearful of losing her, Iskiir kept glancing back. Whenever he turned, she met his gaze with a smile, and for a time he thought himself the most fortunate young man in Tajmengus.

But, as often happened in recent months, his carefree mood did not last. Here and there as he walked, a face caught Iskiir's eye. Thinking he recognized an old uncle, he would stare for an instant at a graybeard carrying a fat orange in each hand; but of course that uncle was gone. Then a plump-faced wood-seller would drive his laden donkey past and Iskiir would have to hold himself back from shouting a greeting. That was not Martulin; the resemblance was not even close. Yet, if he narrowed his eyes, the young man could sometimes believe he was back in his home village.

City-dwellers, mountain-dwellers, we are all Menjians, he

thought, as he tried once more to forget the many he had lost.
For Iskiir, life was far better now than it had been in Dahayart.
For the others of his village, he could not say. Most of their
souls were with the gods.

He and Adeh left the district of shops and passed through
a string of quiet alleys. The walls of the houses, with their
high, grillwork windows, loomed above the walkways, keeping
all in shadow. Sunk in old memories, for a time he did not
speak. Then Iskiir led her out into a broad, bright thoroughfare
and his gloomy reflections were swept away. Near the public
well a crowd of youngsters stood around a comical figure, a
man with white-smeared cheeks who wore a tattered red robe.

"A-sizzle, a-sazzle, and you I will dazzle . . ." said the happy-
man as he pulled a bright coin from one child's ear. Then he
made the piece jump from finger to finger as the small audience
shrieked with delight.

Iskiir grinned. Though eager to reach the market, he could
not help pausing to watch the man's antics. Suddenly the ragged
fellow began to walk on his hands, his robe falling back to
expose bony knees and a red loincloth of absurdly large pro-
portions. Adeh laughed, and Iskiir shook his head at the sight.
They watched a brief time longer, then plunged into the stream
of traffic that was making toward Gahad's archway.

"Tell me how we're going to get in," Adeh asked, slightly
out of breath, as they approached the arch of cut stone that
was the entrance to the caravans' market. "You certainly won't
be mistaken for a merchant."

"Don't you think that someone who can cross the Eastern
Wastes can get past some overfed guards?" The two stood aside
to let a cart-pusher pass. Faded yellow tassels dangled from
the corners of his weathered wagon. Breathing heavily, the
man trundled between the guards at the market entrance who
did not even glance at him.

Iskiir grinned nervously. The Bey's guards were dressed in
short maroon kaftans that exposed their snug camel-hair breeches
from knee to boot. Their hands rested near the leather scabbards
of their scimitars, and Iskiir knew how quickly those weapons

could be drawn. Nonetheless, he started to run toward the entrance, motioning for the girl to follow. "That's our uncle," he told the guards, pointing where the cartman had gone. "We had to go back for his waterbag, but we couldn't find it."

"Then he won't want to see you," said the first guard lazily. "As for you, *bolu,* why don't you go home and grow some hair?"

As soon as you grow back your donkey ears, Iskiir nearly retorted. But he held his temper despite the stinging of his cheeks. "Uncle needs us to help load the cart," he said in a firm tone.

"He's trading for dates," Adeh added. "Honey dates, as long as your thumb." She held up her slender fingers to show the size of the fruit. "We'll give you some when we come back."

"Honeys?" The second guard licked his lips. His expression turned into a leer and he threw his arm about Adeh's waist, drawing her close to him as if she were a *numij* of the streets. Iskiir's fury mounted as the man pressed his grimy fingers here and there, leaving smudge marks on the stripes of the jubbah. He saw Adeh biting her lip with rage, but she made no complaint. "We'll be waiting for you," the guard said. Then, with a smirk, he pushed her toward the market, leaving more smudges on the rear of her garment. She scurried inside, with Iskiir at her heels.

"If I had my knife, I'd gut him for the buzzards," said Iskiir in a low and furious voice as he patted the bare sash at his belly.

"And be gutted in turn by his friend? You should be glad you're not allowed to carry a weapon."

"And what about the dates we're supposed to bribe them with?"

"We'll leave the market by another way. It's a longer walk home, but we *did* get inside."

"We did." Slowly the young man felt his rage draining away. Adeh deserved credit for helping his ruse, he admitted to himself. He grinned, and found that he could not keep silent. "I was right when I said you'd make a good mountain girl. You have the cunning needed to survive in the hills. Come. Now you'll see why we came here."

Then the rank odor of camels reached his nostrils and he glimpsed the long rows of the vendors' stalls. The smells of leather, incense and charcoal smoke all competed for his attention. For a moment he forgot Adeh and Tajmengus and was back in lowly Dahayart. What excitement the nomad traders had brought to his village! The caravans stopped there only a few times a year, bringing with them an unofficial holiday— for who could work when wonders filled the public square?

"Let's go this way," said Adeh. "I want to see the kip-beetles."

"Beware of tricksters," Iskiir warned, not sure she knew about the small illusion-spells that the vendors often employed. An iridescent insect with a soothing song might later turn out to be a dung-colored brute with a grating chirp.

"We're just looking," she answered. "What does it matter?"

Iskiir nodded and followed her toward the displays of tiny cages. Over their russet robes the Karbayra traders wore burnouses of camel hair, the hoods pulled forward, shadowing their eyes. Only their short beards and long thin noses were clearly discernible, and Iskiir could scarcely tell one vendor from another.

Cages of copper wire, or occasionally silver, hung from poles planted in the sandy soil of the marketplace. There were so many kip-beetles that their songs blended into a din that made Iskiir grit his teeth. Though he admired the beauty of the insects, the golds and reds of their wings, he had never been fond of their so-called music. He was about to lead Adeh to another section so that he could complete his errand, when his gaze fell on a cage that was larger than the others. Within, a huge orange-bodied moth spread its silvery wings.

At that moment he felt an odd yet familiar prickling sensation at the back of his neck. Something was strange here; the head of the moth had a tiny human face, a woman's face, full-cheeked and beautiful. Iskiir couldn't help putting his ear to the cage, for the mouth was moving.

"It sings!" he said aloud in his surprise. He strained to listen to the one true song amid the cacophony of chirps. The moth had a tiny voice, but Iskiir could understand its words. It was singing, not in the language of the desert nomads, but in his own tongue!

"Beware of tricksters!" Adeh's teasing words broke his fascination with the insect.

"What do you see?" he whispered, pointing to the cage. She bent closer.

"Only a date moth," she answered.

"And what do you hear if you listen at the cage?"

She touched her delicate earlobe to the thin wires. Iskiir glanced at the proprietor. The shadowed face was aimed in his direction, but he was uncertain if he was being watched. "I hear nothing," said Adeh with a laugh. "Moths make no sound."

"A bit of conjuring then," said Iskiir grumpily. He was not fond of being tricked, but after all, the vendors' illusions were part of the fascination of the marketplace. A serious buyer would bring his own magician, so that the nature of the goods could be verified.

"Come," he said to Adeh. "I have a purchase to make for my cousin Yeniski."

"Yeniski the conjurer?"

"You know him?"

"He's done a few small jobs for my father." She began to smile, but did not explain herself. Iskiir thought it best not to pursue the matter. His cousin still ranked at the lowly fourth level in the Guild's hierarchy, and made his living from such menial chores as setting illusory cats to keep a house free of mice. Yeniski had twice been passed over for promotion to higher rank, and was exhausting himself in his studies so that he might not fail in his final try.

"I have to buy some water from Acurlat wells," Iskiir said. "Yeniski needs it for his work. After that, we can find something for you." He led her past rows of hanging jubbahs, festive wear sewn in the Karbayra fashion from squares of brilliant reds, blues and greens. Iskiir saw Adeh's attention fix on the exotic clothing, but he knew that no *daor* would wear such a garment. Even the Karbayra reserved these robes for special occasions. Next to their goods, wearing black headbands whose flaps covered their noses, sat wide-eyed nomad women in their daily garb of reddish-brown.

Soon Iskiir reached the displays of rare fruits plucked in oases that only the Karbayra visited. Ridged yellow melons the size of his head rested in heaps beside fingernail-sized lemons and oranges. To Adeh he named the fruits he knew. Their scents were like rich perfumes, and their names carried the desert wind.

As Iskiir walked, the noise of the trading was all about him. The Karbayra called to each other from stall to stall in singsong voices, Iskiir comprehending but a few words of their language. Far louder were the men of Tajmengus, the merchants and shopkeepers, who shook their hands vigorously as they haggled with the nomads. Many Karbayra knew only the words for the numbers in the Menjian tongue, and the Tajmengans knew nothing of nomad speech. So the bargain often consisted of single words shouted back and forth, emphasized with many gestures and grimaces.

At last Iskiir and Adeh reached the vendors who specialized in rare substances that conjurers used. On crude wooden tables were laid tiny skulls of desert creatures, some whole, some powdered. Another stall offered preserved hummingbirds in wine, and dried pale-blue flowers from a plant that blossoms only once in a man's lifetime. Iskiir passed over these curiosities until he reached a table holding numerous clay vials, their sides inscribed with short, bent strokes he could not read. "I need Acurlat water," he said to the hooded proprietor. "Twenty drops."

The dark hand swung over the table and a long finger pointed downward. Iskiir picked up the small vial and hesitated. "I have to be sure," he said warily. Karbayra were known for quick tempers, and were not forbidden to carry weapons so long as they remained outside Tajmengus proper. If the man were offended by Iskiir's doubts, he might pull a dagger from beneath his robes.

"So you think me scoundrel like the others?" the vendor said, his voice bearing only a trace of Karbayra accent. "Go ahead. Take one drop for test if you doubt."

Iskiir was tempted to accept the water, but he remembered the trickery with the moth. When had he ever heard of an honest Karbayra trader? He reached inside his kaftan for his purse, and pulled out the prepared piece of cloth that Yeniski had given him. "One drop is all I need," he said. He placed the square of white cloth on the table, pulled the tiny stopper from the vial, and carefully shook out a single drop of liquid. Since the trader did not know how the cloth had been prepared, he could not use trickery to control the outcome of the test. The water immediately produced a stain of brilliant green. Iskiir bent to look more closely and saw tiny yellow flames encircling the stain. The flames vanished almost at once but the green hue remained.

"Satisfied, I assume?" said the trader. "I'm in no mood to haggle, so will make you gift of that bottle. But give me twenty *menos* for trouble of setting up my stall."

Iskiir replaced the stopper, but held onto the vial. "Nomad, your generosity is beyond belief. And if everyone who takes you gift gives you twenty *menos*, you'll be a wealthy man by evening."

"Do you know anything about Acurlat?" To Iskiir's surprise, the trader pushed back his hood and permitted a full view of his face. He was not as old as Iskiir had thought, perhaps no more than thirty years. The desert had hardened his skin, but his eyes were bright and piercing. "There is raider chieftain, Bermegi, who claims possession of well. Do you know this Bermegi?" The vendor bared his teeth like a growling cur. "Fierce. Very dangerous. Only bravest of fools dares slip past guards to draw water at midnight. Of those who fill waterbag, ten are killed for each who returns safely home. In one year, no more than single bag of water is pilfered from Acurlat well."

"I cannot pay more than five *menos*," said Iskiir in a level voice.

"Five does not even pay potter for vial. Do you think every flinger of clay can make such fine piece? Give me eighteen and we can part friends."

Iskiir glanced at Adeh, who was closely following the bargaining, and saw a slight nod of her head. The work of the potter was an expense surely, but the tale of the wells was exaggerated. "I can pay you seven," he countered.

"Seven? My wife will harangue me for week if I take less than fifteen. She'll burn bread just to spite me, and she'll beat children for no reason."

Iskiir sighed. He needed to have some money left over to buy Adeh's present, but the Karbayra was going to fight him for every coin. While considering what his next offer should be, he became aware of a growing commotion behind him. The high-pitched calls of the nomads to each other suddenly had grown louder, he realized. As Iskiir opened his mouth to raise his offer, the vendor unexpectedly began to clear the table. He grabbed the vial of Acurlat water first, wrenching it from Iskiir's hand, then began hastily sweeping the rest of his wares into large baskets. The young man was dumbfounded, thinking for a moment that he had somehow offended the tribesman. But all around him, he saw other traders rushing to pack their goods. Not even the uncommon threat of a rainstorm would cause such panic, and the sky was cloudless.

Adeh turned to a merchant who was hurrying past. "What is it?" she asked. "Why are they leaving?" But the merchant was already out of earshot, making for the nearest exit. Meanwhile, the nomads were hastily bringing their camels to be loaded, and the entire marketplace was in confusion. On impulse, Iskiir took Adeh's hand and followed in the direction the merchant had taken. For a moment, the warm touch of her fingers made him forget all else. Then, above the shouting of the traders came piercing notes of alarm, rams' horns wailing from one watchtower and then from another. The sound made Iskiir weak in his knees, but he plunged on, pulling Adeh with

him under Gahad's archway. He did not see the guards they
had passed earlier.

"What does it mean?" he asked her, as they struggled against
the crush of Menjians who were trying to return to their homes.
Finding an opening into an alley, he led her aside to get out
of the main rush of traffic.

"I've . . ." Adeh was breathing so heavily she could barely
speak. "I've never heard . . . the warning before."

"We can go out this way," said the young man, taking a
less-crowded street that ran parallel to the main way. People
were rushing into their houses, climbing the narrow outside
staircases to reach their rooftop doors. Once there, he imagined, they were stationing themselves with weapons against
whatever dangers were to come. As he hurried along, with
Adeh's hand still firmly within his own, he puzzled over the
cause of the alarm.

Foreign invaders? Not likely. The Menjians had been at
peace with their neighbors for nearly a generation. And though
desert raiders might pick on small groups of travelers, they
had never been known to lay siege to a city. "Adeh," he said
as they neared the high dome of a fire-temple. "We can see
for ourselves. We can learn what the commotion is about."

Adeh chewed her lower lip. "My . . . father will be looking
for me."

"It will only take a few moments. Come this way." The
whitewashed dome of the temple rose before them like the
tapered end of an eggshell. A stairway could be seen spiraling
around the dome to a small round cupola at the peak.

"You can't go up there," she said. "It's sacred."

"I, who have seen Karkilik, cannot go?"

"You shouldn't."

Iskiir grinned. "Come. I'll show you how easy it is." Several
white-robed Keepers stood in the arched portico of the temple,
but Iskiir found the staircase entrance on the side unguarded.
The steps were used only on the twelve Sacred Nights of the
year, when the Keepers climbed the temple's roof to blow their

ceremonial horns. Before Adeh could protest further, he was on the stairs, leading her upward.

Like most staircases in the city, this one had no guard wall. The steps were narrow; a single handspan was the distance from the climber's outermost foot to the steep drop. Making such climbs reminded Iskiir of ascending crags in search of wayward goats. Since coming to Tajmengus, he had enjoyed the view from nearly every temple of the city. But Adeh was unused to heights. After they made their way once around the spiral, she flattened herself against the inner wall and would go no farther.

They were already higher than the dwellings and shops. Only the temples and slender watchtowers of the city rose above them. Iskiir gazed down into the streets and observed confusion everywhere—bucking animals and rushing people all trying to force themselves through narrow byways. Below him a shopping basket spilled, its contents rolling underfoot while its owner screamed after her wandering children. But Iskiir saw no reason for the general panic other than the alarm itself.

Raising his eyes, he looked out over the city that he now knew well, taking in its elongated sweep that followed the sources of water. The red-striped cloth roofing over the spice bazaar caught his gaze, and beyond that he saw piles of broken sticks in a wood-seller's yard. Glancing in turn at the four city gates, he spied no marauders preparing to lay siege. And beyond the walls he saw dry expanses where only low bushes and spiny plants grew. If danger was coming, it was not evident from this height. Perhaps a nervous guard had made a mistake, and all was still well with Tajmengus.

"We must reach the top to be certain," he told Adeh. "Show me that you're the mountain girl I took you for."

Her cheeks were flushed, giving them a ruddy color that Iskiir found particularly attractive. She took a tentative step away from the wall, glanced down over the edge and stepped nervously back.

"Don't look there," he said. "Keep your eyes on me. Watch my steps and don't think about anything else." He began to climb again, slowly this time, with his inside hand holding hers. "One foot after the other," he said. "That's it. I'm holding you so you can't fall."

With much coaxing, he got her around the roof twice more. They halted at the base of the flight that led to the cupola. "You can see . . . from here," she said, her face damp and her breathing rapid.

"Wait for me," he replied, gauging the final climb.

"Have I a choice?" She clutched at a wall that offered no handhold.

"I need to look out in all directions. It won't take long." Iskiir scurried up the last flight and into the open cupola. Quickly he turned, surveying the perimeter of the city. To the east, green farmlands stretched along a row of wells. To the northeast, the caravans' marketplace was almost empty, the long string of camels unwinding from its exit toward the northern end of Taj valley. To the west lay desert. To the southeast lay ruins of a far older city. But what of the danger? Looking toward the horizon, Iskiir at first saw only endless terrain, straw-colored and dry. He squinted, then closed his eyes in disbelief.

"Iskiir! What's wrong with you?"

She had managed the last climb on her own. He opened his eyes, and again confirmed his vision of the distant dark shapes. Was it a magician's illusion? In the market, Adeh had proved herself more resistant than he was to such trickery. "Look out there." He pointed.

She squinted. "They couldn't be riders, could they?"

"So you see them, too? At that distance they're huge. Not riders. Boulders. Great rocks." Iskiir's hand moved to his stomach as a feeling of sickness filled him. Surely he was sleeping, for the nightmare that so often tormented him had come again. But Adeh was too lovely to be part of dark dreams. "Do you know . . ." he managed to say. "Do you know of the village of Dahayart?"

She shook her head.

His thoughts filled with the faces of his lost family, and his old griefs shook him once again. "Dahayart. My village, once," he said hoarsely, abandoning his notion of hiding his origins from her. "Less than a year ago it happened. A handful of us survived, and few believed our tales." He saw again the huge stones, jagged black monoliths that towered higher than Tajmengan city walls. In close formation the demon rocks had lurched out of the wilderness, splintering trees, gutting houses, leaving no opening for escape. He recoiled from his memories of how the few villagers who had withstood the hunger, thirst and disease had been pushed into an ever-diminishing center of safety. "Rocks that move. Great black boulders . . . No one could say where they came from or who had sent them." Iskiir's voice dried up. Dizzy, he leaned against the thin wall of the cupola.

"We must go," said Adeh.

"Go, yes," he said in despair. "Go from Tajmengus. Before the circle closes. If there is time."

"First we must get down from here," she said evenly. "Then we'll hear about those rocks you think are out there. Come." She helped him follow her down the first few steps.

"I've seen it once before, Adeh," he insisted. "I've seen how a village can be crushed and its people destroyed. But why must it happen again? Why here?" He shook his head, trying to clear the tears from his eyes. Now that he had found a new home, and Adeh to fill his dreams, must he lose this all so quickly?

"Even if you're right, Iskiir, remember that this is no village. This is Tajmengus. We have a Guild of a hundred conjurers. Let them put their magic together and they'll stop whatever trouble we face."

"Perhaps," he said, slowly regaining his composure. The two began to descend, and this time Adeh managed well enough on her own. Iskiir said nothing, content to put one foot ahead of the other while he pondered what was to come.

His opinion of Guild conjurers was low. If they were anything like his cousin Yeniski, they could only throw foul powders while the rocks advanced to grind their bones. How, he wondered, could mere tricksters save Tajmengus?

Chapter 2

In a somber mood, Iskiir made his way home through the empty streets. His parting with Adeh had been far too hurried, her father nearly pulling off her arm in an effort to drag her up the stairs to the refuge of their abode. Iskiir had watched them go, hearing her father's angry shouting even after they were out of sight. With a woeful shake of his head, he tried to forget the potter's curses.

At last the young man reached the Yeniskilu house and wearily took the steps. He had to pound on the roof door several times before one of Yeni's young daughters let him in. "Ha. We thought they'd got you," Sar said, sticking out her tongue. "We hoped they had."

Iskiir tried to swat her but she was too fast for him. "This is no time for joking," he said. "I need to see Yeni in a hurry."

"He won't come out," she said, wrinkling her nose. "He's mixing smelly stuff again."

Iskiir raced down the interior stairway to the workshop that his cousin kept in the front part of the ground floor. He put

17

his shoulder to the door at the bottom, but it did not budge. "Let me in," he shouted, pounding his fists against the thin planks. "We've got to talk about the trouble."

Yeni gave no answer. Iskiir pounded again. "Let me in, you spitting camel."

"Do you have my Acurlat water?" The voice was muffled and barely audible.

"The trader snatched the bottle from my hand. Do you know what's happening out there, or have you been locked up all day?"

"I sent you out for water, donkey-brain." Now the voice was louder. "Do I fail my test again because you can't run simple errands?" The bar scraped and the door was pulled slowly back. With his greasy skullcap knocked askew, Yeni looked haggard, his fleshy cheeks sagging, the rings puffy under his eyes. His broad, hooked nose was dusty and his heavy brows carried a coating of powder. Behind him, beams of sunlight passed through grillwork windows to illuminate a yellow haze that filled the room. Iskiir smelled sulfur.

"I had the water," Iskiir said. "Tested true. But then the alarm sounded and everyone packed up."

"I thought I heard something," the conjurer grumbled. He wiped his damp brow with his sleeve, which fell back to reveal his plump forearm. When clean, Iskiir knew, the robe showed green crescents on white; now the green barely stood out from the cloth's grimy background. "I thought it was my hearing going. Too many explosions." Yeni's large sandals scraped the floor as he shuffled toward his workbench, a shabby affair of rough planks nailed together.

Frustrated by his cousin's indifference, Iskiir stomped after him. "The alarm was for good reason. I climbed a temple to look out. You recall what happened to Dahayart?"

"I know what you told me about it." Yeni picked up a charred slab of wood and tilted it to catch the light. Iskiir could see a residue of unburned powder about the edges of the burn.

"The same thing is happening here. The stones I told you

about; the ones that move. They're out in the desert, all around the city."

"Some novice's illusion. A prank against his master." Yeni picked up a small metal blade and began to scrape the residue into a clay dish.

"Prank?" Iskiir slapped the wood piece out of the conjurer's stubby fingers. It fell to the floor, skidded, and lodged in a dusty corner. "Were the stones that destroyed my family a novice's trick?"

Yeni stood open-mouthed, glaring at Iskiir.

"I apologize, cousin," Iskiir said grudgingly when he could no longer stand the silence. He retrieved the slab, blew off some of the dust, and returned it to Yeniski's bench. "But I tell you the danger out there is real. And we need a real magician to do something about it."

"A *real* magician . . . As if the Guild can't take care of this."

"What I've seen of your Guild doesn't impress me."

"Then go have another look," Yeniski said sharply. "Go on. Ride out to your stones, if they're real, and watch my seniors chew them up like goat cheese. And while you're there, find someone who'll part with a little Acurlat water."

Iskiir took a deep breath. Above Yeni's head a design of interlocked black hexagons had been painted on the ocher wall. Staring at the pattern sometimes helped Iskiir keep his temper with his cousin. There was no time for a quarrel now; he must learn the truth firsthand. "I'll go right away," he said quietly, after a moment of grinding his teeth. Then he turned toward the door that led to the stable.

He yanked the warped door open. The workroom's sulfur smell gave way to acrid donkey odor as he crossed the threshold. He kicked a piece of broken harness out of his way while the beasts brayed a raucous welcome. Hanging on the wall were a half-full waterskin and a small sack holding a dried-out round of bread; these he took with him. "Lock up behind me," he called, then opened the door to the alley behind the house and led out the strongest of Yeni's white donkeys.

Once outside, Iskiir was not surprised to find himself alone.

Ordinarily, one risked the wrath of the crowds by riding the narrow streets in mid-afternoon. On this day, the traveling was fast and easy. The walkways were all empty, and even at the public wells and cisterns he saw no queues of young women with their jars.

The vacant thoroughfares made him uneasy since he was used to the bustle and noise, the milling of Tajmengans on a thousand errands. Yet this afternoon he imagined the citizens all trembling in their houses over dangers that no one could explain to them. Perhaps the news criers were still puzzling over what they should say.

The donkey trotted steadily, bringing Iskiir quickly to the Eastern Gate. To his eyes, the high city walls no longer offered protection. The moving stones were taller. He was certain they would smash through quickly and continue their march of destruction until nothing remained of Tajmengus. The thought of where he was heading made his knees shake, yet he did not dare turn back.

Iskiir halted at the gate. The iron-bound wooden doors were shut, and he was forced to throw a coin to the guards before they would open them. Then he was out of the city, hurrying across the belt of farmland that separated the high wall from the desert.

He glanced at the wheat, almost ripened, and wondered whether there would be time for a harvest. The long stalks rippled in the breeze and there was a faint chirping of insects. The scene was peaceful. Except for the lack of people, all seemed well. But then, up ahead on the path, he saw the first black shadows of great rocks. Now his hands sweated and his jaw began to tremble. The monoliths were waiting for him, he thought, closing in to finish the task they had not completed at Dahayart.

Iskiir was so stunned by the sight that he did not slow his mount. Oblivious to the danger, the animal continued toward the towering shapes. And as Iskiir looked up, a single thought held him. *Escape was still possible!* There remained good clearance between the stones; one could drive wagons two

abreast through the nearest gap. At Dahayart there had been
no separation at all on the morning the siege was discovered.

And so, with hope tempering his fears, he allowed the beast
to draw closer. He saw other donkeys ahead, and soon was
near enough to see the red and green fringes on their harnesses.
Then he spotted three white-turbaned figures whose glimmering robes were decorated with gold moons. High conjurers, he
thought, recognizing the garb of the Guild's first rank. The
three stood warily looking up at the great rock. Suddenly the
monolith shook and the men stepped awkwardly backward.
Iskiir had no doubt that the stone had moved.

"No closer!" the young man cried to his mount. He slid
from the saddle. With shaking hands he pounded a stake into
the soft ground to tether his beast. Then he advanced cautiously
toward the magicians until he could observe the rough surface
of the lava rock—a coarse texture he knew well. These demon
stones, now casting low shadows toward the desert, were surely
brothers to the ones that had crushed his village.

The old bitterness rose in his throat. He wanted to scream
at the stones, beat them with his fists, though his knees were
nearly buckling under him. Fists would not help, anyway. But
magic, he believed, might accomplish something. After all,
Iskiir owed his life to a sorcerer of his village. Gradually he
calmed himself enough to pay attention to the turbaned practitioners. These men, he decided, must be the ones Yeni had
told him to find.

The first held a leather flask of liquid, which he periodically
sprinkled in the direction of the stone. The second held a long
staff of carved ivory, which he used to jab at the obstruction.
The third was occupied with muttering a torrent of spells, his
high-pitched voice reaching Iskiir's ears despite a brisk breeze
that stirred the sand. The stone lurched forward again, this
time catching the staff-wielder by surprise. Trying to retreat,
the elderly man stumbled and fell. His friends, preoccupied
with their own concerns, made no attempt to aid him.

Despite the looming stone, Iskiir stepped forward to help
the wrinkled mage to his feet, and then to pick up the fallen

staff. The tip of the ivory piece had a long curve like the beak of an exotic bird. *Like the spout of a Karbayra coffeepot,* the young man thought. The rest of the rod was carved with complex designs—zigzags and diamonds and characters of a foreign alphabet. The conjurer, evidently dazed for a moment, recovered his senses and snatched back the staff. Then he retreated several steps, signaling for Iskiir to follow him.

"You were rabbit-brained to come here," said the turbaned one. A strong odor of unfamiliar spice hung about his clothing. "Perhaps you think you have some wild magic that can stop these things. Believe me, you do not. There are always dreamers around, but I've never known one who could do more than curdle milk."

"I've no magic of my own," Iskiir protested. "I just want to help my friends and my new family."

"Indeed?" The old one showed no hurry to rejoin the fray. His companions continued their exercises, succeeding only in being pushed back another few steps. "What sort of young man are you?" the mage continued. "I see no badge. How do you live without a trade?"

"I have yet to find one," Iskiir confessed. "I came here from Dahayart when it was destroyed, and I stay with my cousin Yeniski. Perhaps you know him."

"Yeniski? No. I don't know your cousin." The turbaned one frowned. Then his eyebrows raised in sudden interest. "But tell me about Dahayart. I've yet to hear a firsthand account."

Iskiir glanced nervously up at the boulder. "I was trapped within a circle, like this one," he admitted. "But at my village, there were no gaps at all between the demon stones. They advanced, pushing us into the center—" His explanation was cut short by a cry of triumph from the spell-casting mage.

"Rilyor, it tipped backward!" the other shouted toward Iskiir's conjurer.

"I saw no change," contended the third practitioner. "Do it again. Let me hear your spell."

"My voice is hoarse. But I know the stone tilted. We'll be

rid of these things as soon as we can get some assistance out here."

Rilyor shook his head when the other had turned away. Then he spoke with his voice lowered so that only Iskiir could hear. "That sheep can't tell up from down, so how would he know which way it moved? I've no need to waste time with him. Now what were you saying about Dahayart?" Rilyor's gray eyes bore into Iskiir's and the young man found his words spilling out unbidden.

"I came down from the pastures to spend a night with my family," Iskiir began. He felt the mage's power, a grip that reached into his thoughts so that his only desire was to speak truthfully. "The boulders arrived while we slept," he continued in a rush. "By morning, there was no escape. Whenever we tried to build a pile of rubble to climb out on, the demon stones would knock it down. Most of us died . . . from thirst or collapsing walls . . . from sickness . . ." He touched his bare head. "But Dajnen saved me."

"Who?"

"An old sorcerer of the village. People laughed at his magic since it usually went wrong. He almost failed this time, too. But he kept working at it all the time the stones were closing in. No more than two dozen of us were alive when his spells pushed the blocks aside and got us out."

"Ha. This Dajnen sounds like another dreamer."

"But it happened," Iskiir insisted. "You're forcing the truth from me. I can feel it."

A tight smile showed on the conjurer's lips. "I can only force you to say what you believe. Truth is altogether a different matter." He held up the staff. "Here is truth. Run your fingers over these runes." He took Iskiir's unwilling hand and guided it to the ivory. Touching the raised surface, the young man felt a weak tingle that quickly spread to his arm. The sensation was mildly unpleasant, and he pulled away. "What do you say to *that*," the conjurer asked with a proud jerk of his head.

"Uhhh . . ."

"Leaves you speechless. I'm not surprised. Well, I think

we have chatted enough, dreamer. You'd better stand back
while I show my colleagues who wields *real* power in the
Guild." He straightened his shoulders, and addressed the lava
chunk that had now been abandoned by the others. He pointed
his staff and briskly began to make figures in the air. Iskiir
watched the tip tracing out runes like those carved into the
ivory. The stone edged forward again, but the old conjurer kept
at his work.

After watching three more unchecked advances, Iskiir had
seen enough. He kicked the sand in his path into small clouds
as he returned to his donkey. The beast snorted, and turned
indifferently for home. "You don't know what's happening,
do you? But I'll get you out, you stupid thing," Iskiir promised
the creature. "I'll chase you between the rocks before they can
close on us ... and maybe I'll go with you. If I don't leave,
then they may as well make me donkey in your stead." Gloom-
ily, he pondered his predicament. He could not abandon the
only family that remained to him. Yet, what if they refused to
flee? And what would become of Adeh and her family? He
shook his head in despair.

By the time he reached the city gate, the sun had dropped
behind the distant peaks and a cool wind swept the valley. He
hurried through the dark, silent streets to the Yeniskilu house,
where he found his aunt Hejan and various cousins already
kneeling on the cushions about the low table. Yeni's pleasant-
faced wife, Rahari, nodded at Iskiir as he took his place, though
her greeting lacked its usual warmth. On his arrival from
Dahayart she had insisted on taking him into the household
despite Yeniski's misgivings. And since then, she had always
treated him well. How could Iskiir blame her today if she was
not happy about having an extra stomach to fill?

The mood at the table was bleak, with little talk. The meal
appeared to be a soupy stew—mostly gravy and *tac* roots with
a few scraps of lamb. Iskiir found that he had no appetite. He
stared listlessly at the table while the others tore chunks from
the small pile of bread rounds and dipped them into the flat-
bottomed communal bowl. The watery food proved difficult

to scoop up, and he watched with disgust as Yeni's fingers grew increasingly greasy.

"There will be long lines at the bakers tomorrow," said Rahari grimly, as if apologizing for the meal. "And who knows when we'll get meat again. We must conserve what we have."

Yeni bent his attention to the bowl. He did not answer as he stuffed more bread in his mouth. Iskiir could not stand to look at him when he ate.

"The criers said we shouldn't worry," commented Sar in a small voice. "The conjurers are taking care of the trouble."

"Who will listen to those criers?" Rahari replied to her daughter. "You'll see tomorrow how nothing is normal. Even to get to the cistern will take a morning's wait."

"Trouble'll be gone by tomorrow," mumbled Yeni, his mouth full.

Iskiir bit his lip to keep from shouting what he knew. By his estimate they had two days before the stones closed ranks about the city. How could one think of food at such a time?

"And I still have no Acurlat water," Yeniski added while he licked his fingers. "I've got to perfect Hadam's Illusion. I'm already behind schedule in my studies." He tore off another chunk of bread and dipped it into the bowl. Then he turned to Iskiir. "Tomorrow, cousin, walking stones or not, you'd better find me that water."

At daybreak the household was awakened by pebbles thrown at the windows and by shouts for Yeniski. The conjurer dragged Iskiir from his rug; the two pulled open the thin shutters and peered through the grillwork windows to see who wanted Yeni.

A forlorn little man in a cobbler's robe was about to toss another few bits of gravel. Beside him stood a tall, dark-bearded man of the weaver's guild. Both tried to speak at once, but the cobbler's voice won out. "My wife can't light a fire this morning," the short man said. "She tells me the demon stones put a spell on the strikers."

"And you want me to undo it," Yeniski replied sleepily.

"For a reasonable fee. I'm a poor man."

"And you? What is your trouble?" Yeni nodded at the weaver.

"We have fire, conjurer. But the water won't boil. It must be the doing of the rocks."

"Ah," said Yeniski, his voice sharpening. "I see this trouble is going to bring me some business." He turned to his cousin. "We can use the money," he confided. "I'll go back to my studies tomorrow."

"But, cousin . . . there's no time to waste. The high mages are helpless. Go out and see for yourself."

"Helpless? Give them a little time," he whispered in Iskiir's ear. "By this afternoon, the stones will be gone. Why not profit while I can?"

"And if they aren't gone? Will you listen to me then?"

Yeni's face reddened. "If the stones aren't gone by evening, then I'll savor your every word the way I savor Rahari's stews. Now get ready to come with me. I'll need you to carry my things." Then he turned to assure his customers that he would attend to them at once.

Iskiir nodded uneasily. Since the start of his stay here, he had served as Yeni's assistant in return for his keep; for now, he would do what was asked of him. But by evening, if the Guild had made no progress, he knew he must leave Tajmengus. And the Yeniskilus, in that case, must also flee. How could he make them see the danger?

With no answer at hand, the young man trudged down to the workroom. While he watched the conjurer take up jars from the bench and pack them in his carrybag, Iskiir's thoughts turned to Adeh. He had not conceded that she was lost to him—not yet. If her family were to depart, then perhaps he could find her again in some distant city. And if, against all sense, they remained in Tajmengus, there was still hope. If only the stones could be stopped . . .

Oblivious to his cousin's brooding, Yeni added a few other supplies to his sack. Then he led Iskiir upstairs, out through the roof door and down to the street. "I'll take care of your problem first," the conjurer said to the weaver, sending the other man home to wait for him.

They began to follow the dark-bearded man. Iskiir muttered to himself, thinking for the first time in a long while of how he missed the mountain life. He felt groggy, and his stomach was empty; he suffered under the weight of the bag as he trudged along behind his cousin. Yeni turned back and beckoned Iskiir closer. "The weaver's wife will surely give us something for our bellies," he whispered.

They reached the weaver's hearth, where a caldron hanging high above a skimpy fire still had not boiled. The wife paced back and forth while others of the family sat glumly on the thick rugs. The walls were covered with patterned cloths in bright reds and rich blues. Polished brass candlesticks stood in neat rows beside the hearth. *A well-to-do weaver*, thought Iskiir. It was no wonder that Yeniski had come here first. The young man, feeling he could not continue without some nourishment, made a show of yawning and grumbling about being called out without his breakfast.

"I've nothing but yesterday's cold bread," said the wife. "The fire's no good."

"It looks hot enough to roast eggs," Iskiir observed.

"Roast? I hadn't thought . . ." She looked about wildly, then shouted a command to a young daughter. The girl hurried downstairs and soon came back with two speckled eggs; she used a poker to push them close to the embers.

One apiece, thought Iskiir despondently, wishing he had eaten more at the evening meal. He tried to get his mind away from food so that he could help Yeni's work.

The conjurer pulled clay jars from his sack and placed them on the floor by the hearth. He took out his thin staff of acacia wood, touched its tip to the water in the pot, then let a drop fall onto the back of his hand. He bent over the pot, sniffed deeply, and finally turned with a look of concern to the householder. "A bad business, here," he said ominously. "I don't know if I can break the spell."

"Twenty *menos*," said the weaver, fingering his purse.

"I'd like to help you," said Yeni, "but if I take less than thirty, they'll expel me from the Guild."

The weaver hesitated. "Thirty, then. But nothing until I see results."

"When have I ever charged for no results?" The conjurer got down on his hands and knees. Sniffing like a cur with his nose close to the floor, he began to crawl about in front of the hearth. Iskiir bit his lip to keep from laughing at the performance. "We'll need to collect samples," said the conjurer, nodding toward his bag. Iskiir knew the routine well. He brought out a tiny pair of ivory tweezers and a square of white cloth. Holding the cloth in his palm, he followed his cousin about the room, picking up bits of lint and dust and loose rug hairs from every quarter. These he gave to Yeni, who folded up the cloth, and with loud incantations tossed the packet into the flames.

While the cloth caught fire, the room was silent as if no one dared to draw breath. "That's the first step toward destroying the influence," said Yeni. He rose and shook his staff, making great sweeps in the air that forced the weaver and his wife to jump back out of range of the stick. He continued chanting until the cloth was fully consumed. Then he took a pinch of powder from a green glazed jar and sprinkled it on the fire.

"Aaah!" the wife shouted as a blue-green flash sent noxious smoke into the room.

"Not good enough," said Yeni, shaking his head. He turned to Iskiir and whispered, "Build up the fire." While Iskiir surreptitiously added sticks from the household's basket of wood, Yeni whirled about with his staff, touching the stones of the fireplace, the brass pots stacked to the side, the braids of garlic hanging from the ceiling. When the fire was blazing well, the conjurer tossed in other powders, making flashes of blue and then of yellow. The room was filled with smoke. The children, coughing, ran to the windows and pulled open the shutters to let in fresh air.

"Now we wait," said Yeni, seating himself cross-legged before the hearth. He used a poker to roll out the blackened eggs, and allowed them to cool on the hearthstones. Iskiir watched the eggs hungrily, but his cousin nudged him with his elbow and nodded toward the fire. The young man added another few sticks; already the flames covered the pot's bottom. Yeni started to peel one egg and Iskiir quickly grabbed the other. It was still hot. He tossed it from hand to hand, then began to crack away the shell.

"I hear bubbling," said the weaver in a tone of amazement. Steam was clearly visible above the caldron.

Yeni smiled as he bit into the egg. "Have you a bit of salt?" he asked with his mouth half-full.

When they reached the street, Iskiir could not contain himself. "How can a man who makes such fine cloth be so stupid?" he asked his cousin in a loud whisper.

"When people are afraid, they don't think," said Yeni. "That woman was trying to save wood, but she cost her husband thirty *menos*."

"And what would you have done if there were *really* a spell on the hearth?"

Yeni smiled. "I've never heard of water that won't boil if the fire is hot enough."

Iskiir shook his head with dismay. This exercise had enriched his cousin's purse but had also strengthened his contempt for the power of the demon stones. At every moment, Yeni was becoming more wrong-headed! They hurried to the cobbler's abode, and the conjurer collected ten more *menos* by the simple expedient of switching dry tinder for the damp char the woman had been using. "When people are afraid," Yeniski said smugly while they walked home, "they blame everything on magic. A man would be a fool not to profit by it."

"The weight of your purse won't matter soon," said Iskiir.

"Ha. We'll see who's right about that." The conjurer rubbed his hands together while Iskiir lugged the heavy sack. "And now I can afford to spend the rest of the day on studies. If others come by asking for spells, send them to Kumni. And be sure to get a commission from him afterward."

As they continued homeward, Iskiir noticed how busy the streets had become since early morning. Perhaps the criers' assurances had been enough to bring everyone out. And Yeni seemed the most cheerful man in the city; he strode along briskly while the burdened Iskiir dropped gradually behind. Suddenly a third-rank magician, his robe patterned in yellow quarter-moons, rushed up to Yeniski.

The higher-ranked mage whispered confidentially in his colleague's ear, and Iskiir, catching up with them, made out but one word in three. They were discussing the stones, he was certain. Yeni's eyebrows raised as the man spoke; his expression became increasingly rapt.

"This is my day of good fortune," his cousin exulted when the other had gone. "What we achieved this morning means nothing compared with what we'll accomplish this afternoon."

"We'll fix a 'dry' well, maybe," suggested Iskiir. "Help someone who can't draw water because his bucket cord's too short."

Yeni, still beaming, seemed oblivious to the taunt. "Even magicians can fall prey to fears," he said. "But this is more than I hoped for. The Guild is offering an incentive to anyone who can deflect the stones. *Advancement* to a higher rank. Ah, day of joy. Just slowing them down is worth my promotion."

"Advancement!" Yeniski, he knew, had been trying for four years without success. But what chance could he have now?

Yeni clapped his cousin on the shoulder. "Think what it means. No examination! No grunting old men to criticize my style! Come on. Let's saddle the donkeys and get out there."

"Out there?" said Iskiir cautiously. He had already seen enough of the walking stones. Only if their jagged presence would frighten some good sense into Yeni did he want to approach them again.

"Wake up, cousin. Show some liveliness. We're going to solve this little problem for the Guild. And then I'll have my quarter-moon robe and I won't have to hear Rahari complaining day and night."

Chapter 3

Arriving by the Eastern Road, they came on the stand of demon rocks sooner than Iskiir had expected. Again the sight made his palms sweat and his thighs shake. He wished this could be the last time he would approach the stones, but knew he would come once more. A glance at the gaps showed him how little time remained; the wall would surely close that night. And Yeni was still laughing at it!

At a safe distance from the nearest monoliths stood clusters of donkeys, and men deep in conversation. Iskiir noted conjurers of several ranks, and also glimpsed the dangling nose chain and lengthy beard of an Appeaser. Perhaps the holy wanderer was hoping to coax relief from the gods. Beside him stood a pair of fire-priests in conical hats. The young man recalled how the priests of his village had made one offering after another to the sacred fire, with no response from the gods. He did not expect priests or Appeasers to save Tajmengus.

"We'll want a stone to ourselves," said Yeni, nodding his head toward his goal and then heading his donkey off the road.

Suffering under the conjurer's weight, nearly that of two men, the animal brayed several times in complaint but gamely plodded on. Iskiir followed on his own patient beast.

"Collect some pebbles," said Yeni while they were staking the animals. "We'll need them to mark the big stone's progress."

Iskiir gathered a handful of flint shards from the sandy ground, then watched his cousin step up to the monolith as if it were a harmless artifact of the desert. The conjurer pointed to a coarse knob on the side at the bottom of the block. "Put something there to mark the spot."

Iskiir hesitated; the lava chunk loomed over him. He tried to shut out his memories, but they forced themselves back— the roar of tumbled walls, the ground shuddering as the boulders heaped up the rubble of Dahayart...

"Come, cousin," Yeni chided. "Must I do your work for you?"

Iskiir measured the jagged mass in his mind, wondering whether it might jump forward just at the moment he leaned close. Quickly he tossed a flint and stepped back. It landed within a thumb's length of the edge that Yeni had chosen.

"Good throw," said his cousin. "Now you watch to see which way the thing is moving. The ride gave me a thirst." The conjurer walked back to the donkeys and returned. Iskiir heard the sloshing of a waterbag, then his cousin's sigh of satisfaction after he drank.

Without turning his gaze from the piece of flint, Iskiir held out his hand for the goatskin. The ride had parched his throat also; he took a long draught of the tepid water. Suddenly he realized that he'd shifted his attention for a moment. He looked down at the sand and saw that the shard was now a hand's-breadth *behind* the rough knob.

"The big one moved," Iskiir said in steady voice. "See."

"Ah, put down another marker."

"Another?" Iskiir unwillingly dropped a second flint. This time he held his gaze steady and caught the moment when the great rock lurched. He continued his tracking of its path until a dozen flints made a demon's tail on the sand. One thing was clear: The stone's trajectory would lead straight to the heart of the city. Glancing behind the monolith, Iskiir saw scant evidence of its passing—only a slight track in the sand that was quickly vanishing under the light breeze.

"Now we have some heavy work, cousin," said the conjurer. He turned to Iskiir's donkey and unloaded the manure shovel that Iskiir had packed. "Take this."

Yeni turned his back to the high rock and paced off a good distance in the direction it was traveling. Then, with the heel of his sandal, he marked a line in the sand. "Dig a pit here," he ordered. "As big as the base of the thing and deep as you can."

Iskiir scratched the bare skin of his head and studied Yeniski's mark. The prospect of such labor under the hot sun gave him no cheer, since the work would only exhaust him and weaken his resolve to escape. For a moment, however, his mind filled with unexpected optimism.

He had long believed that Yeni possessed no talent for magic, yet his cousin's practical approach to matters often succeeded. Perhaps, while the mutterings and staff-wavings and sprinklings of mystical water proved useless, a simple ditch might halt the stone. His cousin's idea was worth trying, though it was through Iskiir's sweat that the testing would be done. With a sigh, he lifted the shovel and set to work.

"Longer," said the conjurer when Iskiir paused to wipe his brow at the end of his first furrow. The young man had only begun the task, and already his arms were tiring. He glanced back, measuring the base of the stone against the length of his narrow trench. "I say it's not long enough," his cousin insisted. Iskiir shrugged and continued. "Now make it broader and deeper," said the conjurer when his cousin halted to lean on the handle of his shovel.

"As you say, cousin," Iskiir answered bitterly after catching his breath. Watchful for the advance of the dark block, he worked until his arms grew weak. Perspiration flowed steadily down his arms and chest, and his breathing grew loud and rapid. Even climbing after goats, he had never worked this hard. And how much had he accomplished? His knees barely reached to ground level as he stood in the hole. The ditch was just wide enough to walk in, and Yeni wanted it as wide as the stone's base. "Now . . . you . . . dig some," he said, panting, as he tossed down the shovel.

"A conjurer can't be seen doing *labor*."

"This isn't . . . labor. It's . . . magical preparations." Iskiir glanced up at the rough surface of the approaching block. "It just moved closer. We're almost out of time."

Cursing under his breath, Yeni bent down to retrieve the digging tool. He looked furtively over his shoulder at the nearby mages. So far as Iskiir could tell, the others were busy with their own spells and contrivances. None would notice what this fourth-rank conjurer was doing. None would care, unless by some chance his scheme succeeded.

The plump man grunted, leaned his weight against the handle, and heaved up a full load of sand. He glanced around again, then dug out a second shovelful. Slowly he worked his way along the narrow trench, widening it but also letting sand spill into the bottom. "Remember," he said as he paused for breath. "All . . . we have to do . . . is slow the thing down. If we do that, I get my reward." He squinted up at the fierce sun. Iskiir noticed that now the boulder cast no shadow at all. "If we prove our point . . . they'll bring others to dig. And I'll be a . . . third-rank mage."

Yeniski tired quickly and Iskiir found himself at work again. The stone had now advanced two-thirds of the distance from the last shard to the pit. "Don't you want to wave your staff?" asked Iskiir while he rested briefly. "Otherwise this won't look like magic." He knew that his cousin would be laughed at for a performance like the one at the weaver's house, but Iskiir needed some relief from the labor, even if it was only a joke at Yeni's expense. With a furtive grin, he returned to the task of shoveling.

"A bit wider still," Yeni called when the block was almost upon them. Iskiir put in a last burst of digging, hoping that the hole had reached the required dimensions. Even if the excavation was slightly small, he thought, the stone could not help but topple as it tried to cross.

The young man jumped from the path of the moving rock and scrambled back to where Yeni was standing. The boulder was speeding up, he thought, as if eager to meet this obstacle. To his surprise, he noticed that a few nearby mages had left work to watch the odd experiment. Perhaps a fourth-rank conjurer was not beneath their notice. The turbaned ones stood behind Yeni, jabbering noisily. While they argued, the stone lurched forward until it teetered on the brink of the digging. The sand below the base flowed like a mountain brook into the trench. The stone slid down gracefully until its front edge touched the pit's bottom.

There was a pause. The next advance did not come when expected. All talking ceased, and the mages watched with tense faces.

Perhaps he has done it, thought Iskiir. He stole a glance at his cousin's smug expression. The higher-ranked Guild members exchanged wordless glances and raised their eyebrows at each other. Had Yeni won his promotion with such a simple trick? As if to give answer, the stone crossed the floor of the digging in a single leap and mounted the opposite wall. A great sighing came from the onlookers, especially from Yeniski. Had he even slowed the thing? The stone rested awhile, its leading edge high, its rear sunk in the loose sand of the pit. Then, with another lurch, it was fully atop the sand again, continuing its progress toward the onlookers. Even Yeni would not dare to claim that its speed had diminished.

The mages grumbled their regrets, then hurried back to their own preparations. "The hole could have been deeper," said Yeni when they were gone.

"Maybe you can hire some farm boys to dig for you," Iskiir suggested unkindly. "Five or six young toughs. Let them dig all day so the stone will have something sizable to leap across."

Yeni scowled. "You are so smart. And what would *you* do if you had your way, cousin *bolu?*"

Iskiir was about to put his head down and butt the conjurer in his fat belly. Then Yeni would know what a shiny pate was good for. "Do you want to know how I got out of Dahayart?" he shouted instead.

"I've already heard your story," Yeni retorted, but Iskiir pressed on.

"Dajnen. That's the name you should remember. He's old and cranky but he must know something that your friends don't know. I *saw* the stones move out of his way. We climbed over the ruins and got free."

Yeniski's heavy eyebrows lifted. "Why should I believe such a tale?"

"Because I'm alive, cousin. Do you think I grew wings and *flew* from Dahayart?"

Yeni rubbed his chin in thought while turning to see how the other magicians were faring. No cries of triumph came from their scattered encampments. "So . . . this disreputable Dajnen knows more than the Guild?" he said at last.

"How else did he succeed? Stay here if you like, but the Guild won't save you." Iskiir kicked up a sand cloud, then turned toward his donkey. Must he now abandon all the Yeniskilus because of his cousin's foolishness?

"Not so fast, cousin. What if your tale is true? How would we find this sorcerer?"

"I know only where he *said* he was going. After Dahayart, we all had to find new homes."

"Well . . ." Yeni edged closer to his cousin. "Whisper. *Whisper*," he said, though no one was in earshot.

Iskiir lowered his voice and named the small village of Lact, where Dajnen's relatives lived. "We've got to leave right away," Iskiir said. "Look . . ." He was no longer certain that a wagon could squeeze between the stones. "The gaps are narrowing. No more time for talk."

Yeni licked his lips. He glanced again at the other mages who were working futilely with colored smokes or drums or trained snakes. "What about my family?" he said nervously.

"They should come with us," Iskiir insisted. "In case we fail."

"All of them?" The conjurer scowled and wiped his dripping brow with his sleeve. "Come on. Let's see what Rahari says about it."

Iskiir did not wish to be part of a family spat, and he had urgent business of his own. After the donkeys were stabled, he slipped out to search for Adeh.

Though the city had not returned to normal, Iskiir noted, the earlier panic had subsided. Some shops that depended on outside supplies were closed, but many merchants and craftsmen sat at their open doorways as if nothing had changed. Why the calm? Perhaps these citizens had more confidence in their magicians than Iskiir could muster. Or perhaps the stones were still too distant to seem an immediate threat. Whatever the reason, he was pleased to find the potters' shop open.

After his last encounter with her father, he was not eager to trade words with the quick-tempered artisan. He stood on the other side of the narrow street and waited to see if Adeh would appear. A glimpse of her red-striped jubbah brought a broad grin to Iskiir's face. Standing behind her uncle's wheel, she turned. Iskiir gave a quick wave, then pointed his thumb toward where they had previously met.

Adeh gave a faint smile, nodded subtly, and he was off. He found the tinker's shop and endured the hammering gladly this time. But he kept watch in both directions so that she could not slip up and surprise him.

"Iskiir!"

He wanted to hug her, but dared do nothing but smile. "Adeh, we must talk."

"You look worried."

"With good reason. I've been out on the Eastern Road." He did not wish to frighten her, but felt he must make her understand the danger. "Come, we'll find another temple to climb. Then you'll see for yourself."

They left the crowded shopping district and reached a fire-temple near the eastern edge of the city. Adeh did not hesitate this time to join him on the spiral staircase. They wound around the dome and stood at last looking out at the demon stones that encircled the city. "Do you understand now?" he asked.

"Like a circle of dark sentries," she said with awe. She reached for Iskiir's hand and he helped support her.

"Our conjurers have been working against them for a full day," he said. "I watched the mages fail. My cousin, too, tried to stop the advance, and I have blisters, for my part." He held up a sore palm for her inspection. "I'm leaving by tonight," he said hoarsely. "I wish you could leave, too. Your whole family should go."

She shook her head. "My father and uncle discussed it this morning. They know a few families who packed up and went away. My father laughed at them."

"Ahh, if it were only a joke. Perhaps somewhere an evil god is laughing."

She put a finger to his lips. "Don't say such things in a holy place."

"But what will you do? What chance do you have if you stay here?"

"My father has decided; there's no more to say. And if I flee alone, my life is finished anyway," she said bitterly. Iskiir could see her dilemma. Leaving would make her a *numij*, outcast from her family. Her life would be worth less than a scavenging cur's.

But a hopeless thought came to him. He had known her so briefly, yet his words tumbled out. "If we were to marry . . ."

Rich color came to her cheeks and she took a deep breath before answering. "Without my father's consent? What priest would agree?"

He shook his head and clenched his free hand in despair. In the mountains matters were less formal. But he knew how rigid were the customs of city dwellers. Her first duty was to her family; she would not bring shame on them even to save her own life.

And if they did marry somehow, how could he provide for

her? At best, they would be beggars wherever they went. The realization made his face hot with anger. "Then I must do what I can for you," he said softly. "For everyone."

"Where will you go?"

"To Lact." He pointed toward the north. "To the high country. I know a man who can help us. Even if the city mages fail, we may have a chance."

She paused with tears moistening her eyes. "I . . . I'll think of you often."

"I won't be away long. There won't be time enough."

"Then I'll watch for you. Every afternoon I'll climb a tower and look out."

Iskiir managed a grin. "I have confidence in you, my mountain girl." Then he threw his arms around her as he had wanted to do in the crowded street. There was no more to say. Her face was wet and hot against his own.

When Iskiir reached home he found Yeni still arguing with his wife and with his mother, Hejan. The conjurer turned to his cousin in despair. "They won't leave the house. They say their friends will never stop laughing at them."

Iskiir wondered how long their friends would live to enjoy their mirth. "Maybe," he offered. "Maybe I should tell them again about Dahayart."

Yeni's face reddened. Iskiir knew that if his cousin were half the tyrant that Adeh made her father out to be, then Yeni's family would already be packing for the journey. "You know nothing of women," the conjurer shouted. "It's enough that *I'm* listening to your donkey-brained scheme. Maybe I should reconsider."

Iskiir's mouth fell open, and he felt as if the wind had been knocked out of him.

"Let's get ready," said Yeni impatiently. "I'll leave my brother in charge. The household will be safe with him. Come. Let's pack up."

In misery, Iskiir turned to Rahari as his cousin rushed from the room. "Go, as you wish," she said in a low voice. "I can't say that you're wrong. But we wouldn't be any help to you on the road. If you're to find your friend, you must travel quickly."

The young man found his words catching in his throat. "We aren't . . . deserting you," he said hoarsely. "We'll bring . . . help. You can be sure of it." Then, before tears could come, he hurried after the conjurer.

He caught up with his cousin in the pantry, where he was stuffing bread and cheese into a leather carrysack. "The water-bag's already full," he explained as they headed down to the workroom. On the way they found Yeni's brother Esen. The conjurer quickly explained his plans and handed over his cash-box key to the younger man. Esen wrinkled his brow, ran his fingers through his hair, and shrugged. Yeniski continued down the stairs.

Pausing before his workbench, the conjurer studied the care-less arrangement of dishes and jars. "Give me some idea of your sorcerer's technique," he said. "Then I'll know what equipment to take."

"There was no smoke, no smell, no waving of wands . . ."

"Then what, in Karkilik's name, did he use for magic?"

Iskiir closed his eyes and tried to remember. He had paid little attention while the old man was working. After all, no one had expected him to succeed. "I remember a bell tinkling," he said suddenly.

"Bell!" Yeni began rummaging through a large chest that lay beside his bench. He pushed aside cloth scraps, empty jars, skins of desert animals. "Here," he said, triumphantly pulling out a small bronze bell crudely marked with wavy lines. When he struck the clapper it made a dull sound.

"It may do," said Iskiir skeptically.

"It will have to. That's all I've got. Now tell me what else you recall of Dajnen's magic."

"He held something between his teeth."

"A stick?"

"Flat . . . I think. White. Maybe ivory or bone."

Yeni ran his hand over his brow and knocked his skullcap

askew. "Whatever it is, I don't have it." He tossed the bell
into his equipment sack, which still held all the supplies from
his morning calls. Then he shouted for Esen to come down
and lock up after them as they went out.

They threaded their way through the late afternoon crowds,
the pedestrians making way sullenly for their passing. Had it
not been for Yeniski's robe, the strollers would have hurled
curses and jeers. Those who left the city at this time of crisis
were not popular. But grimy as his clothing was, people recognized Yeni's guild; few citizens would anger a mage, even
one of fourth rank. And so the passage was tedious but quiet.

The sun was low as they reached the city's outskirts and
continued on the road that ran north. The monoliths rose ahead
of them in a wall of black stone—at that distance, Iskiir could
see no gaps between them. He wondered if there would even
be room enough to squeeze the donkeys through.

The road dipped and for a while they could see only the
tips of the stones. The ground in this region was sandy and
barren, with only a few spiny plants dotting the landscape.
Iskiir found his thoughts straying to Adeh as he began a gradual
ascent. Facing the prospect of a fruitless journey, he recalled
again their last meeting. He should have pressed her to flee,
he told himself, regardless of the consequences. Her fate now,
so far as he knew, rested with a cranky old sorcerer. And if
Iskiir could not locate the man . . .

"Someone should get rid of that ugly old ruin," said Yeniski,
disturbing his cousin's reverie. His finger pointed to a sand-
covered rubble pile on the brow of the hill.

"The demon stones will take care of the ruins for you,"
replied Iskiir irritably. "Everything will be swept clean. But
who'll be here to look?" Only a few blocks of pitted limestone
remained exposed. The young man saw worn outlines of carvings, but could not tell what they represented. He noticed a
dark patch that might have been a shadow or an entrance, but
gave it no further attention.

"Old places like that bring bad luck," said Yeni with a visible shudder. "For all we know, our troubles came from an ancient curse in those carvings."

"Ancient indeed," Iskiir retorted, his teeth knocking together while the donkey lurched over a rough section of road. "After centuries of peace, why would the curse choose to bother us now? And why would Dahayart suffer first?"

Yeni shrugged. "Nobody understands such matters."

They reached the crest of the hill to find the monoliths almost upon them. Men on donkeys were milling about while mages called to each other in anguished voices. Iskiir rubbed his eyes, but what he saw did not change. The worst had happened; the blocks had closed up, leaving no gaps at all!

"It can't be," Yeniski shouted. He swatted his donkey, urging it off the road to follow the forbidding line of rocks. "There's a break down that way," he called back. "Hurry and we can still get through."

But Iskiir saw no opening. The monoliths were arranged in two circles, he saw, one just outside the other. Those in the front ranks did not touch each other, but each gap was covered by a stone from the second circle. This was exactly how the attack on Dahayart had begun.

"They've slowed, thank the gods," called one harried-looking priest as Iskiir rode past.

"Now they've got us trapped, they can take their time," answered another.

Iskiir could not believe his own stupidity. How had he been so careless as to miss his chance for escape? Tears of regret filled his eyes, but he could not lose Yeni; the two had cast their lots together. He swatted his own mount and held the pommel tightly while the beast caught up with his cousin. "It's no use. Why kill your animal?" he said. The other donkey's flanks were wet with perspiration.

Yeni jerked the reins and his mount halted. The conjurer scratched at his ear and furrowed his brow. "And what do you have in mind, cousin?"

Iskiir looked helplessly at the huge dark wall. Suddenly the stones made a grating sound and he felt the ground tremble.

The front ranks advanced, and the second ranks followed on their heels. He saw no space between them, even during the instant of motion.

"I have a way," said Yeni. "We'll put a big ladder up and climb to the top. Then we'll lower ourselves down the other side with a rope."

"Do you have a ladder or a rope?"

"We'll build the ladder. We'll need to cut down a tall palm tree."

Iskiir looked behind him. He knew that the nearest palm would be in the wells district, and that they could not ride there and return before dark. And he knew also that Yeni was not carrying, perhaps did not possess, enough *menos* to buy such a tree. But he would not mention those problems. "What will you do for carpenters' tools?" the young man asked. "And how will you coax the donkeys up the ladder?"

Yeniski sighed. "Then we might as well go home and give the women something to laugh about."

"I'm not going home," said Iskiir. He sat still for a moment, remembering the ruins on the hill. Suddenly he turned his donkey.

"Then where are you going?"

"I want to look at something." Iskiir gave no explanation as he returned toward the road they had recently left. Along the stone front, the work of the mages had become more frenzied. Violet smoke blew from a bubbling pot into Iskiir's face. He coughed, gasped for breath, pulled his robe up over his head. The donkey brayed and Iskiir felt a blow.

A shrill voice struck his ears. "Out of my way, ox dung!" Iskiir slid forward, clutched his mount's neck, but did not fall. When he regained his equilibrium, he pulled down his robe and glanced back at a man in a white turban sprawled in the sand.

"My apologies, sir," Iskiir shouted at the senior magician. "My donkey has poor eyesight."

"If I had time, I'd blind him for you," the fallen one howled. "Finish the job that someone left half done."

Iskiir ignored the threat and concentrated on steering his beast back to the road. He had to work around an arriving procession of wood-laden carts. Was someone hoping to burn the stones, he wondered. Or perhaps crack them with heat? He was not planning to stay to find out. After turning to see that Yeni was following him, he made for the ruin they had passed on their arrival.

"You long-eared eater of weeds," said his cousin when he caught up. "Because I told you the place was full of bad luck, you came right back here."

"I want to look at the opening," the younger man answered.

"Opening?" They halted near the old monument. "You want to crawl in?"

Iskiir studied the rise and fall of the landscape. "The rocks will slide up the far side of the hill," he said, moving his hand parallel to the ground, "and then down this side. They'll push these old temple blocks away, but we can be safe underneath."

"In *there?*"

"We can stay below until the demon stones pass. Then we'll be *outside* the wall." He grinned at the simple brilliance of his plan.

"But the space is too small. We can't get in, and even if we could, we'd have to leave the donkeys."

"Small?" Iskiir stood half a dozen paces from the gap between the limestone blocks. He stepped closer, scrutinizing the dark shadow under the overhanging slab. A prickling sensation began at the back of his neck and spread quickly to his shoulders and arms. Was he sensing unfamiliar magic, he wondered, or just reacting to ordinary strangeness. Perhaps the opening was larger than he'd first thought. If the light was not playing tricks on his eyes, then steps led down from the entranceway to an underground chamber.

"There's not room enough to get so much as my head in," Yeni complained.

The prickling feeling now covered Iskiir's legs as well. He heard a hiss like that of a steady wind against tentcloth, but felt no breeze.

"Come away from there, cousin," said Yeni, his voice faint against the unexplained sibilance that filled the entranceway. "Maybe the ladder is not such a problem as you think. We can leave the donkeys and *walk* to Lact."

Iskiir could not answer his cousin's foolishness. He saw now that the opening was wide enough to permit even the animals to enter. "Bring me my donkey," he said. "Then do what you want." He held out his hand, but did not turn his head.

"I don't know what's wrong with you," Yeni said.

Iskiir remained in place, his eyes fixed on the entrance.

"Let's be done with this," said Yeni. "Try to squeeze your melon through a keyhole, and when you've given up we can think of something sensible to do." Iskiir heard footsteps, then felt the donkey's moist breath on his hand; he grasped the halter. Slowly he stepped beneath the overhang, and there he saw three steps leading down to a sand-covered floor. The beast brayed and balked. "I promised to save you from the stones," he told the donkey. "You're young still. Do you want to feed the buzzards so soon?"

"He can't fit," Yeni protested.

But Iskiir was already inside and the creature was following him down the steps.

"Where'd you go?" came Yeni's shout. The ruin smelled of ancient dust; from inside Iskiir could see only the daylight about the entrance. He felt he was in a sizable chamber, but until his eyes adjusted to the light he would know no more. "Come closer," he called to his cousin.

Then he saw Yeni's face at the opening. "What an illusion!" the conjurer exclaimed as his sandal rested on the first step. "Until you put your foot in, it looks like a mere crevice. I don't know how you found it."

"Bring your beast," Iskiir said. "We haven't much time."

"But what if the thing falls in on us?"

"There must be a solid roof here. It's been holding up the sand for all these years."

"It could be a trap. Old magic."

"No worse than the trap we're in already." Iskiir wondered, however, what had been happening to him. The tingling was fading, and he could no longer hear the hiss. Nonetheless, he felt unreasonably safe in a place that might be filled with dangers. He shrugged, opened a saddlebag by feel, and pulled out a mat. Then he sat on the floor, with his back against the donkey's flank, and waited for Yeniski to make up his mind.

"Can you see anything in there, cousin?" the conjurer asked.

"Light's too dim."

"Could be full of scorpions." Yeni scratched at his cheek, then vanished. Soon Iskiir heard a few sharp taps and guessed that the conjurer was striking fire. The young man was only mildly curious to see the interior of the room. He leaned back, content in the cool solitude of the place.

Soon Yeniski appeared carrying a cylindrical lantern that shed light unevenly through a lattice of holes. He stretched his arm into the room and looked about. "Old magic!" he said with disgust when the walls became visible. The surfaces were covered with carved images of beasts—camels with the tiny wings of birds, goats with scorpion tails, sheep with jackal heads. The ceiling held only a huge human face, its lips tight, its wide eyes staring down.

"I don't see any danger," said Iskiir.

His cousin began to mutter conjurer's oaths. He set down the lantern and held up his hand with his fingers splayed while he finished his incantation. "Maybe that will protect us," he said without conviction. "Whatever is in here can't be worse than facing Rahari." Then he led his donkey down the steps, alternately coaxing and tugging until they were both inside.

Chapter 4

In the Demilu household that evening there was little talk until the meal was finished and the first coffee served. Adeh's father Demid and her Uncle Nomidi toyed with their empty cups until her mother was forced to make excuses. "No more tonight," said Passela. "There were no beans in the market today. And if the traders can't reach us..."

Nomidi coughed, but looked at his brother to make the rebuke.

"Am I as poor as a dung-sweeper?" Demid asked. "That tonight I'll thank the Fire for my single cup?"

"Demid, you know what's happening," his wife replied.

"City of donkeys!" He clenched his fist. "What do we have out there? A few stones that nobody noticed before, and the brayers turn that into a siege."

"It's worse than you think," Adeh blurted out, ignoring a chilling stare from father and uncle. "The gaps are getting smaller. By tomorrow we'll be walled in."

Demid raised his eyebrows. "How do you know so much about it?"

Adeh felt her face flush and saw her father's redden in response. "Ahhh," he said. "Must be that sheep-loving *bolu* filling your head with wool. I told you to stay clear of him."

"But..."

Demid brought his fist down on the serving platter, rattling the small cups and shaking the coffeepot. "Your three sisters. You see how well they live." He ticked them off one by one on his fingers. "A miller, a cattle-butcher, a lamp-maker. Three sound husbands. Three sons-in-law I don't have to whisper about. And what about you, last-born daughter?"

I should have gone with Iskiir, she thought fiercely. *If I'd had more courage...*

Demid turned to his wife in disgust. "She got rid of the Rejiku boy quick enough. Nobody else I want to know will bother with her."

Passela gave her daughter a secret sign, a twitch of her eyebrow meaning: *let me handle him.*

"He's gone now," said Adeh bitterly, ignoring her mother's advice. "Iskiir's gone. You won't have to chase him from the shop again."

"But who'll be next?" Demid began to smirk. "There's a blind beggar in Coppersmith's Street who needs a wife..."

"Demid!" Passela began to collect the cups. "Now's not the time for this." The ugly smile faded slowly and Adeh wondered which her father thought more important, his daughter's future or his coffee. "If the traders come tomorrow," said Passela, "then you can have five servings for all I care."

Eager to escape the attention of the men, Adeh hurried to help her mother. But while she was lifting the tray, a rapping sounded at the roof door. Demid and his brother shot puzzled looks at each other as if to ask: "Who is so desperate for an oil jar that he can't wait until morning?" Again the knocking came, this time louder. Curious, Adeh set down the tray while Nomidi went up to learn who was troubling them.

Her uncle came down the stairs followed by a gray-robed

acolyte from the fire-temple. Nomidi rubbed his short goatee and frowned. "Says some priestess wants to see Adeh," he told his brother. "I thought that was settled long time ago."

"Myranu..." said the cowled messenger to the daughter. "She asked me to bring you. At once."

Adeh felt her lips tighten; a call to the temple was a serious matter. And Myranu was a priestess she knew well. It was from Myranu that Adeh had received her religious education. Out of a class of one hundred girls, the priestess had invited only Adeh to join the Women's Order.

"I, too, thought it was settled," her father grumbled to Nomidi. "But maybe we were too hasty. Maybe she should join up with 'em after all. They'll feed her and keep her out of trouble. If she won't take a decent husband..."

"I must go," Adeh said nervously. Demid had opposed the idea of temple service when it first came up a year before. And at that time Adeh expressed no wish to take the Oath. Though she respected the Keepers, she had always felt uneasy within the confines of a temple. Perhaps it was the nearness of the gods that troubled her, the feeling that they were staring directly into her soul. Must they see again and again, she had wondered, how she chafed under her father's rule? Might they not take her rebellious feelings as a sign of impiety?

And yet, if it was the rule of men that she sought to escape, the Women's Order of the Fire offered shelter. This contradiction she had never fully resolved...

"Go and be quick," her father said. "Find out what your priestess wants and then I'll decide."

"And have 'em send someone back with you," Nomidi added. "Don't know that the streets are safe anymore with these troubles."

"I'll escort her home," the acolyte answered.

Her uncle snarled at the youth. "And why should she trust *you*? Even if you're a temple boy, they didn't cut yours off, did they?" He made a vulgar gesture with his thumb.

The boy turned his face away from the insult and kept his

eyes averted from Nomidi. "Uncle, have some respect," Adeh shouted.

Her uncle waved her away; hurriedly she climbed the stairs.

"He cares nothing for temples and Keepers," Adeh said apologetically to the boy as they hurried down the dark street. "Don't fault him for his ignorance."

The acolyte shrugged. "He doesn't understand," the youth said in a low voice. "Just 'cause we don't marry, doesn't mean we never..."

She felt her face redden. "You don't have to explain. Myranu told me about the rituals."

"The life is better than you'd guess. Better than being married," the acolyte continued. "For one thing, it's quieter; no kids bawling."

This was a matter that Myranu hadn't spoken of. But Adeh had never heard of a priestess with children. A brew of mountain herbs, appropriately taken, might explain that... or Karkilik's intervention.

"Other comforts, too," he added. "Thick sleep-rugs. Coffee every morning. The freshest bread in the city."

"I've never thought that I was suited for the temples." But if she were not to choose the Fire, then she must serve a husband. Until Iskiir had come into the shop, that prospect, too, had held no appeal. Now all she could feel was confusion. For if the crisis ended and Iskiir returned, then he was but a *bolu* with no profession. And if the crisis did not end, then what would any choice matter?

"Maybe," said the youth. "Maybe it's not about the Order. She might have something else to see you about."

All the streets they passed were empty, and Adeh recalled what her Uncle had said about danger. Even at the public well there were no women drawing water. The lamps that normally burned along the wider thoroughfares had not been lit.

Ezla Fire-temple lay just ahead. A single light burned on the steps of its portico. They passed under the arch, then made for a small door to the right of the entrance to the domed hall. Here another lamp burned, its orange light pale against the black-and-white mosaic set into the door. She could just make out Karkilik, breathing sacred Fire as he stood above his enemies, with one forepaw on the cobra's hood and the other on the scorpion's stinger. The acolyte rapped softly with his knuckles against the wooden panel that framed the tiles.

The door slid aside. Within stood another acolyte who beckoned them forward. Adeh had been down this narrow corridor more than once, but the thought of being in the heart of the temple produced her usual goosebumps. Along the walls, bronze oil lamps burned, their flames too dim to show the nature of the painted tiles on both sides of the hallway. She saw shadowy hints of beasts and gods—Mirzapur, Uzurek, Itarsus—as she followed her messenger up two steps and then into a corridor that branched to her right.

A dark woolen hanging covered the entrance to Myranu's cubicle. The youth put his face next to the cloth. "Lady Priestess," he said shyly. "I bring Adeh Demilu as you requested."

"Send her in," replied the familiar husky voice. The acolyte bowed, pushed aside the hanging. Adeh came into the tiny room and saw that it had not changed since her earlier visits. On the small writing desk near the front stood two candelabra, each holding three burning candles of dark wax. To the rear, Adeh glimpsed a thick rug for sleeping and a chest that undoubtedly held the priestess's garments and belongings.

The soft footfalls of the youth vanished down the corridor behind her. Adeh brought her attention to Myranu, who sat on a stool with one elbow on the round-topped desk, the other arm free at her side. The priestess was not wearing her hat. Her hair, as Adeh had seen before, was shorn close to the scalp. Her chin was narrow, her face thin. Adeh did not find Myranu's features repulsive, but she recalled with discomfort their past conversations and lowered her gaze.

"I've not asked you here to discuss that matter we spoke of a year ago," said the priestess. "The problem I have now is more immediate."

Relieved and puzzled, Adeh glanced up from the terra-cotta floor and waited for Myranu to continue.

"You know about the walking stones . . ."

"I . . ." She could not say that she had committed the sacrilege of climbing a temple to look at them. "I have heard too much about them."

"This is an issue, I fear, not between gods and men but between men and men. Perhaps I should explain."

Adeh nodded weakly as a feeling of despair gnawed at her belly.

"Some citizens are looking to their priests and priestesses for aid. We must tell them not to expect help from sacrifices and prayers. The gods don't interfere in matters such as this. It is for the magicians and the soldiers to find our enemies and put an end to them."

"Then if there is no hope from the gods . . ."

Myranu held up her hand. "Wait. Because we can do nothing through the Fire doesn't mean we sit idle in the temple while the city suffers. You know it's the duty of the Bey and his guards to keep the civil peace." The priestess lowered her voice. "But I can tell you in confidence that many of those guards have run away. Escaped, before the wall could trap them."

"Then that's why people are afraid in the streets."

"It will be worse. This is the reason I called you. Each of us who knows bright and energetic people is speaking to them tonight. We want you to be part of our Binding of Allies. We must hold the city together until the problem is solved. Food, water, public safety. Wherever we're needed, we will help."

"But who will listen?"

Myranu smiled. "There is strength behind us. If something must be done, and an official or a merchant stands in our way, we will deal with him; do not fear. Now tomorrow you'll be needed in the grain fields. We'll be holding an early harvest, and a quick one. The crops must all come to the temples so they can be fairly distributed. And after the harvesting is done, we'll have other work for you."

"Then the stones . . ."

"If they have not closed already, it is but a matter of hours."

Adeh did not know precisely when Iskiir had departed. Was it possible, she wondered, that his escape plan had failed?

"You are thinking of something else?" the priestess asked.

"Only of a friend. Someone who means much to me. He . . . planned to go for help outside."

Myranu's thin eyebrows raised. "Help from outside? Tell me about this friend."

"He is . . . not like the others. Wilder, rougher, I think. I sense unusual strength and will in him." She paused and frowned. "Sometimes I'm puzzled by what he says. Is it likely, do you think, that he once saw Karkilik in a pool at Wej oasis?"

"*In* the pool?"

"A reflection."

"I don't know. Tell me. I've judged you to be unusually perceptive. Does this young man lie to you?"

"Not often. He misdirects sometimes. But in this matter I sensed some truth, though not all. He said the god roared and burnt off his hair. Of course that part was a tale. But of his vision, I'm not certain."

The priestess leaned forward. "I'm interested in meeting this friend."

"If he comes back . . ."

"If?"

"He will come back."

Myranu smiled. "Then I'll ask him myself what he saw. And now, one last matter." She reached inside her robe and brought out a flat amulet on a chain of silver links. The amulet was of polished greenstone, with the fire-and-hand symbol of the Order carved in its center. "Wear this. If you need help, show it in any fire-temple. That's my mark beneath." She pointed to a jagged line near the bottom edge of the piece.

"But . . ." To Adeh's eyes, this was the amulet that was given to probationary novices. "What will I tell my father?"

"There is no obligation to keep it. When the troubles are over, give it back."

Could she refuse? Myranu had made her feel that others depended on her. She would be aiding her family and friends by joining the Binding. Otherwise she would have nothing to do but sit in the shop and listen to Nomidi's grumbles and curses.

She turned the greenstone over. With the smooth blank side showing, the amulet looked almost like an innocent piece of jewelry. Seeing it this way made her acceptance easier. She quickly pulled the chain over her head and dropped the stone inside her jubbah.

The priestess showed a faint smile. "I'll send you home with my acolyte," she said as she pulled on a rope that connected through a hole with some unseen mechanism. Breathing heavily, the youth burst into the room moments later.

"It is finished, Lady Priestess. The ring has closed." He knocked his fists together in midair.

Adeh drew a deep breath.

"I hope your friend was quick," said Myranu in parting. Adeh could say nothing more as she hurried from the room.

Sitting on the floor of the underground chamber, Iskiir *felt* the approach of the demon stones before he could hear them. The ground shook gently and Yeni, seated nearby, began to mutter to himself. Moments later the floor shook again; this time the lantern's dim light wavered.

"They are coming, gods curse them," said the conjurer in a tense voice. Then Iskiir heard the first deep rumble of stone against stone.

"We're safe here," the younger man said with a nervous voice. But in truth, his earlier feelings of security had fled. The thought of the great bulk that would pass overhead was making cold droplets of sweat trickle from his armpits. "Cousin," he said to assure himself. "Did you notice the shallow track the stones made in the desert? Some force buoys them up; I don't think our roof will suffer their true weight."

"You may think so, *bolu*," replied the conjurer, "but I noticed that this evening the stones bit deeper into the ground than they did at noon." He lifted his hand, palm outward. "Now they're pushing little dunes ahead of them. We'll see if your roof can take *that* extra weight." He glanced up and Iskiir followed his gaze to the ceiling's wide-eyed face.

Another shudder came, followed by a deep scraping directly overhead. *They've reached the old blocks,* thought Iskiir, recalling the exposed portions of the ruin. Now the ancient slabs would be pushed aside. He tensed, waiting for the coming tremor.

The next sound of grating Iskiir felt in his teeth. "The ceiling will fall next!" shouted Yeni as he crawled beneath his trembling donkey for protection. "Enough!" shouted the conjurer. "Why don't they pass?"

Iskiir tried to time the stones' progress, counting breaths between each advance. But his breathing was not steady. "If their march has slowed," he said, "then be thankful that Tajmengus has a bit more time." Even anticipating the sound, he could not help jumping when the next shudder came. There was no way to tell how much longer the crossing would take. Nothing was visible through the ruin's opening; either night had come or the entranceway was buried. The shaking and grinding continued, accompanied by a constant braying from the donkeys.

In the center of the floor the lamp still burned, its light flickering with every jolt. The air was filled with dust shaken from the ceiling. Iskiir coughed. "That flame is burning up our air," he said.

"Leave it," his cousin insisted. "It's keeping us safe from *them.*" He pointed a thick finger at the beasts on the walls.

"If we can't breathe, it won't matter . . . *Ach!*" A loud crack made Iskiir think the shelter had been breached. With his heart racing, he lifted the lantern to look for damage.

"See the crack!" shouted Yeni.

A jagged gap had opened high on one side wall. Another rumble sounded above and small fragments began to tumble. Iskiir took shelter under his donkey and listened to the patter of falling shards. When the storm from the ceiling ended, he looked up and noticed that pieces of the beard and nose of the carved face were missing.

"Now the old gods are having their vengeance on us!" Yeni groaned. "And all because I call you kin. My uncle should have wed a camel before choosing such a wife as your mother."

"But, Yeni," Iskiir replied in kind, "I fear we're not cousins after all. People tell me that *your* mother took on a herd of goats while my uncle was out buying her a knobbed stick."

"Compared with your grandmother's habits..." Yeni stopped in mid-insult as the chamber rocked again. The crack lengthened to reach the floor. The donkeys' braying grew more frenzied.

Iskiir grasped the halter and tried to calm his animal. The mount bucked and twisted. *"Hisss,"* Iskiir soothed while trying to avoid its dangerous rear hooves. He heard his cousin calling to his own mount. *"Hisss. Hisss."*

"L-Look! Wall!" shouted Yeni just as the donkeys began to quiet. "Moving! M-moving!" He pointed a shaky finger at the frieze of exotic creatures. Iskiir thought the flickering light was to blame, but then he saw that the wall itself was trembling. Thin slabs began to fall away from the facing. The donkeys grew frantic again.

"Back," said Iskiir, pulling his crazed mount away from the cascade of limestone toward the one wall that still appeared solid. He did what he could to control his animal, clasping its neck and whispering sweet words into its ear. The shattering continued, and Iskiir feared collapse of the entire structure, but he kept his attentions on his donkey.

The room pitched twice more and another layer of carvings disintegrated, filling the air with heavy dust. But the grinding noise was no longer overhead. Now the sounds softened at each repetition as they moved toward the entranceway, toward Tajmengus. The scraping still jarred his teeth, but shook nothing more loose within the chamber. The dust began to clear.

Slowly his donkey calmed, and Iskiir was able to examine the damaged section of wall. To his surprise, he saw another frieze that had lain hidden beneath the first. Where a camel had stood, there now sat a cross-legged woman. A jackal-headed sheep was replaced by a priest, a goat by a kneeling child.

"Old magic!" Yeni complained when he noticed the change. He began to shout protective incantations. But to Iskiir, the newly exposed figures showed no signs of hostility. As the scraping continued to recede, the young man puzzled over the carvings. Was it possible, he wondered, that one temple had been built inside the ruins of an even older building? He would learn nothing from Yeniski, whose Guild banned study of ancient lore. But if he managed to find Dajnen, perhaps he might ask about the fallen frieze.

For the moment, an awesome silence reigned. He wondered if the demon stones were resting at the brow of the hill, surveying the city they would soon claim. Iskiir heard only the labored breathed of Yeni and the donkeys.

"What's that?" asked the conjurer when the quiet was broken by an unusually sharp rumble. He cocked an ear toward the entrance. The noise this time, Iskiir realized, had come not through walls but through the opening itself. And the entrance-way faced the city!

"They're past us," said Iskiir triumphantly. He wiped his dripping face on the sleeve of his robe, then took the lantern and walked gingerly to the steps. Underfoot, all was thickly coated with dust. Beyond the doorway he could see only blackness. Then he smelled the cool fresh air of evening. "*Aiiii!*" he shouted suddenly, trying to cover his head as a torrent of sand spilled down on him.

"Cousin?" Yeni called nervously from behind him. Iskiir was busy shaking sand from his hair and brushing off his robe. The lantern had fallen and gone out; he felt in the pile of loose grit and pulled it free.

"I'm all right, cousin," said Iskiir, peering outside. Ahead he could see only darkness. The backs of the walking boulders were before him, almost within reach. But by craning his neck he could see the moon, almost full, above the eastern horizon. "Bring the donkeys," he said. "We can squeeze out now and travel by moonlight."

"What are you saying, whelp of my uncle?" Yeni came cautiously up behind him and then looked out. "You mean we got past those demon stones?" He scratched his head in wonderment.

"They got past *us*. Now hurry." Iskiir extended his hand to receive his donkey's rope.

Complaining about having to return to the dark chamber, Yeni padded back inside. In a moment, Iskiir heard the beasts straining to reach fresh air. "Don't let them touch the sides," he warned. But Yeni's donkey lurched against the edge of the entrance, dislodging another pile of sand left by the passing rocks.

The beast kicked in fright at the cascade of grit that poured onto its back. It pulled free and ran out into the night with Yeni in awkward pursuit. After the long entombment, Iskiir needed nothing more than some amusement. He could scarcely keep from laughing aloud as he watched his cousin stumble, rise, change course and run again. The donkey dodged one way and then another, and finally stopped to shake itself off.

"Hold still, you polluter-of-water-holes," said Yeni as he rushed forward to take charge of the beast. The creature waited until he had almost grasped its lead rope, then turned and trotted briskly a short distance farther. Once more, it stopped to shake itself.

"I'll roast you . . . on the first cookfire," Yeni shouted between gasps for air. "And make your ears . . . into a wristlet . . . to show my next donkey . . . what he can look forward to." Panting and wheezing, the conjurer paused to catch his breath.

Iskiir tried to maintain an expression of concern as his own mount carried him closer.

"Catch that ungrateful . . . sack of hay, for me," gasped Yeni, waving his hand at his animal.

"I think he'll be happier if you catch him," countered Iskiir.

Yeni shuffled forward, this time slowly. The donkey's attention seemed to be elsewhere. Step by step, the conjurer drew closer. As he reached for the rope, the beast shook its head and tried to repeat its earlier escape. But Yeni threw himself at the baggage, caught a strap and clung. The donkey dragged him a few paces and then halted in resignation, its head down and its legs firmly planted.

Iskiir laughed silently behind his sleeve, tears of mirth streaming down his face. "When you recover, cousin," he said as soon as he could speak soberly again, "we must find the road." He turned his mount and headed the way they had come. But when he looked out and saw the scraped and gouged floor of the desert, his good spirits vanished. Nothing was left of the track that had been beaten hard by years of travel. And the cairns that marked the route were also gone; not even a tiny bush remained for landmark. "Yeni, we must use the heavens for a guide," he cried in dismay.

"Then you should have no trouble, my young goat-boy. You must have spent your whole life staring up at them." Mounted at last, Yeni rode to his cousin's side.

"To the north, then," said Iskiir, ignoring the gibe. He turned to put the moon at his right shoulder. "With luck, we'll hit the cross-route before dawn. From there, it should be easy to find Lact."

Iskiir was not happy crossing the ruined landscape, a place where nothing remained but the marks made by passing mono-liths. Where, he wondered, were the small holes made by lizards and hares? Where were the thorn bushes that sometimes sheltered a desert grouse? The region had been scoured of every form of life.

Their ride through the wasteland was not long, however. Soon Iskiir noticed strips of ground where stones had not passed. It pleased him to see a small cluster of brush. *Something here has survived,* he thought. The untouched areas widened. Then, suddenly, all signs of destruction ended. "Here's where a de-mon stone first appeared," he said to Yeni, pointing to what seemed to be the start of a track.

"Show me the road," countered his cousin. "At least that's good for something."

"I don't see it. But if we continued north . . ."

"Yes, yes. Well, let's get going, then."

Iskiir was curious whether anything might be learned by studying the initial placement of the great rocks. They had seemingly arrived from nowhere, but that wasn't possible. Something might be learned by examining the border of the disturbed sand. Yet he understood his cousin's haste. If the city's mages hadn't scrutinized these markings while they could, then so much the worse for them. He slapped the donkey gently and went on.

The moon was in the west when they sighted the first cairn, a marker for the cross-valley road. Iskiir whooped his delight as he neared the jagged pile. He dismounted and poked about the desert floor to find a sizable rock, then added it to the tower in gratitude. His direction-finding had been accurate. Here lay the road to the mountains, the path that would take them to Dajnen.

"An hour's sleep, cousin," begged Yeni as he rode up.

"Sleep in the saddle," Iskiir advised. "I'll tie your beast behind mine. Let's not waste the moon."

Yeni swatted his donkey's neck. "This spiteful thing has learned how to twitch just when I close my eyes."

"Then wait until the day heats up and we'll have a real rest."

Yeni grumbled and turned left onto the road. Iskiir could not let himself wonder if he also was too weary to continue. He sighted the next cairn and began to travel. The moon was so bright that he could make out the hoof marks of earlier travelers.

"I see light," said Yeni some time later. Iskiir had noticed a gradual change in the sky from black to gray. But it was the flickering fire on the ground ahead that his cousin had meant. Then Iskiir caught a scent of smoke and his mouth began to water.

A party of four men examined them warily as they neared the cookfire. The hoods of the strangers' robes were thrown back. Their beards were hacked short, bristly and uneven. Iskiir judged them to be mountainfolk driving sheep to be sold on the opposite side of the valley. The bleating creatures, kept in place by a pair of curs, milled nervously near the side of the road. Whatever the travelers had been eating was gone, but a pot of dark liquid still sat on the rocks above the coals. From the smell, Iskiir recognized the brew of dried twistgrass, which bore poor resemblance to coffee. He would eagerly have downed a cup, however, if it were offered; for years he had known nothing better.

One man, the tallest of the lot, stepped forward. The others held their hands close to the curved knives in their belts. Iskiir had placed his own weapon in his sash on leaving the city's jurisdiction, but saw no profit in showing he was ready to use it. "We're peaceful travelers to Lact," said Yeniski. "Do you offer no hospitality to the weary?"

"And what's y'r business in Lact?" the tall one said with a twitch of his shoulder. Iskiir thought he saw the man's hand creeping close to his blade. His own hand touched his weapon's bone handle.

"We're looking for . . ." Yeni glanced at his cousin.

"Dajnen . . . recently of Dahayart. He told me he had family in Lact."

"Dajnen?" Turning to the others, the spokesman shouted the name and waited for a response. "Do we know him?"

The three muttered among themselves. Iskiir thought that these shepherds, too, must have ties in the mountain village; otherwise, why should they be so wary of travelers seeking the place? "You won't find him," said one herder suddenly. "Crazy old fella . . ." added a stubby man who had a wandering eye.

"There . . . ya see? You're not goin' to Lact after all." The spokesman lifted his blade's hilt enough to show the glint of metal.

"As you say," replied Iskiir with a dry tongue. "But tell us, friends of the road, what's happened to my companion Dajnen."

"Why such interest in the codger?" The tall one strode closer.

"I knew him in Dahayart," said Iskiir. "Dajnen . . . helped me once. Now I need to talk with him."

"You? Dahayart?" The herdsman grabbed an edge of Iskiir's kaftan and rubbed it between greasy thumb and forefinger. "Ya look like *city* to me. Sound city, too."

"Dahayart born," he insisted, but his questioner spat into the road in disbelief. *Sound city, too*—what could he do for that? Having unlearned the mountain manner of slurred speech, Iskiir was not sure he could convincingly bring it back. But he knew another way that might prove his kinship with these herders. "Do city folk play the *lailu?*"

The other smiled. "If ya can play 'Woadar's Journey' I might believe you." He snorted to one of his companions, who reached inside his robe and produced a short flute carved from hardwood. Iskiir viewed the grimy instrument with distaste, but quickly brought it to his lips. He had not held a *lailu* since the last day he had cared for his goats; his own flute had vanished in the rubble of Dahayart. He tried his fingers on a few holes of this one and found the fit comfortable.

"'Woadar's Journey,'" the tall one reminded him.

Iskiir nodded and began to play. The tune rose and fell as it told of the ancient herder's quest for the cave wolves that preyed on his flock. Here was the canyon with icy water foaming at the rocky bottom. Here was the crag where the wanderer slipped and tore his leg. Here was the mountainside, lush with wild olives and junipers. And then came the ominous tones at the lair, where sheep bones lay in piles outside the entrance. The music told how Woadar entered the deep cave armed only with a club; within, the whole pack was waiting for him.

Woadar feinted, retreated, and the beasts lunged. The scuffle sounded in a quick melody. They came at him from all directions. He swung the heavy cudgel around and around. Each wound he suffered was a high trill of pain. Each smashed wolf body meant another dying howl. Iskiir blew the dozen death songs that suggested the hundred of the legend. The pack was beaten; not one beast survived. But Woadar, too, was dying, his final cry of victory trailing off into silence.

The former goat-boy held out the instrument to its owner. "So you are a mountain fella after all," said the tall herdsman, showing his yellow teeth. "We do the last part a bit different. Show him, Evey."

The other began to play while Iskiir shifted impatiently in the saddle. This version was at least twice the length of his own. The battle in the cave was unduly prolonged, the former goat-boy thought. He lost track of the number of howls. "A good variation," Iskiir said with little enthusiasm when the song was done. "And now, brothers of the hills," he added, trying to maintain a casual tone, "will you tell us what you know of my friend Dajnen?"

The men stared at the ground and none replied at once. One coughed, raised his eyebrows, and glanced at another. At last the herder with a wobbling eye spoke up. "That codger wasn't long in Lact," he said. "My uncle's a fire-priest; that's how I know about him."

"Priest?"

"Old Dahayart man came to my uncle to take vows. Uncle thought he a strange fellow. Raving about demon stones all the time. Tales to make a peddler blush. But Uncle, he heard his vows and sent him to the smith for his chain."

"Vows . . . chain . . ." Iskiir shook his head in astonishment. "You mean Dajnen's an Appeaser now?"

"Makin' the holy triangle." The man's good eye shifted to the side as he jerked a thumb over his shoulder. "You folks do like pilgrims and ya might find him." The four began to laugh.

"We'll start at Amonib's Tower," said Iskiir, undaunted. The shepherds were already turning their backs to him. He watched them settling around their pot of twistgrass tea. Then, when it was clear that no invitation was forthcoming, he slapped his donkey's flank and rode on past them.

Chapter 5

Following the priestess's instructions, Adeh went out early to the wheat fields. The sun had just risen above the dark stones that stood in the desert beyond. The long shadows pointed ominously toward her and she imagined she could see them creeping ever closer. How long, she wondered, before the barren stretch was crossed? If the grain was not harvested today, she was not sure there would be any left for tomorrow.

She looked at the others who had come for the harvest. Some wore the coarse robes of farm people. This group, all men, stood sullenly together. The others were *daor,* city folk, young people in red-striped jubbahs or indigo kaftans. All these she assumed had been recruited at the temples.

What a strange sight this harvest would be! The farmers did not permit their women in the fields, she knew, holding that they brought bad luck to the land. Yet now there was no time to honor old superstitions.

"Gla!" Adeh recognized a former schoolmate in the throng

that had gathered to receive instructions. She tapped her friend on the shoulder and received a welcoming grin.

"Myranu said you'd be here," said the shorter girl, tossing back her head. "Come, we have to learn to use the reaping knife." She pointed at a thickset man in front who held a short curved blade above his head.

"Grab the sheaf in your left hand and cut like this," he said, bending with a fluid motion and deftly slicing through the tawny stalks. "Tie the bundle like so . . . then lay it aside." He made the job look easy. "Again . . . watch." He went through the steps once more, then asked for someone in his audience to come forward.

Gla quickly volunteered. Adeh wondered if her eagerness had anything to do with the fact that the dark-eyed teacher was coarsely handsome. Gla took the knife and bent to the wheat. Stalks fell in a jumble, leaving no neat sheaf to tie.

The farm people jeered. "Watch more carefully this time," said the instructor. "Now let me take you through it." He placed his hands over hers and guided her through the motions. Gla did better on her second try, losing some stalks but binding up most of them.

"Someone else." The teacher beckoned for another volunteer. One by one he tested them. Adeh, when her turn came, felt her palms dampen with sweat. The knife slipped from her fingers, and she was obliged to hunt for it in the stubble.

"Your grip is wrong," said the dark-eyed one. "Look. This way you won't drop it."

Her face reddened and her palms felt even more slippery. But with the new grip, the knife did not slip. On her third try she tied a near-perfect sheaf.

Soon the newly trained harvesters were strung out in a long line, advancing slowly up the field. Even the farm people had joined in, after much grumbling, but their line quickly moved ahead of the others. Adeh began to feel the strain on her back as she bent time and again to the wheat. When boys came along the row with buckets of water, she was as grateful for the respite as she was for the drink.

Noon came and found her dusty and tired. Her nostrils twitched with the scent of ripe grain; the ache in her back and shoulders was growing worse. There was no shade, and the meager wind carried hot desert air. Never, after this, would she complain about her work in the shop.

All labor stopped briefly as the water boys handed out stuffed roundbreads. Adeh nibbled at the offering, barely tasting the greens and fried dumplings within. Gla, sitting beside her in the field, took a few bites and rested her meal on her knee. "What's next?" asked Gla. "Myranu had no time to explain."

Adeh looked over the sheaves that lay where they had been dropped amid the stubble. "She didn't say much. The threshing will be done, I'll guess, as soon as we're finished here."

"Under the priests' eyes for certain. The threshers will steal half otherwise." Gla took several bites more from her round. "Anyone who can, will steal. Later . . . who knows what a loaf will buy. Better save what you don't eat." The rest of her meal she pushed into a pocket inside her robe and Adeh followed her example.

"Then you believe it, too?" said Adeh. "That we'll all starve in the end?"

Gla interlocked her fingers in her lap. "Myranu said it might happen. It's up to the conjurers now. All we can do is buy them a little time. And sometimes I wonder whose side they really are on."

"Whose side?" Adeh would have liked more of an explanation for Gla's remark, but shouting and waving from the others convinced her that the rest period was over. She turned again to her task, and felt herself slowing down against her will. Her arms felt heavier as the hours passed, her various pains merged together into a single broad ache, and it seemed no longer to matter whether she worked or rested. The farm people finished reaping, then began to gather up the sheaves and pile them onto carts. Yet ahead of the line of city volunteers lay a broad swath of uncut grain. Behind her, the sun was already low. She shook her head, wondering how they would continue.

The dark-eyed leader Haraj urged them on. "Bend and cut, bend and cut." The farm people, almost done with their tasks, were singing harvest songs in low voices. Adeh knew some of the words, but her tongue was too dry for her to join in. Haraj took the knife from her hand and gave her a few moments of relief before passing on to help Gla. It seemed to Adeh that he worked far longer at Gla's station than he had at her own. Bend and cut. The songs of the farm men droned in her ears until she wished never to hear them again.

She worked on, as did the others, and the reaping ended shortly before sunset. The last sheaves went directly from her hands to the gatherers, so that the carts were all loaded by the time the field was cleared. Shielding her eyes against the sun, Adeh glanced back to see what had been accomplished. The cut field, to her surprise, seemed larger than when full of grain. And something else seemed odd. Along the far corner, away from the road, many sheaves lay in heaps, uncollected.

"Gla," she said, pointing out the bundles to her friend. Gla squinted toward the sun. "We've forgotten some."

"Forgotten? It's picked clean," said Gla.

"But it isn't!" Adeh rubbed her eyes and looked again.

"You'd better go home and get some rest," said her friend, turning toward the city road. "Come. Walk with me."

But Adeh shook her head and cut diagonally into the field. When she was halfway across, several farm men began to shout at her. "Off the land, off the land," they said, waving their hands, as if suddenly determined to enforce their old law again. Tired as she was, she quickened her pace. Two of the men began to run after her.

She reached the far corner and swept up a sheaf from the uncollected pile. At her feet lay at least a quarter of the harvest; yet the wagons were leaving this bounty behind. Who had arranged the deception and why had the others ignored it? Determined to ask Haraj, she turned and ran for the road. But the farm men were almost on her; she heard their panting and their grunted curses. She called out to her friends, and waved the rescued sheaf. There was little more she could do, for she

could not outrun the farmers. Suddenly she was tumbled to the
ground, her wind knocked out of her, the men shouting ob-
scenities in her ear. One put his hand inside her jubbah.

Rough fingers clutched at her thigh. Adeh bit deeply into
an arm. A man screamed, and for a moment the pawing ceased.
But the two on top of her, stinking like donkeys, did not give
up the struggle. They twisted her arm, then pulled the wheat
from her hands so roughly that the skin was scoured from her
fingers. Others joined the fray, dark robes and homespun all
in a tangle. Adeh was at the bottom, feeling elbows and knees
and rough hands. She gasped for air as she clawed and kicked
her assailants.

The potter's daughter did not join the threshing that evening.
Bruised and sore, she was taken to Myranu by two acolytes
who had pulled her from the fight. The fire-priestess, seated
at her desk, eyed her with weary curiosity. From appearances,
Myranu had not had much sleep recently. "I want to know
more about what happened," the priestess said.

Merely recalling the incident was enough to set Adeh trembling with both rage and anguish. "I . . . I saw sheaves . . . left
behind," she said, knotting her fists. "I told Gla but she saw
only a clean field."

"All our people saw what Gla saw," said the priestess.

"Then how . . ."

"They hired a second-rank conjurer."

"*They?*"

"The farm people. They weren't satisfied with the fair price
we paid them for the grain. So they had an illusion set up to
cheat us. We know who was responsible; the conjurer will be
disciplined by his Guild. As for you . . ."

"I did something wrong?"

"Not at all. But the fact that you saw through their illusion
will give the magicians something to think about. It shows
their magic is less powerful than they'd like to believe."

Adeh's fingers began to loosen. "I don't think it was much
of a spell."

The priestess shook her head. "I can tell you on good authority the magic was well-laid. Tell me. Have you been able to do this before?"

"Before?" Adeh's thoughts were racing first one way and then another. How could she concentrate on her past? "I . . . I don't see much magic. Just spells in the house to scare off mice. Anyone can see those cats aren't real."

"Not anyone. No. I've seen very convincing false cats." Myranu tapped a long fingernail against the desktop. "I don't know what to say. I'm pleased with you but I'm also worried. There will be others tempted to use trickery to profit from our troubles. One with your perceptions will surely prove valuable. Yes. But there are people who will want you out of the way so they can get on with their treachery."

"Then what . . ."

"Let me think about it. We have some special tasks for you if you've the courage to take them. Now you'd better stay here tonight. We'll put ointment on your bruises and we'll send word home to your family."

"Stay here? But my father . . ."

"He'll understand. I'll send someone to have a talk with him."

"And tomorrow?"

"Tomorrow we shall see. But for tonight, you must stay here for your own safety."

Too weary to argue further, Adeh nodded agreement. The priestess signaled for an acolyte, and the potter's daughter followed the girl down a long corridor to the acolytes' quarters. This was a place that Adeh had hoped never to see, yet now it was a refuge. Tonight she did not even mind her proximity to the temple's heart; indeed, she found comfort in the nearby presence of the Fire. Had the walking stones, she wondered, changed her that much already?

To reach the nearest point of the pilgrims' Triangle, Iskiir and Yeni followed the cross-valley track westward a short way, then turned back to head south. Iskiir ignored his cousin's complaints and pressed on, promising rest when they reached their destination. At mid-morning, the travelers caught their first sight of Amonib's Tower.

"There it is," shouted Iskiir, pointing at the round building that stood a mere three stories tall, and wondering if it had somehow gotten smaller. He recalled his one previous visit to the site while accompanying an old uncle on the holy Journey. To his eyes, the structure had indeed been a tower. But that was before he had seen Tajmengus.

Despite its small stature, Iskiir understood that this lime-stone structure was a wonder of the desert. The blocks had been meticulously shaped, and fitted together without mortar. Even upon close inspection, he knew, it was difficult to find the seams. The Tower's original purpose was to protect the well it covered. In early times the top floor was filled with soldiers, who stood ready to bar the doors against raiding tribesmen. The ancient doors had vanished long ago, and Iskiir doubted there was other than an aged caretaker in charge.

About the building, the young man expected to find Appeasers, for ritual touching of the forehead to the Tower's stone was required of all who wished the gods' favors. As he approached, however, he came first on the queue for water that extended far past the entrance to the well. He saw boys arriving with empty waterskins, while others emerged from the square doorway burdened with filled bags—glistening goatskins that quivered in their arms.

It was not until Iskiir passed the Tower's side that he spotted a single Appeaser, a bent and sunburned man whose nose chain dangled to his waist. Iskiir's pulse quickened with hope, but at once he saw that the man was not Dajnen. The holy wanderer stepped up to the wall and stood before a smooth indentation in the stone. He recited a brief prayer, bent forward to touch the worn surface, then backed away.

Iskiir watched the man depart and wondered where his companions might be. Probably resting from their long walk, he guessed. Should he follow the Appeaser, he wondered sleepily, or first see what lay behind the well.

"Where do we pitch the tent?" asked Yeni with a whine. Startled from his deliberations, Iskiir looked up to see pilgrims, city-dwellers on visit to the holy places, stretched out on their mats in the Tower's short shadow. The cool stripe would soon vanish and leave the travelers to bake in the desert's heat. Only a half-dozen palm trees clustered near the well; the rest of the place was barren. "Wherever you want," Iskiir said. "Everywhere's the same. And I've got to go look for Dajnen." He sent his cousin off with a wave of his hand.

On the far side of the Tower, Iskiir found a large, noisy crowd about the water troughs. Donkeys brayed, camels growled and drivers cursed, as all grew impatient to reach the basins. A dusty youth in a nomad's russet robe stood at the troughs, supervising the watering and collecting his small fee from each driver.

Iskiir took a quick survey of the animal handlers. The small, dark men in skullcaps he knew to be southern traders, Aken. Karbayra comprised at least half the crowd. The remainder were pilgrims—mountainfolk in sheepskins or coarsely woven kaftans, city-dwellers in finer robes.

Finding no other holy men by the well, Iskiir continued toward the scattered travelers who had camped in the sand. A nomad with a bandy-legged camel was hawking rounds of bread. "Fresh-baked. Fresh-baked," he cried. Skeptical passersby shouted in response, "Sandcrack, sandcrack," referring to the hard crusts that travelers made in the embers of their fires. But the vendor pointed to a distant pile of stones that he claimed to be an honest oven.

A second vendor offered soured camel's milk from a skin slung over his back. He seemed to be doing a good business among the city-dwellers, providing a cupful of milk for a small coin.

Another man who caught Iskiir's attention was selling nothing. His head was wrapped in a pale blue cloth; he walked in a slow, fluid motion, staring straight ahead as if in a trance. And close behind him followed three creatures such as Iskiir had never seen—men who seemed both young and greatly aged. On their faces grew fresh beards of youth, yet they walked stiff-legged, one leaning on a staff and the others staggering as if badly in need of aid. Their cheeks showed a youngster's smooth skin, but their hands were gnarled and veined. These awkward three were evidently attached to the sleepwalker, for they clutched often at his robe as he made his unswerving way through the throng.

Iskiir turned from that odd sight to survey the campsites around the Tower. Here, as he had expected, scattered about the fringes of the area, he found Appeasers in number. Most squatted, or sat cross-legged on the sand, robes wound about their legs, backs to the sun. Their headcloths hung down over their faces so that their features could scarcely be discerned. Iskiir had been told that the holy wanderers did not sleep at all, but he had also heard that they slept sitting up with their eyes open. Where the truth lay, he could not learn from atop his mount.

Quickly he found Yeni's white donkey, which stood tethered now beside a frayed black tentcloth. While Yeni snored within, Iskiir staked his animal beside the tent. Then the young man stepped out to make his rounds.

Squatting before one still figure after another, peering into shadowed faces, he did not find his friend. This was no surprise; Dajnen might be anywhere along the Triangle. If Iskiir was to find the former sorcerer, he knew he must make inquiries among these unsociable men.

"Greetings, holy one," he said, bowing slightly in a gesture of respect. "May you know the peace of the Journey . . . and the hospitality of the road." When the wanderer nodded his head almost imperceptibly, Iskiir felt greatly pleased with himself. He had recalled the proper greeting. Now he felt bold enough to press his question.

"I seek one of your fellows—newly sworn. Dajnen of Dahayart and lately of Lact."

The old one, his face cracked and dark, stared wordlessly at Iskiir. His nose chain hung down into his lap, the small brass links piling atop his gray robe.

"Have you seen or heard of my friend?" Iskiir asked again.

The holy one continued to stare. Perhaps this man had taken a vow of silence, or perhaps he had lost his voice from disuse.

"Please, my esteemed one. If you know of Dajnen, will you nod your head?"

The wanderer made no gesture at all. Iskiir sighed and took his leave. One by one, he accosted the other Appeasers and found that several indeed appeared to be sleeping while awake. Many ignored him. A few responded to his pleas, speaking in hoarse whispers but conveying no useful information. Only a single man gave him hope. Whispering the name "Dajnen" he pointed with his thumb in the direction of Karkilik's Throne, the outcropping that preceded the Tower in the pilgrims' route.

This piece of news cheered Iskiir doubly, for he knew that the Journey was taken only in one direction. If the man was correct, then Dajnen could not be far. By heading toward the Throne, Iskiir would meet the former sorcerer along the road.

By the time he finished his questioning, the young man's eyes were falling shut. The sun was nearing noon and he was tempted to take a brief nap in the heat of the day. But the demon stones were not resting. No, he would not linger.

Iskiir was returning to the shelter to wake his cousin when he noticed again the odd group of travelers—the blue-turbaned leader and the three who hobbled after him. The first sickly one wore a nomad's garb. The other two appeared to be Menjians, mountainfolk. This, in itself, made a strange association. And what sort of person was the leader? Iskiir was too weary to bother his head further with the matter. He returned to the tent and crouched beneath his donkey to check its belly band. Regardless of the heat, he was determined to find Dajnen that day.

"Holy traveler . . ." came a chilling voice from behind him.

Iskiir looked up into harsh eyes whose pale blue matched the man's head-cloth. The turbaned one had come after him, and the young man could not break away from the stranger's gaze. He rose slowly, and faced the visitor.

"You ask after someone called Dajnen," the stranger continued, his words spoken carefully and with a subtle accent that Iskiir could not place. "A traveler from a mountain village."

Iskiir had felt the truth spell's grip before, but never with such strength. The force frightened him. There was no resisting; he could only open his lips and answer.

"I . . . seek the one you named," Iskiir replied humbly. He felt the grip grow tighter, like a cheesebag squeezing out whey. Yet his mind was not totally paralyzed; in one part of it he wondered why this magician would use such means to get his answer. Was he trying to aid Iskiir's search? More likely, he had a darker purpose.

"And this traveler claims to be from Dahayart?"

Iskiir was about to explain all, but he held himself back. He could speak no lie, but he might avoid saying more than he must. "He does. He comes . . . from that place."

"And what do you know of his life in that village?"

The young man felt perspiration rolling down his forehead. The question was too broad to miss the essence of the matter; Iskiir could only stall. Yet he feared for Dajnen if he should reveal too much. "He was . . . laughed at in the village."

"And why was that?"

Iskiir sought frantically for a way to break free. His mount, loosely tethered, stood between himself and the shelter where Yeni lay snoring. "The old man was . . . a fool," he said as he began to lean against the donkey's flank.

"Tell me." A throbbing began in Iskiir's temple. He felt dizzy with pain. "Tell me."

"Daj . . . nen. He . . . muttered spells that didn't work. Nobody paid him, so he begged food from the households. The women took pity on him sometimes." A stronger push. The donkey resisted.

"And now tell me why you seek this fool."

In a moment, the stranger would know all. "Because . . . because he did me a service once." He could speak truth and avoid the issue, but soon he would run out of evasions. Iskiir gritted his teeth and shoved the beast once more. Then the donkey brayed, plunging forward to topple the shelter, at the same time kicking out with its rear hooves. One of the blue-turban's followers cried in surprise. Yeni bellowed as poles and cloth fell on top of him. Distracted, the mage looked away from Iskiir, and for the moment his spell was broken.

"Whelp of my uncle!" shouted Yeni as he crawled out from under the wreckage. The kicked man was lying on the sand nursing his leg. Iskiir kept his back to the visitor and tried to approach his fuming cousin to offer a warning. Yeni threw handfuls of sand in disgust, and Iskiir could not get close. Around them he noticed that the commotion had attracted a small group of onlookers.

"Yeni, listen." Iskiir knelt and knocked his cousin's arm aside. "Watch out for the turbaned one," he said in a loud whisper. "He's got a truth grip to squeeze words from the dumb."

The stranger was shouting at his fallen follower, and Iskiir watched cautiously from the corner of his eye. Evidently the mage did not fancy having an audience, for he pulled the man to his feet and retreated, allowing the injured one to lean on his arm. As Iskiir turned his head cautiously to watch their departure, he felt a prickling at his nape. The sensation spread to his shoulders and suddenly a startling change took place in the mage's appearance. The robes and blue headcloth vanished; the one who had worn them was gone, and in his place . . .

Iskiir's mouth hung open. A hulking thing, with a head that was half its body, and talons as long as fingers, was leading the hapless young-old man across the sand. The creature's head was lumpy and misshapen, covered with coarse, pale hair. The body was compact, with a short neck and thickly-muscled legs. Iskiir thought of the frightening tales of his childhood. "Jinn" was the word that formed silently on his lips. Then the vision passed and the turbaned one, in his earlier guise, vanished into the crowd with his charges.

"Y-Yeni, did you see?" He clutched his cousin's arm.

"See what? See the donkeys? You'd better go after them."

"No . . ." Iskiir pointed, but he dropped his arm in despair.

Had Yeni watched the change, he could not have concealed his shock. And none of the other onlookers showed more than curiosity in their faces . . .

On a few earlier occasions, Iskiir had observed what others did not see. Sometimes the visions had proved out, as with the opening into the old ruin. But this time? Iskiir shook his head. No, he was mistaken; the man was dangerous, but not a jinn.

Iskiir's heart still raced from his vision, but he got to his feet. The donkeys had run off in a direction opposite to that the strangers had taken. After a brief search, he found the creatures wandering aimlessly nearby.

"We're leaving now," he announced to Yeni on his return. Hastily, he began to fold the fallen tentcloth.

"You've had too much sun," said Yeni. "Put up the poles again and get some sleep."

"And wait for *him* to come back? He knows we're looking for Dajnen. He still wants to know why."

Yeni scratched at his neck and blinked his eyes sleepily. "What can he do to us?"

Iskiir continued to fold the tent. "I'm not waiting to find out. Dajnen is already on the road from the Throne. I'm going to meet him along the way."

"But I've had no rest!" The conjurer's tone rose in complaint.

Iskiir tied the poles to Yeni's mount and secured the fastenings of the baggage. "Did you see how his followers walked? Not long ago, you can be sure, they were frisky as young goats. He can do that to us . . . and who knows what else."

His cousin still sat on the bare sand muttering. He held out his palm. "Feel the sun. We'll cook."

Iskiir smiled grimly. "I can think of worse deaths." He finished his packing and climbed onto his donkey. "Are you coming?"

At last, his cousin nodded.

They wrapped their heads against the blaze and began the harsh trek southward, traveling in the opposite direction to the pilgrims' route. Yeni looked back often, each time pointing out the absence of pursuers. "That magician friend of yours isn't following us," he reminded Iskiir for the fourth time. "He's probably sitting in the shade now laughing to himself." Then Yeni's eyelids drooped and soon he was asleep on his donkey.

Despite the heat and his own exhaustion, Iskiir did not nod off. Every time his eyes closed, the vision of the jinn jolted him awake. Often around the campfires, the goatherds had vied at telling tales. There were creatures who killed a man quickly, and there were those who enjoyed prolonging the process. And perhaps once he had heard of a creature who sucked life slowly, over weeks and months, but he could not recall the details. Had he seen such a being today?

The road ahead was empty. To the side, the sands shimmered in the heat, the faces of the low dunes rippling as the wind shifted the grains. The air blew as from a baker's oven. No one with sense crossed the desert at midday. No one but a blasphemer rode the Triangle in the wrong direction.

Yet Iskiir pressed on, driven now by fear of the turbaned one's pursuit as much as by his need of the old sorcerer. He hoped that Dajnen would have an explanation of the odd events at the Tower.

From time to time the young man sighted Appeasers, a few walking doggedly through the heat of the day, others sitting in their customary poses by the sides of the road. They seemed to stop anywhere, not even seeking the modest shade of a bush. He halted to question each, though he expected that each in turn would be questioned again by the blue-turban. How else to learn if he had ridden too far? But no wanderer gave news of the man from Dahayart.

In the afternoon sun, Iskiir felt faint from heat. At a brief stop, he drank sparingly, not knowing when they would reach water again. He had not realized how badly their goatskin was leaking, and now regretted passing up Amonib's well. Yeni was asleep on his donkey and Iskiir recalled the old proverb: "Sleepers don't thirst." He did not waken his cousin.

Ahead the dunes grew steeper, and the road more winding

as it found a path between them. The sands were of two colors, silver on the exposed ridges and gold in the deeper pockets; the brightness burned his eyes. It was no use looking back. The dunes blocked his view of the road; a pursuer might be just behind him and remain unseen. He pulled down the head-cloth to shade his face again.

Soon the sands took on new colors. The long, sharp-edged dunes gave way to smaller crescent-shaped piles, some of dark-red or even coffee-colored grains. The road climbed, crossed a limestone ridge that was blown free of sand, then descended to another expanse of gleaming sword-dunes. The heat rising from the brilliant landscape drained the last of Iskiir's strength.

He slumped in the saddle, feeling the donkey's pace slackening. He lacked the will to attend to the beast. His eyes closed. Even the jinn's image could not rouse him now. *What if you miss Dajnen?* a voice whispered, but too late. Succumbing, he slipped into a dream filled with jinns, each grinning at him with dark, knifeblade teeth. They came at him one at a time, jaws spread wide, but each taking just a small piece of his flesh. His fingers went bit by bit, then his arms in many separate slivers. At last the creatures brought out a huge soup pot and lowered what was left of him into it. He hung upside down, his head splashing first into the warm water.

"He's coming 'round," said a throaty voice. "Don't waste any more of that."

Iskiir opened his eye a crack and saw faces, human faces. Wizened features, leathery skin, a jingling of nose chains... *Appeasers!* He lay on his back looking up at them while one wiped a damp cloth across his face. How had he fallen from his mount, Iskiir wondered. Now he was a spectacle, a casualty of the Journey; a third holy man leaned over to peer at him.

"Let me see that one," said the new arrival. "I've met that *bolu* before." The head was hooded in gray, his short chain swinging.

"Daj..." Iskiir winced at the pain of his cracked lips. Yet a long-faced old man he knew was staring at him. "Dajnen!"

"You!" The tired eyes widened.

"I . . . need your help," Iskiir rasped.

"Help?" The voice was suddenly angry. "Why did you follow me here? I'm pledged now. Can't you see?"

"But . . . the stones. New ones around Tajmengus. The city . . . doomed."

"Doomed it is, then."

"But you . . . you had a spell."

"Spell? I think you lost y'r wits when you lost y'r hair."

Iskiir tried to speak again but could not. Someone moistened his lips with the cloth and he gathered what strength he had. "You pushed aside . . . the demon stones. I saw."

"Only 'cause *they* were finished with 'em. Thought we were all smashed meat by then so they put aside their magic."

"*They?*"

"Hethi. Didn't you know?" The other holy men looked at Dajnen and made clucking sounds of concern. Dajnen shook his head. "Nothin' can be done against Hethi sorcerers. Tajmengus attacked, you say? Then forget the place. You might as well take vows and join with us."

Chapter 6

Iskiir had heard Dajnen's words, but refused to believe them. The old one, he was certain, knew how to help Tajmengus if he wished. But before Iskiir could press the matter, he became aware of Yeni's absence. He sat up slowly, then peered about. "My cousin . . ." he said hoarsely. "Where is he?" Aside from the three Appeasers and his own mount, nothing lay before him but bright sand.

The wanderers furrowed their brows at his question.

"A plump man riding with me. He was asleep on his donkey the last time I looked."

"We found you in the road," the tallest Appeaser answered with a shrug. "Nobody else around."

"We were heading in your direction," Iskiir insisted. "You might have seen him first."

The holy one shook his head. "Who travels the wrong way on this road? We'd remember him."

"Then he's lost!" Iskiir considered whether he should hurry after his cousin or first explain the oncoming danger. But if

81

Yeni's donkey had turned back toward the Tower, then surely he would be the blue-turban's next victim. The young man still felt dizzy, but he staggered to his feet and managed the few steps to his donkey.

"I'll have to find him," he said as he awkwardly swung into the saddle. "And when I come back, Dajnen, I have something to tell you. A warning. I don't like bringing such news."

To Iskiir's relief, the holy men decided to rest. By the time he turned his beast about they were squatting by the roadside. With their headcloths pulled around their faces, Iskiir was no longer certain which man was Dajnen. What if he lost the old sorcerer after taking so much trouble to find him? But the wanderers were on foot and the sun was still high. Even if they resumed their traveling, they would not get far.

The young man turned his attention to searching for tracks. Besides his own beast's marks, he saw only footprints of the Appeasers. He and his cousin had separated earlier, but where? He tried to think like a donkey, imagining Yeni's weight on his back as he trudged toward Karkilik's Throne. The line of high dunes ahead offered no promise of food or water. In the opposite direction lay patches of forage and the drinking troughs at the well. Without guidance, the beast would surely turn around.

Iskiir noticed how his own mount quickened its pace as he headed back north. The donkey would be far less eager, Iskiir thought, if it knew about the turbaned man and his group. But, despite his fears, Iskiir urged even more speed.

After a ride that seemed too long, Iskiir spotted no one. Nor did he see on the ground any signs of a second donkey's passing. At last, hoping a view from the heights might resolve the mystery, he left his mount at the base of a dune. Climbing its gentler face, he sank to his calves at every step. Halfway up, he began to pant; the air parched his tongue and seared his throat. He reached the top, fell wearily to his knees, and felt the sand scorching his skin through the cloth. Still breathing heavily, he shaded his eyes and peered out over the desolation.

The images shimmered in the heat, but something caught

his attention. "Ahhh," he shouted with satisfaction. Not far ahead, a donkey was carrying a broad, slumping rider. And beyond the errant beast, he had a good view of the road.

His feeling of relief at locating his cousin vanished at once. Four riders were approaching from the Tower, the first well ahead of the others, the remaining three bunched tightly. Iskiir imagined he saw a flash of blue about the first figure's head. He blinked, but the color was gone. No matter. As the Appeaser had asked, who travels this path in the wrong direction? Only desperate men.

In his haste, Iskiir lost his footing and tumbled down the last part of the slope. He landed in a cascade of sand that sent his donkey scurrying for the safety of the road. Spitting grit and curses, the young man staggered after the beast. Then he was riding, shouting to waken his cousin as he went.

When he caught up with the conjurer, Yeni stared at him groggily and almost fell from his mount. He pointed to his tongue and rasped a request for water.

"No time," said Iskiir, but he untied the slack skin and handed it to his cousin. "The blue-turban!" he said, pointing down the road. "I saw him from the top of the dune."

Yeni almost choked on his drink. "Him again? The sun's got to your eyes." He calmly tilted the sac and took another long drink. Before he could wipe his mouth, Iskiir snatched the bag from his plump hand.

"It's true, you cud-chewer. What's more, I met my old sorcerer. He's not far down the road."

Yeni's eyebrows rose. "Now I do have something to ride for." He reached behind him and slapped his donkey's rump. "Show some life!" he shouted at his mount.

The Appeasers were still sitting as Iskiir had left them, their wrapped faces seemingly lifeless. Dajnen appeared to be in a trance, his eyes fixed on his leathery toes. "So you found him," the wanderer said, without looking up. "Bad luck to ride the wrong way."

"There's someone else coming, too," Iskiir said in a hushed

voice. "He used a truth grip on me at the Tower. A mage with a blue turban, and three sickly followers."

"Blue turban?" Dajnen's head jerked up. "Followers?" he asked in an agitated tone. "What did they look like?"

Iskiir hastily described their youthful faces and aged limbs. The old one's frown deepened with every word. "What did you tell 'im?" he demanded. "Anythin' about me?"

"He . . . found out I was looking for you. Someone told him, I think. He wanted to know what happened in Dahayart, but I didn't say."

"Didn't? How could you help yourself?" Shaking his head and clucking to himself, Dajnen began to rise.

"I said other things. Told him your spells didn't work. Usually."

The old one's mouth popped open and he fixed Iskiir with a furious stare.

"It was true. Most of the time. Otherwise I couldn't have said it."

"What else did you tell the breath-stealer?"

"I . . . I made a diversion. Pushed the donkey into Yeniski's tent. It kicked one of the followers and we got away."

"But *he* knows you were holding back. The Hethi knows. Ahh, what a sheephead I was to get you out of Dahayart." The Appeaser clapped his hand over his brow. Then he moved his gnarled fingers to his nose chain and pushed the small links toward Iskiir. "D'you know what this means?" he asked bitterly. "Fifty links, I'm pledged for. If the buzzards get me first . . ." His voice trailed off.

Iskiir nodded penitently. He was aware of the Appeasers' beliefs. If Dajnen fulfilled his vows by traversing the Triangle fifty times, then his soul after death would rest on Mount Topias. But if he failed, then his spirit would be enslaved to jinns, and misery would be his eternal lot. "I meant you no harm," the young man said in a quiet voice. "But you won't earn your place on the mountain if that mage catches us."

"I saw the blue-turban," Yeni said to the old one in a con-

ciliatory tone. "He looked harmless to me. My cousin's imagination . . ."

"Demons take both of you!" shouted Dajnen. He turned to
look at his companions of the road, but all seemed engrossed
in their own thoughts. "I've got to leave the Triangle," he
called to them. The tallest of the wanderers broke from his
trance to stare at the old sorcerer. "And none of ya can know
where I'm going," added Dajnen. "So tell me three routes
where there'll be water and I'll choose one. But quick. We've
got to get off this road."

The other holy one nodded his head. Iskiir tried to guess
the number of links in his long chain, surely more than a
hundred, enough for an exalted place on Topias. "Three ways
I know," the rough-voiced Appeaser said solemnly. "Go north,
then west to the mountains. Go south to Koloo village. Or east
to Jalween oasis."

"The mountains I can find," said Dajnen. "Tell me land-
marks to Koloo and Jalween."

The other closed his eyes and started to recite. He pointed
one way and then the other, naming peaks on the two sides of
the great valley, describing outcroppings and terrain and sources
of water.

"Enough," said Dajnen. He raised his hand in a cross-fingered
sign of blessing. "Know the kindness of the stranger," he said,
"and the peace of the journey." Then he turned and began to
walk the path toward Amonib's Tower.

"Not that way!" shouted Iskiir. "And you'd better get up
here and ride with me."

Dajnen seemed not to hear. He kept walking steadfastly as
if he were continuing his holy travels. Iskiir trotted alongside
him on his donkey, berating the stubborn man for his folly
until they were out of sight of the others.

"Enough," said Dajnen with disgust. "Get off the path and
I'll ride with you. And when I come back, I'll start my walking
from this very place." He turned around slowly, as if memo-
rizing every wrinkle in the sand. Then he stepped out toward
the unmarked desert.

"They'll see our tracks if we leave the road," Iskiir complained as he reached down to pull the old man up behind him. Fortunately for his donkey, the Appeaser was light. Between the two of them they didn't equal Yeni's weight.

"We'll have to fool 'em," said Dajnen. "What do you say to that, conjurer?" He turned to Yeniski, who sat glumly in his saddle, looking at the ground. "Any tricks in your sack?"

"None for your purpose," Yeni answered testily.

"Can't handle a Hethi?" Dajnen clucked his mocking disapproval. "Thought you city mages knew everything."

"I should be third-rank by now," Yeni said. "Then I'd have bigger illusions."

"We don't need *shopkeepers'* magic," the Appeaser roared. "The illusion's got to have size, but if it lasts till dusk that's good enough."

"I can make a cat that lasts a month," Yeni countered.

Dajnen sighed. He reached out to one of Iskiir's woolen saddlebags, pulled open the drawstring, and fumbled through the contents. "Nothin' but food here," he said grumpily. "But a decent magician could do something even so." He held up a quarter round of dry bread. "This . . . could be a dune to sit on our tracks while we run."

Iskiir stared at the bread and saw no dune. Yet, for a moment, his attention was so drawn to its mottled surface that he lost sight of his surroundings. Then a prickling at the back of his neck warned of an odd vision coming. How, he wondered, could the crust be something else? The prickling spread to his shoulders, to his arms; had he not felt this way while watching the moth in the nomads' market?

Suddenly a tent of goatshair cloth appeared floating in the air, its poles skewed at different angles as it stretched like a huge, black wing. Tassels of yellow thread dangled from its margins. Its doorway was covered by a rug of reds and greens. Yet the tent was incomplete, its ends ragged, as if a huge hand had torn the rest away.

"What's that?" shouted Dajnen in surprise. But by then the tent was gone. Only broken bread remained between the old man's fingers. The sorcerer peered at Yeni and scratched his short beard. "You sure you've got no magic, conjurer?"

Yeni frowned. "Did you see something?"

"Thought I did." He shook Iskiir's shoulder and stared into the young man's eyes when he turned. "What about you?"

"It . . . looked like a tent," Iskiir confessed. "Sometimes I imagine things."

"Karkilik's mane! Maybe we've both had too much sun."

"We can't stay here talking," said Iskiir. "They're coming for us."

"Then ride," said the wanderer. "Let 'em follow us awhile. Maybe we'll have a surprise for them later." He pointed toward the east and Iskiir's mood brightened a bit. Tajmengus lay to the southeast. They would be backtracking rather than leaving the city behind. He had not abandoned his purpose.

"Keep that notched peak in front of you," said Dajnen as they followed the base of a dune. He pointed to the far side of the valley where the gray mountains were barely visible. "Got to get clear of this sand. Just keep riding."

The sun was halfway down from noon, beating on Iskiir's back as he fled its glare. The young man wrapped his cloth around his face, leaving only eyeholes and a space for breathing. Behind him, he heard the Appeaser grunting whenever the donkey lurched. "Easier to walk," Dajnen complained. But he did not climb down to tread the sand.

Iskiir kept looking back at the obvious trail they were leaving. Soon the breeze would rise and blow sand over the hoof marks. But the Hethi mage, as Dajnen had called their pursuer, was probably close behind. Unless they reached hard ground, they could not hope to lose him.

As they rode, Iskiir's lack of sleep made his eyes heavy again. "Watch the peak," Dajnen reminded him, digging his knuckles painfully into the young man's back.

"I had no rest last night or today," Iskiir complained. Groggily, he pulled the donkey back on course.

"If the Hethi catches you, he'll swallow a thousand of your sleeps. You saw the cattle he dragged after him."

"The followers? They could barely walk."

"His spells eat up their lives. That's where his power comes from. A boy goes gray in a month, is bent like me in a few days more. That Hethi will want a strong fellow like you to replace someone he's used up."

"He'll have to look me in the eyes again," said Iskiir. "I won't give him the chance."

"He's got other ways to snare you, *bolu*. Now watch your mark."

Iskiir felt another sharp jab at his back and hurriedly glanced up at the horizon; he corrected his course slightly. "But what do Hethi have against Tajmengus?" he asked. "You said they sent the big rocks."

Dajnen sighed deeply. "I thought you goat-boys told tales. Don't know what else you do nights up in the hills."

"I can tell you a hundred tales of jinns."

"And not one about the Hethi and the Menjian conjurers? The clash at Yag Ravine with a thousand mages on each side?"

"I've heard of Yag," Iskiir admitted. "Our mages against the dark ones. That tale can cost me a night's sleep if I think about it. But we never called the fiends *Hethi*."

"Heth was their leader. What's it matter how they call themselves?"

"But they were all destroyed in the end. Their secrets, too."

Dajnen snorted. "Tell that to the folks we left in Dahayart."

"Then the Hethi have come back?"

"Come to revenge the beating they took at Yag. And this time there won't be any Menjians left when they're through."

Iskiir frowned. "Tell me why the Tajmengan conjurers know nothing of this."

"Ha. Shopkeepers' magic is all they know now. The other arts, what they used at Yag, they locked away. Forbidden arts, they made 'em, 'cause the knowledge was so powerful. But your Guild mages won't believe the Hethi have come back. I know their kind. You can truss up one of those blue-cloths and carry him through the streets of Tajmengus and they still won't believe it."

Iskiir turned to see if Yeniski was listening to the sorcerer's tirade. His cousin's face was covered, so he could read no expression. "What do you say, Yeni?" the young man asked.

"Old magic!" his cousin shouted hoarsely. "No Guildsman will touch it unless he's tired of having a livelihood. They take your rank away if they catch you."

"There's your answer," said Dajnen smugly. "Now swing toward that rusty patch over there."

At last they were coming out of the sands. A field of reddish lava lay before them. Soon they began to climb gently, the donkeys picking their way between the jagged chunks. "From here we could turn down to Koloo," said Dajnen, "or head north to meet the road to the mountains. They won't know which we chose. But we can fool 'em even better by going straight through to Jalween. They won't think we'd go back into dunes again."

"But when can we rest?" whined Yeniski.

"Should be a spring on the other side," Dajnen answered. "Water the donkeys there if you want."

"Water..." The word seemed filled with longing as it fell from Yeni's mouth.

They climbed awhile, occasionally startling lizards whose colors closely matched the rust and charcoal of the rocks. Then they came down the far slope, reaching at last the edge of the lava field. Before them lay an expanse of dry soil marked with sparse vegetation, spiny camel-thorn and a few small acacias. Farther out, Iskiir saw a patch of thick, green herbage. "There's your water," he shouted.

The mounts seemed to scent what lay ahead. They sped forward, pausing at the border of the greenery to lap at a trickle of water that flowed from the ground. About the spring, Iskiir spied footprints of foxes and hares as well as many animal droppings. He dismounted, then helped Dajnen to his feet. The donkeys soon abandoned the meager flow and fell to cropping the coarse grass.

On his knees, Yeniski bent to touch his lips to the water. He made a slurping sound; when he sat up his face was smeared with mud. "Good!" he declared as he carelessly wiped his mouth.

Iskiir saw no way to fill the waterbag from the meager spring. Rather than use what remained in the skin, he, too, bent to sip from the ground. The taste was mildly salty, but better than the goaty flavor the other had taken on. Dajnen merely dampened a finger, pushed aside his chain and moistened his lips.

Yeni, seemingly refreshed, stared at the Appeaser. "Now, what about Tajmengus?" he said suddenly when the old one was done. "You're supposed to tell us how to stop those demon stones. Why do you think we came after you?"

Dajnen glared at Yeniski. "Hethi magic!" he growled. "Do you think you can fight it?" He turned angrily away, put a hand on Iskiir's shoulder, and began to walk. "You . . . come along with me," he said in a gentler tone. "Might find somethin' useful around here."

Leaving the waterbag with his brooding cousin, Iskiir followed the sorcerer across the narrow patch of grass. Grasshoppers crawled between the thick blades, and a green, banded snake slithered across their path. Dajnen seemingly ignored these creatures, but stopped to probe here and there in the black soil with his bare feet. When he found nothing of interest he moved on a few steps. "Look," he said at last, flipping a fallen twig of acacia up with his big toe.

Iskiir bent to pick up the piece, a wrinkled fork covered with dirt.

"Maybe you can see something else in it," said Dajnen. "Remind you of anything?"

"Maybe . . . the staff that one of the Guild mages was waving. But his was made of ivory. And it didn't really look like this . . ."

"Could it be an ivory staff?"

Iskiir stared at him in confusion. "How can one thing be another?"

Dajnen gripped Iskiir's shoulder roughly. "How can a crust of bread be a black Karbayra tent?"

"But..."

"I still got my wits, goat-boy. Yeniski there had nothing to do with the tent we saw in the air. And Karkilik knows, I didn't either. That leaves you, *bolu*. You made the thing appear."

"I..."

"Now I want you to do something with this twig. The same way you made the bread change."

Iskiir threw out his arm in exasperation. "I don't know what I did. All I know is that sometimes I get a prickly feeling. There was a moth in the caravans' market. I saw a face on it and I heard it singing. Adeh saw only a date moth."

Dajnen reached inside his robe and brought out an amulet that hung from his neck, a flat triangle of copper inscribed at its center with tiny black letters. "Look at this," he said, turning the piece over. The back side carried a broad cross-hatched design. "First it looks like this, then it looks like this." He flipped from one inscription to the other so quickly that Iskiir could not see the movement of the copper. "Now take that crust you were holding. It has an ordinary back side that looks the same as its front. But it has *another* side, a magical side, that's a tent. You can't get to that one by flipping it with your hand. You've got to grab it in a different way. Grab it with your mind and flip it over."

Dajnen leaned his arm against Iskiir's back. Suddenly the young man was pitched forward, tripping over the sorcerer's outstretched leg. He shouted with surprise as he landed headlong in the dirt.

"Now look at your twig," the Appeaser shouted.

Iskiir wanted to to do something unkind to Dajnen with the forked stick, but he fought his temper. The old man was trying to teach him something, a trick that might help fight the Hethi. With a groan, Iskiir opened his hand, which was now filthy, and saw that the piece had split through the joint. *Two donkey tails,* he thought.

"Find the *other* side," said Dajnen. "Reach out. Take it with your mind."

Iskiir waited for the sticks to turn into tails but nothing happened. He sighed and stood up, leaving the uncooperative pieces on the ground.

"*Aiii!*" Another blow. Iskiir was suddenly on his back, staring at the cloudless sky. He sat up, this time prepared to attack the holy one with his fists. Grinning cruelly, Dajnen bent over him holding one piece of the broken twig. Iskiir suddenly thought of a long quill pen that Yeni used for writing incantations. For a moment he saw clearly the gray striping of the vane and the ragged tip of the feather. "Satisfied?" Iskiir asked, thinking he had succeeded in the task set by the sorcerer.

"With what? Did you *feel* anything?"

"The hard ground." Iskiir knew that wasn't the answer he wanted. The prickling hadn't been there, and despite his wish to bring it back it would not come. *Enough,* he thought. *I'm no magician.* He was about to rise again, but saw Dajnen tensing for another attack. "Let me try it when you're not watching me," Iskiir said, grasping the stick. As soon as Dajnen turned, the young man flung it away and ran off to catch his donkey. The sorcerer cursed at him, but there was nothing more he could do.

Iskiir insisted that the old man ride the saddle while he perched behind. He wanted no more surprises. And he could bear no more talk of magic that afternoon. Grumbling, Dajnen took the reins and prodded the donkey with his bare heels. They followed their shadows across the plain into drier and drier country. The vegetation dwindled to occasional lifeless stalks. As sunset neared they sighted dunes again.

"Now we can rest until moonrise," said the holy one when they had put several dunes behind them. Yeni fell from his beast and was asleep at once. Iskiir took the trouble to unroll a mat and lay it on the sand. His eyes closed, but it seemed only an instant later he was being shaken roughly awake.

Night had come. A faint light fell on Iskiir's robe and a hand held something oblong in front of his face. "What do you see, goat-boy?" rasped a familiar voice.

"Fleas!" Iskiir shouted, reaching to rub the back of his neck.

He felt tiny things crawling onto his shoulder, but he could not scratch them off. And above him hung a tall palm tree. Had he reached the oasis already? In the moonlight, he thought he saw bunches of dates hanging from the branches. The fronds were still, but he heard the whistling of wind.

"You did it," shouted the old man. "Look. You found the *other* side of that egg."

"Which side? What egg?" The itching vanished and the windy noise ceased. The palm tree disappeared as well. In Dajnen's hand lay a roasted egg from Yeni's provisions.

"Bring it back," Dajnen insisted.

"Bring what?" Iskiir was still groggy from his brief nap. The sorcerer had startled him out of a dream and then tricked him with an illusion.

"The tree, you belching camel. You could've climbed up to pick the dates, and now where is it?"

Iskiir shook his head. "I had nothing to do with that."

"And I had nothing to do with *this*." Dajnen smashed the egg onto Iskiir's pate, rolled it down his forehead, then began to flake away pieces of shell. "Your trouble, *bolu*, is that you've no control. The talent sneaks up on you."

"Talent? I see things sometimes. That's all." Iskiir brushed burnt eggshell fragments from his robe.

"Seeing's the first step. Can't do anything without it. Once you glimpse the *other* side of a thing, you can pull it over. It's the seeing you've got to master first." The sorcerer bit the egg in half.

"How is it possible?" Iskiir tried to recall his other odd experiences. Only at the mouth of the ruin had he heard the windy sound that had recurred this night. Had he made something change back there also? Yeni first saw only a crack, yet Iskiir found a broad entrance with steps.

Iskiir thought of another vision and felt his stomach tighten. "Sometimes I see things I wouldn't want to be real," he said with a shiver. "At Amonib's Tower, the blue-turbaned mage looked like . . . a jinn."

Dajnen sucked in his breath. "You *saw* that? Thank the Fire you didn't drag him across."

"But..."

"A Hethi can make that change for himself. It costs his followers plenty, but he can do it. All the more reason to keep ahead of our friend." He hooked a thumb over his shoulder.

"I need more sleep," said Iskiir.

The old one shook his head. "Sleeplessness will be good for you," he said, clapping Iskiir on the arm. "Now get up. We can reach Jalween before dawn." Then he stood over Yeni and jabbed a toe into his belly until the conjurer, swearing, came awake.

Chapter 7

When the roof door opened, the acolyte who had accompanied
Adeh took a step backward, leaving the potter's daughter to
face the magician alone. The pinch-faced man at the doorway
took her in with a single glance. "Ah, you're the one Myranu
told me about," he said with a faint smile. The red half-moons
of his robe showed that he held second rank with the Guild.
His narrow chin and thin brows left Adeh with no doubt that
he was Myranu's brother. "I am Salparin Jethlu, as you undoubtedly know already. Are you coming in?"

His short beard was neatly trimmed and showed no gray
hairs amidst the black. Had he been dressed otherwise, she
might have taken him for a jewel merchant or a trader in rare
spice. Adeh had studied few mages at close range. This man
was nothing like the clumsy Yeniski who kept rats out of her
father's house.

"I must get back," said the acolyte uneasily. The girl had
guided Adeh to Jethlu's dwelling, but now seemed eager to

return to the temple. With a parting glance, Adeh stepped down into the dim interior of the house.

"Will you eat something?" asked the magician when they reached the central chamber. Adeh saw two women clearing away the remnants of breakfast. Tiny porcelain cups rattled on a silver tray. Behind the women, the walls were covered completely by fine tapestries. And the rugs, with swirling patterns of reds and golds, were far richer than any in her own modest abode.

"We breakfast early at the temple," Adeh explained, after thanking him for his generosity.

"Then let me show you my workroom. We'll talk there about what is to come." He led her to a dark chamber on the ground floor of the house. "We can have light," Salparin said, as he walked along the outer wall pulling cords attached to small hinged panels. Once opened, the row of grillwork windows admitted dappled shafts of daylight. Adeh could now see many stoppered clay jars, some as tall as her waist, lined up along the inner walls of the room. From pegs above them hung narrow strips of copper, iron and lead. On the tidy workbench lay fine tools and several polished gemstones alongside a round bronze mirror.

But her attention was suddenly drawn to a soft chattering noise that came from a corner of the room. Adeh approached several wire cages that hung there, and saw that each held a large moth whose silvery wings were patterned with tiny black dots. She listened to the creatures, certain she heard them whispering. Then she recalled her visit to the market and shouted, "Iskiir!"

The magician turned to her with a puzzled look.

"My friend . . . Iskiir . . . saw a moth at the caravans' market," she explained. "He asked me if I heard it talking. Of course, I laughed at him." In the cage that swung just above her head sat an orange-bodied moth with a tiny woman's head. She could see the mouth move as it sang softly.

"A Karbayra was selling such a creature?" Salparin lifted his fingertips toward the cage. "I would not think so."

"Iskiir said he heard it speak, but I heard nothing. To my eyes, there was only a date moth in the cage."

"Perhaps your friend fell victim to a simple trick. The nomads have conjuring skills. And you, if Myranu is correct, are immune to such illusions. That would explain why you saw the common moth."

"But I can see these . . ."

Salparin smiled. "My *buris* are not illusions. But it puzzles me that a nomad would make such a creature appear." He frowned for a moment. "No matter. Let me tell you why I keep these creatures here. With their aid, I can communicate rapidly with my colleagues in Permengord." He lifted his hands toward the cages once again. "I've already sought advice about our problem with the stones."

Adeh's eyebrows raised at the mention of the capital city of the Sultanate. *Permengord*. The mere name was enough to raise goosebumps. In that distant place resided not only the Sultan of the Menjians, but also the greatest magicians of his realm. "Have . . . have you learned anything?" she dared ask.

"I was told to suspect foul play from within our city. Someone may have created this threat of stones merely to profit from it. Later, when the boulders vanish, a certain unscrupulous person will be both wealthy and a hero."

"How could such a trick be done?"

The conjurer shook his head. "So far, I can only guess. But I assure you that the stones are solid. They push aside whatever's in their path, and they will crush us all if they aren't stopped. Whoever is behind this uses knowledge that the Guild has long kept hidden."

"Hidden?" she asked uneasily. Iskiir had spoken of a disreputable sorcerer he once knew, hinting that the old one possessed arcane lore.

Salparin lowered his voice. "I tell you this in confidence. A handful of men in Permengord have studied the old texts. One was my mentor, and he passed to me a few of the ancient practices. But even my longtime teacher hesitates to name the source of our trouble. At first, I, too, suspected city mages, but now I'm far less certain."

"Then what can we do?"

"If a city mage is to blame, then we must find him. And even if outsiders have sent the stones, they may well have an agent within Tajmengus. So we must locate everyone who stands to gain from this crisis, and that's why I need your help. Conjuring has been used to steal grain and will be used again. Together we must catch these culprits, and learn if they also are involved with the demon stones. But if no one within the city can explain the stones, then we'll notify Permengord at once."

"Notify . . . the Council?"

"I gather you've heard of Permengord's Council of Mages. If I achieve nothing else, I'll alert them to the true nature of this attack. The other cities must be prepared." He picked up the mirror from the workbench, stared at it briefly, then placed it in a new position next to a cluster of carved jade beads. Adeh noticed how carefully he adjusted its alignment. "Come," he said. "I want to show you something in the stable."

The conjurer lifted a heavy bar and pulled open a thick door at the rear of his shop. Three well-fed donkeys greeted him with a chorus of braying. He could not make himself heard until he delivered a mound of hay to each stall. Above the beasts, a row of narrow windows similar to those of the workroom admitted light and air. "Look over there," said the mage, when at last the animals were busy chewing. He pointed to the wall by the outer door. "Do you see anything?"

"Saddles hanging."

"Look in front of them."

Adeh caught a movement, then suddenly stepped back in surprise. By the doorway stood a creature, nearly transparent; now she could see its yellow shaggy hair, its stubby forelegs with their huge claws, its fanlike ears and blunt snout. The beast reared up on its long hind legs, opened its mouth and blew a tongue of flame at her face. Feeling a blast of warm air, she threw herself against the opposite wall.

"Have no fear," said Salparin. "It's an illusion and harmless. Most people panic at the sight of the creature. I have no trouble with thieves here. But you'll notice that I've kept it odorless, so the donkeys barely pay attention to the thing."

"To me . . . it's almost invisible."

"To most of us, it appears far too real. And your reactions prove that you're not fully immune."

Adeh remained with her back firmly against the wall. The creature's mouth opened again, and she shuddered at the length of its fangs.

"There are other illusions you'd find more convincing," Salparin added. "But I'm not trying to discourage you. I know you have a rare talent. What I hope to do is develop it further."

"Must we . . . discuss it here?" To Adeh, the longer she watched the beast the more solid it became.

Salparin gave a quick smile, then led her back into his workroom. "You've learned something already," he said. "Once it catches you, the image draws you in. You have to look past it, concentrate on the edges until they start to fade." He picked up the bronze mirror from his bench and held it in the palm of his hand. "This has been charged from a spell set into the jade. Come. Sit over here and tell me what you see." He pointed to a stool that stood before a low bookstand. With one hand he closed and lifted a slim volume set there; with the other, he placed the reflector on the stand.

"I see only the mirror," said Adeh. She heard a sharp ringing noise, then turned to see the magician bringing a lit oil lamp. "How?" She had heard the mages could strike fire in an instant, but she had missed her chance to observe how the trick was done.

"Not important," said Salparin, waving away her curiosity with a pass of his hand. "Keep your gaze on the table. *Now.*"

Adeh screamed as a cobra leapt up from the bookstand. She felt tied to the stool, as if she could never get free of it. The hood flared and the scales glistened. The neck swiveled, first turning to display a pattern of eyes behind the hood. Then the true eyes found her as the fangs whipped around. The snake struck; she broke from her trance and kicked free of the seat.

"It should be no more convincing than the stable beast," said Salparin.

Adeh did not look back until she collided with the tall jars that lined the walls. "Maybe . . . not," she admitted, feeling the quick drumming within her chest. "But the surprise . . . was greater."

"Surprise always benefits a weak illusion," the mage replied. "But now, you must go back to it. Study the edges. Try to make them fade."

"I can study the thing from here," Adeh replied. The cobra lay coiled around the mirror now, its head only slightly raised.

"Please," said Salparin, his hand on her shoulder gently pushing her toward the stool. "You can be sure that Myranu won't let me harm you. Now find the thinnest parts of the image and scrutinize just those."

As the serpent's hood flared again she tried to pull away, but Salparin was holding her firmly in place. *What would a mountain woman do on meeting such a snake?* she asked herself, hoping for courage from Iskiir.

"I see something," shouted Yeni, who had taken the lead. Dawn had come, and now the conjurer rode a dozen lengths ahead, eagerly seeking the promised oasis. "Feather palms. Look!" he said, pointing east.

Iskiir groggily raised his attention from the long morning shadows. Dajnen still rode in front of him, blocking the view. The young man leaned out and squinted; perhaps his cousin was right this time.

"It's Jalween," said Yeni with conviction, slapping his donkey's rump. "Hurry up, you weed-eater. There's food and water waiting for you."

The other mount also seemed to sense the message. As the creature picked up speed, Iskiir was forced to grip the beast more tightly with his legs. His muscles were cramped and the skin of his thighs rubbed raw. Never before had he ridden so long in such an uncomfortable manner.

"Don't get careless here," warned Dajnen. "We'll stay on the outskirts as much as we can. Too many people pass this way."

Iskiir shut his eyes and tried to ignore the donkey's bouncing and the growing heat of the sun. Soon he would have fresh water and maybe even a patch of shade for the tent. He would sleep . . . if Dajnen let him. But after that he must squarely face this Hethi problem. Surely the old man knew more than he had admitted.

When Iskiir looked out again, he saw scattered clusters of green poking through mounds of sand. The stalks were more numerous ahead, and farther out he saw heads of palm trees, their boles half-hidden by the terrain. Yeni's donkey stopped to crop at spiny leaves. "Not yet," fumed his rider, but the creature ignored the threats and blows until it had reduced the coarse plant to stubble. Iskiir's donkey caught up with Yeni's, and the cousins continued side by side in silence.

The ground had been dropping gently; suddenly the contour changed, sliding quickly into a broad depression. Iskiir shouted with surprise when he looked down at the long bowl of Jalween, its sandy bottom thickly dotted with greenery. Date palms of various ages grew everywhere, some with tall trunks that were bare beneath the crown of fronds, others with short cones topped with feathery clusters.

"Look!" said Yeni, pointing to a small compound surrounded by a fence of tied twigs. Several crude dwellings lay within; the rest of the space was so crammed with plantings that Iskiir wondered how the occupants could come and go from their houses. He recognized bean vines twining on a tripod of poles, saw small golden fruits dangling from a branch that hung out over the fence. He was tempted to ride by and pluck those within reach.

"Bear away," whispered Dajnen. "No need to give 'em a good look at us."

Iskiir gritted his teeth and swore softly. The taste of the fruit had almost been on his tongue. But Dajnen's advice was prudent. He turned to follow the rim, advancing along the eastern periphery of the oasis. Here the dwellings were spaced irregularly, each surrounded by a similar fence and each a center of lush growth. Perhaps, Iskiir mused, a private well lay hidden within each enclosure.

Soon the riders passed a small herd of goats being driven by two boys to forage farther out. The animals had just been watered, Iskiir suspected. With his eyes, he followed their tracks back down into the bowl. Did Jalween have surface water, he wondered, or only wells? If the latter, then someone would have the chore of pulling buckets for the donkeys.

At last Iskiir saw below him heavily beaten paths and a crowd of animals and nomads. The shouting and singing of the people about the public well was a sound that many travelers would welcome after hours of desert silence. But the young man knew nothing of the local tribes and by now was leery of all strangers. Perhaps Hethi lived among them.

"I'll take the donkeys," said Dajnen. "You two stay off the paths. Pitch y'r tent over there and stay inside."

"But . . ." Iskiir wondered whether the aged one could handle the heavy bucket.

"Someone'll always help a holy man," said Dajnen. "And nobody takes a good look at one of us."

Iskiir shrugged, climbed down and leaned against the saddlebags for support. His legs were so shaky that he could barely stand. Yeni slid from his own mount and pulled the short tentpoles free of their wrappings. Iskiir fumbled with the ties, let the tentcloth drop to the sand.

Here, most of the bushes had been eaten to the roots. He looked in vain for any source of shade, finally flopping down on open ground to wait for Yeni. As if working in a dream, the two raised the cloth and crawled beneath. A brisk wind might pull up the hastily set pegs, but Iskiir could not worry about that now. If he was lucky, Dajnen would be long at the well . . .

It was not the old man who woke him. "Come quick, come

quick," said a child's high-pitched voice while mischievous hands tugged at Iskiir's legs. Before he could rouse himself, he was pulled out into the sun. Iskiir shaded his eyes and saw a pair of dark-skinned young boys, one in a tattered robe that dragged along the ground, the other wearing only a loincloth. "Your friend in trouble," said one youngster. "Say you pay me come get you."

Iskiir's mouth was parched, and the waterbag had gone with the donkeys to be filled. He groaned, rolled to his knees, and stood up painfully. There was a commotion by the well, and he could see that Dajnen was in the middle of it.

"Say you pay me," insisted the youth, tugging at his arm.

Iskiir reached for the small purse within his robe and took out a coin. The boy in the loincloth snatched it from his fingers, and the two ran gaily back down the slope. Iskiir made sure his knife was in its usual place, then did his best to hurry down after them.

As he descended, the acrid scent of camel urine rose from the heated sand below. Small boys guarding full waterskins stood back from the well while older boys led goats or camels in to drink. The animals bleated and moaned as they clustered about a long leather trough hung on a wooden frame. The cistern was merely a hole ringed by a single course of stones. Leaning over the edge, a half dozen Karbayra youths, two of them girls, took turns dropping and pulling buckets to keep the trough filled.

Dajnen stood arguing loudly with another youth, a tall, lean fellow who held the halter of Iskiir's donkey with one hand while pushing the open palm of his free hand at Dajnen's middle. Iskiir had heard of nomad disrespect for Menjian beliefs, but hadn't imagined such coarse treatment of a holy man. As he approached, he was unable to comprehend a word of the tirade.

"*Bolu!*" The sorcerer glanced up with relief. "This one hasn't heard of charity. Says he'll keep the donkey if I don't pay f'r using his trough."

"I should've guessed," said Iskiir. Appeasers, he knew,

forswore the use of money. By using the nomads' basin, Dajnen had tripped his own snare.

The youth turned to Iskiir and began to jabber in the Karbayra tongue. Quickly Iskiir took out a coin, but this failed to satisfy him. The nomad continued to shout and gesture, pointing first at one donkey, then the other, and then at his friends working the buckets. He went through the motions of drawing water, wiped imaginary sweat from his brow, and pretended to pant. Iskiir was outraged at the demands, but far too tired to continue the argument. He placed another coin in the brown palm and his donkey was released.

Then, as he turned to press his way through the throng and back up the slope, he was met by a piercing pair of eyes. *Not possible*, Iskiir thought as he vainly tried to turn away from the blue-turbaned head and its fierce gaze. He had not seen this man in the crowd before. How had he hidden? And was this the same mage he'd met at the Tower? The answers did not matter.

The Hethi held him with a force that seemed unbreakable. This was more than a truth grip; Iskiir's whole body was rigid. He felt his mount's lead rope slip from slack fingers, but could do nothing to retrieve it. He saw youngsters turning to stare at him. The one in the loincloth who had pulled him from the tent grinned broadly, showing his missing front teeth. And the mage advanced, stepping slowly, his long, narrow features showing no emotion.

Stop him! thought Iskiir furiously and without hope. At the Tower he'd been able to move enough to unbalance the donkey; now he felt like a sheep trussed for holy sacrifice. He watched the Hethi come closer. Children scrambled from his path, one dropping a toy made of two bent twigs.

"You come with me," said the mage in a compelling voice. The man's lips did not move, and he stood a dozen paces away, yet Iskiir heard his words inside his head. The blue-turban halted and the voice came again. Between the two men lay bare beaten ground, a zone that neither animal nor human dared enter now. Iskiir felt his foot move forward of its own accord.

"Come," said the throaty whisper. "Your destiny is to serve me, and that is all you will ever care to do."

Another foot advanced. Was there no weapon he might turn against this demon? The knife was within easy reach, yet it might as well be lodged in the distant mountains. "Closer!" demanded the mage. Iskiir thought he would scream aloud with his efforts to disobey, but his legs moved again toward the turbaned one.

Would no one aid him? Yeni lay asleep in the tent. Dajnen, among his vows, had forsworn any practice of his meager magic. And the onlookers, the rowdy nomads, viewed the scene as a spectacle. None would care to help him, he knew, nor would any risk the mage's wrath.

Iskiir helplessly stepped forward again. His eyes remained centered on the Hethi's, but he could see somewhat unclearly the space around the man. His thoughts turned to the toy that had fallen near the mage's feet; the twigs had been tied into interlocking hoops. Seeking to break the compulsion, he tried to shut out the mage and see only the bent sticks. "Be pleased I have chosen you," said the voice. "I have passed up many others." The young man felt his neck prickling as he kept his attention on the toy.

What of Dajnen's strange ideas? Suppose one could seize this simple piece of handicraft and turn it to something else? As Iskiir continued to concentrate, the prickling spread to his shoulders, and suddenly the Hethi began to frown. "Now you must come..." said the voice, but another sound, a whistling of wind, rose and the words trailed off.

Iskiir found he could keep the voice at bay if his attention remained with the tied twigs. The eyes still stared into his, but they no longer mattered. Something was changing; the toy appeared to grow. The droning became louder, and suddenly the Hethi was no longer visible, his figure blocked by a fence of narrow planks.

Iskiir's mouth hung open as the nomads set up a clamor. A compound, similar to those at the edge of the oasis, had sprouted beside the well. Tall plants rose thickly above the top of the

fence, some bearing spiny black leaves while others were mere
stems surrounded by barbed thorns. Iskiir had never seen so
unpleasant a garden. From within he heard a frantic rustling
while branches shook. Someone—surely the Hethi—was
caught in the enclosure and trying to break out.

The young man was slapped out of his daze by Dajnen,
who pushed him forward and thrust his donkey's rope back
into his hands. "Quick," said the Appeaser. "Unless you brought
some demons over along with the garden, he'll be after us."

There was no time to ponder the strange apparition he had
loosed. Iskiir stumbled up the slope, then knocked down the
tent with a single blow. By the time Yeni had untangled himself
from the wreckage, Dajnen had arrived with the second donkey.
Iskiir still heard the strange wind in his ears, but the sound
was dying. And now the Hethi had evidently recovered from
his surprise, for he was beginning to speak again. "Come back
to me," the coarse voice demanded.

"No time to pack," said Dajnen as he pushed the young
man into the saddle. "Catch up to us if you can," he told
Yeniski. Hastily he climbed up behind Iskiir.

The fat conjurer looked wildly about, first at the shambles
of the tent and then at the commotion by the well. Seeing the
others departing, he mounted his beast as if he were sleep-
walking.

"Your service is mine," said the Hethi voice. "I have only
to claim you." Iskiir felt alien sensations, frigid hands that
touched him in places he could not name. Something was
pulling him back; he felt an urge to climb down and run to the
mage.

"Help me with this accursed fence," said the voice. "A few
blows with a heavy stone and I'll be free." The young man
saw himself battering at the planks. He imagined his joy as
the turbaned one emerged from confinement.

"I'm coming!" he shouted, as he tried to pull his foot from
the stirrup. But a hard hand clamped down on his leg.

"Ride, you camel's bladder," said Dajnen. He swatted the
donkey and the beast began to trot.

Chapter 8

The power of the voice faded and Iskiir no longer needed restraint to stay in the saddle. Dajnen, riding behind him, relaxed his grip.

For a second time, Iskiir realized, he had managed to evade a Hethi. How long he could keep ahead of the turbaned ones he didn't know, but for now the donkeys were moving briskly. And if he could escape the sorcerers, then perhaps he might even learn how to stand and fight them. If only he could get enough sleep to clear his head . . .

"How was the blue-turban traveling?" Iskiir asked the Appeaser as they followed a track into the desert. He glanced back, but saw no signs of pursuit. Perhaps the mage had been confused by the multitude of paths about the well.

"By camel. He was bringin' the beast in to drink when he trapped you."

"Then he wasn't the mage I saw before. That fellow was on a donkey. And you say this one's mount hadn't been watered yet?"

"Was bringin' 'er in," Dajnen said. "She was moaning with thirst, too. Otherwise, I . . ." His voice trailed off.

Iskiir noticed the hesitation in the old one's voice but did not pursue the matter. For at the mention of water his long thirst asserted itself again. "Did you . . . manage to fill the skin?" he asked throatily, dreading the answer. He turned back to see the old one shaking his head with regret.

"Then we've got to find water along the way. And soon."

"You've got a choice," said the wanderer. "Go back and face the Hethi. There's plenty of water there."

Iskiir wondered if the gods would punish him for pushing Dajnen off into the next clump of thorn bush. "If I knew how to fight him, maybe I'd chance it," he said defiantly.

"You might stand against him. Look what you did with the twigs."

"I don't know what I did back there," the young man complained. "I was lucky. What if I'd found myself inside the compound with him?"

"That's why, when you reach for the magical side of somethin', you've got to *look* first. Have a peek so you know if you want it."

"You might as well tell the donkey to grow another tail. I don't understand this magic of yours."

"Can't be as bad as all that. Listen to me. We'll practice again as soon as we can stop."

"Practice? I can't even keep my eyes open. I've forgotten what it is to sleep." He gazed out at the dry terrain. Only a few leafless acacias and prickly bushes broke through the nearby sand. Small red crescent dunes showed in the distance, and far beyond them rose the dark tips of the Ajur range. His mind began to wander as he nodded, woke with a jerk of his head, then dozed again. "It's the prickling at my nape," he muttered the next time the donkey bounced him awake. "I always feel that first, just before the vision comes. It creeps down onto my shoulders. Then I sometimes hear whistling."

"Stop your ears," said Dajnen.

Iskiir scowled and wondered if the sorcerer had understood.

"Like this!" The young man suddenly felt a horny thumb in each of his ears. "That'll keep out the noise so the change doesn't come till you're ready. That way you can *look* first and then decide what to do."

"Maybe. But the trouble is . . . I still don't know how to bring on the prickling." The donkey bounced onward and Dajnen offered no advice on that matter. Iskiir felt himself nodding once more.

"Tell me about every one of 'em," said the Appeaser with a slap that brought Iskiir miserably awake. The young man did not want to talk; his lips were dry and his tongue was thick. Dajnen handed him the near-empty goatskin and he limited himself to a tiny swallow. "Now," the old one insisted. "Talk and then you can sleep."

Iskiir rubbed at his eyes. Within his robe, he was coated by perspiration. His body felt as if it were suffocating, yet he knew that the day's heat would parch him if he opened the garment to let his skin dry off. Dajnen poked him in the ribs, and at last Iskiir tried to gather his recollections. He thought he would do anything to keep the old man quiet awhile.

There had been the moth at the market, the entrance to the ruin, the bread that became a tent . . . Iskiir described every detail he could recall, and mentioned also a few earlier incidents. But none of his visions had come before Dahayart's siege, none before the illness that had stolen his hair.

"It seems your magic came with your shiny head, *bolu*," said the former sorcerer with a laugh. "A fair bargain, I'd say."

"I'll give you both," said Iskiir, "if you rid us of the demon stones."

"The talent'd do me no good," said the old one wistfully. "Not after my oaths. And you won't get any use out of it till you learn some control."

Iskiir's eyes shut again. "How . . ." he said, half-dreaming.

"Chew on this while you're driftin' off. It all has to do with your concentration. Focus. Attention. That's what you're going to practice."

"After my sleep we'll talk about it." Iskiir glanced back

once to check that Yeni's donkey was following, then closed his eyes. The holy one seemed to need no rest at all. Let him keep watch for the Hethi, Iskiir thought. Let him keep Yeniski from getting lost again...

When the former goat-boy came awake, noon was long past. Dajnen now went on foot, holding a donkey rope in each hand as he trod a path that was now barely discernible. The ground was no longer sandy, but hard and thinly graveled. The beasts' heads hung low, and each of their steps seemed labored. Yeni snored on.

How far had they traveled while he slept? To Iskiir's eyes, the jagged Ajurs seemed no closer. And the likelihood of finding a well before they reached the mountains was not good. He reached back and felt the goatskin, shaking it in hope of dislodging some water from its folds. There was enough for each traveler to have a swallow; he must save that for now.

Along the path Iskiir saw occasional clumps of gray-green saltbush. Dajnen was permitting the donkeys to browse when they wished, even making small detours toward the greener patches. This was necessary, Iskiir realized, for the beasts had not been adequately fed. He would have climbed down to ease the load, but he did not think himself capable of walking.

Ahead, the hilly landscape was varied by occasional rounded outcroppings of limestone. Here and there a lone acacia offered a small patch of shade, but Dajnen showed no inclination to stop traveling. The sun still burned mercilessly, and Iskiir could think of nothing but water. The camel-riding Karbayra were known to travel ten days between wells when necessary. Following a nomad path, one had no assurance of finding anything to drink along the way.

Iskiir thought he might fall from the saddle. He tried to clutch the pommel, but felt himself slipping to the right, then to the left. He had heard tales of drought, of men without water feeling their blood thicken until it no longer flowed. In Dahayart he had known thirst, but never with this intensity. At his besieged village there had been rainwater to catch, and shade...

He tried to force his thoughts elsewhere. He studied the contours of the boulders along the way, their edges soft and their surfaces scoured smooth. In some he thought he saw faces, inhuman visages that seemed to mock his plight. *No comfort there*. He turned from studying the rocks to the small bushes and trees that dotted the area. In hollows he saw bunches of coarse grass. Tamarisks, occasionally showing feathery flower clusters, appeared in increasing abundance as the riders descended a gentle grade.

Iskiir rubbed his eyes and looked around again. The plant life was surely more abundant here, in the small gully, than anywhere in the surrounding land. The eroded bottom must have carried a watercourse at one time. Perhaps a shower had fallen not long ago and a few puddles remained.

Suddenly he noticed three fire-blackened stones in a triangle, remains of an old pot fire. Someone had camped here. There were camel droppings scattered over the sand, and more pellets lay to the side of the path . . . "Water?" he rasped, trying to get Dajnen's attention. The Appeaser halted and looked around skeptically.

Iskiir could ride no longer. Where the droppings were thickest he saw a white crust on the sand. He slid from his mount, took a few steps, staggered and fell. To stand again required more effort than he could spare. He crawled forward on hands and knees towards a salt-encrusted slab of rock. Only a few steps away, he thought, but his crawling made such slow progress! Then he was crossing the white stain, feeling the salt stinging his scraped palms. At last he fell forward, his hand dangling over the edge of a hole cut into the exposed limestone.

Was it possible? He felt the solid edge of the well and no longer doubted. "Bucket!" he tried to shout, but only a whisper emerged. Once more he pulled himself forward, this time to hang his head over the narrow shaft. The air from below felt cool on his face, and he smelled brackish water. *An ancient cistern*, he thought, as he noticed grooves worn into the stone by countless bucket cords.

"You've got good eyes, *bolu*." Iskiir could not turn to watch

as the Appeaser unpacked the leather bucket and dropped it
into the shaft. He heard a soft splash far below, then reached
down and did his best to help with the rope. Dajnen took merely
a sip. "All I need," he said.

Sitting up slowly, Iskiir tipped the bucket to his lips. His
hands trembled and the container nearly slipped from his fingers. He took three great swallows before he noticed the bitter
taste. Beyond his control, the contents of his mouth sprayed
onto his robe and dribbled into the sand.

"Water?" said Yeni sleepily. "You found some?" Iskiir was
debating with himself whether to risk another draft of brine.
His cousin dismounted heavily, reached down a meaty hand
and lifted the bucket to his mouth. Saying nothing, Iskiir awaited
his reaction.

To his surprise, Yeni sniffed cautiously before drinking. He
dipped his finger in, set down the bucket, then scrutinized the
water dripping from his fingertip. At last he touched his tongue
to a single drop.

"No!" shouted the conjurer. "We can't drink this." He looked
around fearfully, as if expecting hostile company. Then he
untied the waterskin from Iskiir's donkey. "Help me fill it,"
he said. "We'll be rich."

Iskiir wondered if the sun had cooked his cousin's brains.

"Quick," said Yeni. "We've stumbled on the Acurlat well.
I'm sure of it."

"Acurlat?" asked his cousin in disbelief, his tongue still foul
with the water's taste. "Then where..." he asked weakly,
recalling the tales from the market. "Where are Bermegi...
and his guards?"

"Asleep?" Yeni suggested. Iskiir watched the conjurer fum-
bling with the mouth of the goatskin and could not think what
madness possessed him.

"We'll need that skin," the young man argued. Somehow
they must search on for another well. Even the poor donkeys,
he was certain, would not drink this water. He leaned on his
hands, gathered his strength, and managed to rise. If he could
reach his mount, perhaps they might continue...

Then Iskiir saw a sudden motion; he felt something sharp pressing against his back, at the same time saw a dark hand bring a blade to Yeni's throat.

As Adeh followed Salparin through the alley behind the temple, they came upon armed men who did not resemble the Bey's guards. The youths, talking together in low voices, seemed ill at ease with the curved swords that hung from their shoulders. They stood at each side of a doorway that opened into a side chamber of the temple. A steady procession of grunting men were unloading sacks of grain from carts that clogged the alley. Adeh recognized a few faces from the wheat field.

A tall man with slate and chalk tallied each sack as it was wrestled past him. He nodded when he saw Salparin, and the guards paid no attention when the mage led Adeh inside. What this room had been used for in the past, she could not guess. The ceiling was vaulted, and the plastered walls bore large rectangular patches that were white against the gray background; possibly tapestries had recently hung here.

The room was slowly being filled, with sacks piled as high as Adeh's head. "See how they leave space between the rows," said Salparin. "That way, they can inspect later for vermin and rot." The air was heavy with the scent of laborers and coarse sacking. Adeh would have preferred to hurry back outside, but Salparin took her down one of the narrow pathways. A man with a fat stick of charcoal was marking crude figures on the bags. "Those numbers will help us discover if any are missing," the mage explained as they squeezed past.

In the center of the room, near the doorway, Adeh noticed that the bags had been stacked to make a rough stairway. Several of the workers were demonstrating its usefulness by climbing to the top of the heap, waving, then quickly coming down. To Adeh, this seemed a game with no serious purpose. "The inspectors can get a good view from up there," the mage said. "We're taking no chances on thievery. Even if the demon stones are stopped, the grain we're putting away will have to feed us for a long time."

Adeh nodded. She knew that the outermost farms had already been scoured by the monoliths. And without the goats and sheep supplied regularly by nomads, meat was becoming scarce within the city. The wheat must be preserved. But she wondered how thieves would get past locked doors, guards and inspectors. By trickery, perhaps. Any of the sweating men unloading sacks might be an impostor, a mage in disguise or someone working under a conjurer's orders.

"We'll return when the outer door is sealed," Salparin said. "Then we'll know the full tally." He led her back outside, nodding to the guards in passing. Small children in the alley were dodging about the feet of the laborers to pick up whatever loose bits fell from the sacks. One guard shouted at them, but the youngsters doggedly continued with their scavenging. Adeh doubted that any would come home with more than a handful of kernels.

"What sort of person would steal from the temple?" Adeh asked when they were clear of the noisy crowd.

Salparin walked with his head down and his hands behind his back. "Someone who misjudges the seriousness of the situation," he said. "Someone who feels he has plenty of time to make amends to the gods later."

Adeh glanced at his downcast eyes. She was aware that even now most residents viewed the stones as a temporary inconvenience. But only a wealthy person could afford to hire the magical services needed to carry out thievery. Who might that be?

The conjurer caught at the wheat field, she knew, had revealed no clues to the identity of his employer. He'd been found rigid—poisoned—when the Guild's questioners reached his cell. So the mystery continued.

"There are families whose fortunes have fallen in recent years," continued Salparin pensively. "And don't forget the vicious rivalry between the Tarkilus and Reenenus. One clan may think the other conjured up the stones for its own profit. The first then rushes to gain the early advantage." He shook his head. "Who can account for greed?"

By the time they reached Salparin's street the shadows were
lengthening, and people were scurrying to reach their homes
before dark. "More practice," he informed her. "You'll try to
master the cobra. And tonight you can stay with my women."

"I've seen enough of that snake," Adeh answered irritably.

"I want you to see *less* of it. That's your task." They trudged
up the stairway to his roof and the mage tapped at the doorway
until a servant admitted them. "Down to the workroom," he
said firmly.

Adeh hesitated near the threshold while the mage used his
fire trick to light three lamps. She stared up at the moth cages,
hoping that Salparin would question her interest. When he said
nothing, she gathered her courage and spoke. "You say you
send messages to your friends with these insects. I would like
to send a message to Iskiir."

Salparin's brow furrowed for a moment. "What do you want
to tell him?"

The two nomad captors spoke not a word of Menjian. They
roughly bound the travelers' wrists and ankles, treating the
holy man no more kindly than the rest. Then the Karbayra
dropped to the ground, to loll at the base of the bushes that
had concealed them. From time to time they chatted in low
voices and pointed at the motionless landscape, but Iskiir could
make no sense of their words. They were waiting, but for
whom he could not say.

As the wind came up, the captors pulled up the hoods of
their burnouses and tied the cords loosely at their throats. Iskiir
had seen many nomads at markets, and at the watering places,
but these seemed a different breed. Their skin, stretched tight
against their cheekbones, looked tough as saddle leather. The
man who seemed to be the chief bore a scar that ran from his
forehead to the bridge of his broken nose. He was the one who
glanced at Iskiir most often, always muttering the same unfamiliar word. Perhaps, the young man thought miserably, it
was the Karbayra term for *bolu*.

The guards had with them a small black and white goatskin.

Each time they passed it for drinking, they made a point of smacking their lips and muttering what sounded like praises to their gods. The chief seemed to enjoy pausing as if about to offer the bag to Iskiir, then laying it aside with a grim smile.

The captives said nothing. Though he lay on the ground like a trussed goat, Iskiir managed to twist his head for an occasional glance at the others. Dajnen appeared to be in trance, his lips moving in silent prayer. Yeniski glowered at his cousin with such an intensity that the young man could feel the force of his rage.

But far worse than the conjurer's gaze were Iskiir's pain and thirst. The salt water had left his lips and throat even more parched than before. And the growing cramps in his belly from the foul water threatened other unpleasant effects. For comfort he tried to think of the Tajmengans, and especially of Adeh. For her, he had willingly risked everything, even the wrath of the well-keepers and the sickness from their water. What did his own suffering matter? Somehow he must get free or the city was lost.

Again the nomads drank, and the young Menjian could not keep his eyes from their waterbag. He could feel its weight in his hands, taste its soothing contents. Suddenly the back of his neck began to tingle and he was startled so that he quickly turned his head away.

At once he recoiled from the thought of doing magic here. He was yet a novice at this trick of causing changes, and Karkilik alone knew what the *other* side of the goatskin might be. What if it brought harm to himself and his companions as the spiky garden had nearly done? He must *look* first, but with his hands tied, he couldn't try Dajnen's suggestion of stopping his ears if he didn't like what he saw.

Yet, he could not remain idle while the nomads chose his fate. Iskiir brought his thoughts back to the waterbag and reflected on what he'd learned from his visions. There seemed to be a relationship between the common and the magical side of a thing. The piece of bread that looked like a folded cloth had turned into a tent; the tied sticks had become an enclosure whose fence was bound with cords. As for the egg, he could only think of the vague resemblance between its shape and that of the dates that hung from the tree. He wondered if he might guess the nature of the *other* side of the waterbag.

Too many possibilities arose. The shape suggested an out-cropping of weathered stone. The contents made him think of a water hole. And the patches of white goat hair amidst the black suggested snowcaps that sometimes appeared on mountains above Dahayart. None of these alternatives struck him as plausible, but he could rule none out.

Another idea came to him. He might focus on the skin and let the change begin. Then, when he heard the rising wind, move his gaze and thoughts firmly elsewhere. That way, he would have a glimpse of the *other* but the change would be undone. Iskiir wished he could consult with Dajnen first, but dared not chance that the guards might understand. He did not even know if he could work the spell again.

The waterbag lay at the chief's side while the nomad relaxed. Iskiir studied the sac, noting every crease and wrinkle. The ends were tied off with thick black thread; the neck was closed with leather thongs. The young man tried to forget his thirst, his aches, his misery. In his mind he stroked the skin's matted, dirty hairs. The prickling began...

The whining followed, and he braced himself to turn away as soon as he got a glimpse. But instead of a dramatic change, the bag merely puffed up and turned a ruddy color. Its surface, slick and moist, suggested a bloated internal organ of a beast he could not name. The fleshy bladder pulsed as if something were trying to get out. Its sides fluttered first in one small place, then in a dozen.

He had forgotten to stop himself! Now he was caught by the thing, as incapable of turning from it as from the Hethi's gaze. The wind droned in his ears, and he thought that if his hands were free he might still win back the original goatskin. The blood-colored sac was parting, tearing. A rush of dark fluid poured onto the sand, and a multitude of black squirming limbs showed through the breech. A smell of burning sulfur fouled the air.

Suddenly the scarred nomad leapt to his feet and pulled out his weapon. A few of the crawlers had latched onto his russet robe, but he knocked them off and then began hacking at them with a long blade. The pieces kept squirming, and some uprighted themselves for a new attack. Each creature's leg was paired with a huge pincer that waved in the air, and even a broken body looked dangerous. Iskiir tried, but could not turn away.

The crawlers were emerging from the sac in greater numbers. The other nomad staggered forward with a heavy rock. He avoided one cluster of pincers, then managed to smash the rock down on the transformed goatskin. He howled with pain as dark fluid splashed his feet. A half dozen mutilated creatures were already swarming at his middle. And the chief was dancing in the sand, slapping at spidery limbs that now covered his arms. One creature had reached his throat.

Iskiir felt a blow. His head was knocked sideways and then he fell facedown. Freed of the sight that had held him, his instincts took over. He began to twist from side to side, moving through his furious efforts only a hand's-breadth at a try. Maybe the nomads would satisfy the demon-crawlers' appetites. Tied as he was, he might squirm far enough to be safe . . .

The sounds of the battle were suddenly drowned out by Dajnen's voice. The old one began roughly crooning a watering song, and the nasal voice kept Iskiir from hearing even the whining wind. What was wrong with the old sorcerer? Why waste his breath when he could be trying to escape? The perspiration flowed thickly down Iskiir's face, but for all his efforts he had barely moved himself.

Then he realized that the tingling was gone. Dajnen's singing stopped; the whistling sound, too, was gone. Did that mean the spell had ended? The enclosure he had brought over had remained, at least long enough to permit the escape from Jalween. Fearing he might be entranced again by the sight, Iskiir dared not glance back to see what had happened to the ruddy sac. Once more he fought his bonds.

"Enough, *bolu*." The sorcerer spoke in a low whisper. "It's gone back. Look for yourself."

"Gone?" Iskiir felt his blood pounding in his ears, but there were no more sounds of struggle; reluctantly, he turned his head. The nomads were cautiously pulling their squashed waterbag from beneath a rock, and the sand was wet with its contents. Clucking to himself, the leader held up the ruined skin. The other guard, looking equally perplexed, put his foot on the rock and studied a large red welt that reached to his ankle. He spat a gobbet of saliva onto the discolored skin and rubbed it gently. The first guard began to inspect the swellings on his arms and hands.

Iskiir turned and realized that Dajnen had squirmed close enough to kick his head with his tied feet. Had the Appeaser not found a way to distract him, the creatures would have finished their work. And Yeni would have slept through it all, waking perhaps only as the black limbs swarmed over him. The young man glanced once more at the remains of the goatskin, then closed his eyes and fell forward with relief.

"There's no doubt you have a talent, *bolu*," the old one said. "Next time, be careful how you use it."

Chapter 9

The guards did not return to their places near the captives, but squatted instead beneath a clump of tamarisk. They spoke to each other in low voices, and frequently rubbed at bites on their legs and arms. Their discomfort, thought Iskiir, was meager repayment for their ill hospitality.

From time to time, the guards glanced nervously at the Menjians. Whether the nomads attributed the strange attack to their captives or to some malicious passing jinn, Iskiir didn't know. But the two kept their distance. And Iskiir was not tempted to try his magic again. Later, perhaps, if he could get his hands free...

The afternoon passed and no one else appeared at the well. How long, the young man wondered, would this waiting continue? Just before sunset, he saw the nomads rise; from behind, he heard footfalls that grew louder. Raising his head, Iskiir caught sight of a caravan approaching and thought that Bermegi's raiders had arrived and that now he would learn his fate. Yet Iskiir was puzzled. The nearest camels appeared sturdy but not built for speed. From their saddles hung bulky sacks, baskets and tools. He could not imagine these laden beasts racing across the sands.

The lead rider dismounted and unpacked a small bucket and a stout, narrow-mouthed clay jar from his baggage. Throwing back his hood, he displayed his untidy mane of gray, and a bulbous nose that seemed to cover half his face. He strode with the strength and assurance of a far younger man.

The guards' chief, with hostile wariness, followed the visitor as he approached the well; the two greeted each other coolly. Surely this was not the raider chieftain who had just arrived. Perhaps the caravan had merely happened by, and its leader would take no interest in the Menjians.

At the well, the two began a conversation of quick phrases and replies. At first they spoke calmly, but after some time the newcomer became angry. Leaving his equipment, he stalked back to his camel and returned carrying a curved sword in its scabbard. The chief guard drew the blade and studied it in the failing light.

The newcomer kept touching the hilt, pointing back to his caravan, and waving his arms. Whatever he was saying seemed to make little impression on the guard. The latter sheathed the weapon, laid it by his side as if accepting it, then pointed to Iskiir and the others. He uttered what sounded like additional demands.

The gray-haired one turned to call angrily at his men. He paced and fumed about the well, then began to beat his chest with his fist while he waved his hands in the air. The scar-faced one stood firm.

At last the visitor turned to Yeniski and shouted, "Menj? Menj?" He opened his mouth and gestured at his tongue.

Yeni, who still lay where the nomads had dropped him, did not answer.

"You go us," called the rider. Turning, he gestured at the caravan and watched while several men slipped down from their camels. "For Bermegi, I keep you," he continued to the captives. "Keep you till he come." Iskiir raised his eyebrows.

So this was how the guards would rid themselves of the tres-passers and still fulfill their duties. He wondered how long it would be before the raider chief caught up with the caravan.

A half-dozen men advanced on the captives. Two bent to work on Iskiir's wrists and ankles; he felt the knots loosen. The nomads lifted him onto his donkey, then pushed his face forward and tied his arms tightly around its neck.

His chin was pressed against the stubble of mane and he could not see ahead. With difficulty, he turned to watch Dajnen being led away, perhaps to be placed on a camel. From Iskiir's other side he heard grunts and words he took to be nomad curses. He twisted his head and saw the Karbayra struggling to put Yeni on his mount. Three men fell back under the weight. Then one stood up, drew a knife, and began to shout at the conjurer.

Yeni lay in the sand, slack-faced and evidently dazed. The leader came over to assist with his modest knowledge of Men-jian speech. "Up, you. Up," he said. Yeniski did not budge until another caravaner brought the tip of his blade close to the conjurer's stomach. Then, with his lips pursed and his eyes half-closed, Yeni heaved himself to his feet and into the saddle. With a chorus of calls, the nomads closed in to tie him down.

The men, all but the leader, returned to their mounts. Iskiir's attention remained on the large-nosed one, who lowered his bucket into the well. He drew it up carefully and waited until the guard was holding the jar over the cistern before he began to pour. The gray one gave the bucket three quick shakes to extract any lingering drops. Then he twisted a cloth-wrapped stopper into the jar's mouth.

By the time the caravan was moving, dusk had come. Iskiir found himself in the rear, his donkey led by a frizzy-haired youth who kept jabbering at him, occasionally stepping back to poke his fingers into the captive's ribs. Perhaps the youth was merely curious, or possibly he was showing a harsh form of friendliness. Iskiir did not know the nomad word for "water," but he thought he might try to communicate his need. He opened his mouth and stuck out his tongue in imitation of a dog's panting.

The youngster came closer. In the gloom, Iskiir could barely make out his rounded features. "Ergar," said the boy, pointing to himself.

Iskiir did his best to gesture with his chin, then hoarsely said his own name before repeating his pant.

"Iskiir *kest*. Iskiir *kest*," the youth shouted as if he understood the Menjian's thirst. But he merely clapped his hands, then grabbed the donkey's rope and hurried to catch up with the rest of the party. As he alternately loped and walked, he repeated the phrase with evident delight.

"Ergar *kest?*" whispered Iskiir in a moment of silence.

"Ergar *ekest*. Ergar *ekest*," came the singsong reply.

The ride continued through the cooling evening air, and Iskiir did not know how much time had passed. His face kept bouncing against the donkey's mane until he was certain his skin had all been rubbed raw. His back and arms ached more at each step.

All sense of time had fled. The caravan had stopped, but Iskiir couldn't guess how long his donkey had stood at its tether. Around him were the sounds of pitching camp—the pounding of stakes and the cries of the tent raisers. He smelled smoke—cookfires.

"Iskiir *kest?*" said Ergar's voice somewhere behind him. Suddenly the bristly neck of a goatskin was thrust against his mouth. In his awkward position, as much dribbled down his chin as reached his throat, but what did that matter? The water was mildly salty, and stank of its container. Never had he known such a welcome drink.

At last several nomads freed him from the donkey. They allowed him to squat to relieve himself, then led him to a small, unfurnished tent where again they tied his legs. Dajnen and Yeni had arrived ahead of him; in the flickering lamplight he saw their limp forms stretched out on the bare sand.

The ones who had brought him stood aside, while a brawny

man with thick lips and a lopsided, rounded face entered the
tent. In the near-darkness, Iskiir thought the man resembled
young Ergar. "I am Odeema," he said, poking his chest with
his thumb. "I keep you safe for Bermegi." Iskiir's eyebrows
raised at the nomad's Menjian speech. "You. You. You." He
pointed to each captive in turn. "You try get away, I cut off
the less important parts first." He grinned as he pulled a short
knife from his belt. "So long as you still can talk, Bermegi is
happy."

"But . . ." Yeni's voice came out in a hoarse whisper. "We'll
pay for the water. My . . . my cousin thought it was for drinking.
How could we know?"

The nomad scowled and sheathed his knife slowly. "If matter
of payment only, the buzzards already feast on your eyes." He
looked behind him and muttered to someone outside the tent.
Turning back, he added. "Instead, it is *you* feasting at *our*
expense. But thank Bermegi for that when you see him." He
smiled and backed outside.

A wide-eyed young girl brought in a bowl of pale liquid.
Timidly, she held it before Iskiir. Under the gaze of his new
captors, the young man sipped. *Soured camel's milk*. The taste
was unfamiliar—mildly bitter, salty and cool. His thirst and
hunger drove him to sample it again. Then the girl moved on
to Yeni.

The conjurer pushed himself up to a sitting position, took
a deep draught of the contents, and smacked his lips. She
moved again, and Dajnen, too, found the strength to sit up and
drink. The girl made three rounds, then hurried from the tent.
Iskiir heard breathless chatter at the entrance, and then a second
girl came in carrying broken pieces of bread.

Even the bits of sandcrack loaf, overcooked and smoky,
tasted good to Iskiir. Dajnen took only a few bites, but the
plump conjurer devoured all that remained. Finally Ergar, chattering incomprehensibly, gave them briny water from a goatskin. The meal was done.

The guards tied the captives' wrists together and laid their
bodies out like spokes of a wheel about the center tentpole.

Then the nomads took their oil lamps and withdrew. Iskiir watched the tribesmen settling down before the open doorway of the tent, their broad backs to the captives, their faces toward the flickering cookfires.

For a few moments there was silence within the tent. Then the young man heard a soft shuffling as Dajnen twisted his body, snaking slowly closer to Iskiir. The Appeaser swung his hobbled legs, then heaved his middle, until at last he could whisper in Iskiir's ear. "You can get us loose," he said, "with your magic."

Iskiir grimaced. "After what happened at the well, you want me to try again?"

"I told you. Before you bring the *other* side of something into this world, *look* first."

"But I can't stop myself if I don't like what I see. And I can't see anything at all in the dark."

"At dawn then. But think about it. We'll leave 'em somethin' to remember us by." Dajnen began to hitch his way back to where he'd been placed.

"Whelp of my uncle . . ." Yeni hissed. "May jinns clean their teeth with your bones." But by then Iskiir was too weary to be kept awake by any talk.

It was not Dajnen nor his cousin but the sound of hammering that woke Iskiir. From outside the tent he thought he heard the rush of air from a bellows and the rhythmic pounding of an anvil. He tried to shut out the noise, but despite his concentration he could not recall his vanished dreams. In his sleep he had been with Adeh; that much was certain. And now he could not even picture her face.

Swearing softly, he lifted his head to gaze out past his captors, who still sat at the doorway. Other nomads were stirring in the early light, several carrying long, snakelike roots dug from the hollows. Ergar trotted by, then retraced his steps to peer in at the captives. "Iskiir, Iskiir!" he shouted cheerfully. Even that loud call was not enough to wake the others.

A shout came from outside and the boy scurried away. Iskiir could not hold his head up any longer. The sand beneath him had turned cold, and he shivered in the morning air. Suddenly, Odeema's deep voice startled him.

"My pigeons sleep well?" The Menjian looked up at the round-faced nomad. Now a smith's hammer dangled from Odeema's sooty hand.

"Tell us what you want," said Iskiir. "If not money . . ."

"I want nothing. Bermegi wants."

"It's not about what happened at the well?" Iskiir had intentionally framed his question to include the trespassing as well as the magic.

The sturdy man shrugged. "He gives orders. We want his water, so we do what he asks."

"But he must have a reason."

Odeema frowned and pursed his thick lips. "He has trouble with Menjians. Soldiers, maybe. He thinks you can tell how he lost twelve men." He gestured with his hammer. "Poof. Gone. Not even bones left behind."

"Soldiers?" Iskiir knew how the Bey's patrols were laughed at in every village; no one believed they had any effect on raiders. Yet twelve of the desert warriors were gone. The Menjian suspected that only sorcery could explain such a disappearance.

"If you tell what you know," said Odeema, "maybe he lets you die quick." Seemingly in thought, the nomad tapped the hammer against the back of his hand. "Think well, my pigeons, and spare yourselves pain."

As soon as Odeema was gone, the young man saw Dajnen stirring. "I can guess what happened to those raiders," Iskiir muttered.

"Don't bother your head with it, *bolu*. Worry about gettin' us away." The former sorcerer evidently still had hopes for Iskiir's questionable talent. He lifted his bound arms. "What can you do with these ropes?"

"Make a donkey tail and put it on your backside," replied Iskiir testily. "For all the good it will do."

"If my hands were free, I'd teach you how to answer." The old man breathed heavily and Iskiir could feel his angry eyes.

"But instead," said the Appeaser, his tone shifting from gruff to persuasive, "I'll show you how to stop a change you don't want. Even though you're trussed like a sheep."

"All I care about is magic to help Tajmengus."

"You're a long way from y'r city, *bolu*. And Bermegi's got other plans."

Iskiir sighed, admitting to himself the truth of the old one's words. "What do you want me to change?" he asked in a more docile tone. The sand in the tent was bare. Should he try the tentcloth or the poles? Could these things be turned into weapons?

"There's a scorpion sleepin' next to Yeni," Dajnen said hopefully. "Might do somethin' with that."

"I . . . might . . ." But first Iskiir checked about his own body for the pests. Finding none, he wriggled closer to the holy man until he, too, could see the scaly, pale-green creature nestled in a fold of his cousin's robe. What sort of "other" side could he expect of such a small and dangerous thing? A sword with remarkable powers, perhaps, encrusted with green jewels and gold? Or a beast a hundred times larger and more venomous than the scorpion? These thoughts filled him first with hope and then despair.

Dajnen proceeded to narrow the gap between them until he lay beside Iskiir. "Here's how we'll do it," said the sorcerer. "When you feel your pricklin' start, you say 'hold' and I'll count ten heartbeats. Then I'll kick you like I did at the well."

"How do I know that'll get my attention?" Iskiir's skepticism lasted only a moment. "Ow!" he cried as Dajnen demonstrated his technique. The sorcerer was surely related to a donkey, Iskiir decided.

"Try it now," Dajnen insisted. "That raider could come any time."

Iskiir admitted to himself that the scheme might succeed. He began to perspire despite the morning chill. Focusing on the scorpion, he tried to shut out the sounds of his cousin's snoring and the banter of the guards as they shared a meal outside the tent. But the camp held too many other distractions.

The nomads hurrying by cast long shadows that flickered across Yeni's robe. Camels moaned and coughed. A child began to sing. Iskiir put the sounds aside and thought only of the sharp tip of the stinger. He imagined the tail uncoiling, rising, preparing to strike. His prickling started . . .

"Iskiir! Iskiir!" The boy raced into the tent. Seeing the object of Iskiir's attention, he reached down fearlessly, plucked the creature from its bed, and flung it out over the heads of the guards.

"No!" Iskiir shouted.

Ergar seemed to take Menjian's word "no" as his name for the scorpion. *"Asit* no! *Asit tebr!"* the boy cried gleefully when he saw the pest spitted at the tip of a guard's knife. Then, when the excitement was over, he sat down next to Iskiir and looked up expectantly. He held out his thumb. *"Heff,"* he said, then pointed to Iskiir's thumb and waited to hear the word in Menjian. *"Heff."* The former goat-boy shrugged and replied.

The language lesson was brief. A morning meal, identical to that of the previous evening, was served by a new pair of girls. When that was done Ergar departed, and the guards again tied their captives to the pole.

"Now we have somethin' else to try," said Dajnen when the nomads were gone. He rolled his body, then dug at the sand with his toes until he pushed out two crusts he'd secreted. "One of these may work."

Iskiir eyed the remains of the meal dubiously. What could come of bits of bread, he wondered. But his thoughts returned to Adeh. He dared to hope that the stones were not yet past the city walls, that he still had time to halt the demonic attack. But first, he must free himself. "Get ready," he told the sorcerer.

"Whelp!" said Yeniski in a cold whisper.

"Enough from you," Dajnen warned. Then Iskiir tried to regain the feeling of intense concentration he had nearly attained with the scorpion. What might he find on the other side of Dajnen's crumbs? Perhaps a mist, or a sandstorm to cloak an escape. He fell deeper into his trance.

"Iskiir, Iskiir!"

Dajnen spat a curse. Wearily, the young man let his cheek fall onto his hands. He let out a deep breath and waited to see what Ergar's interruption would be this time.

"Iskiir, man look you," the boy told him in a combination of words and signs. He stood tall and strutted in place, stamping his feet three times. "Bermegi come."

The guards hurried into the tent. There was no time for the Menjian to prepare his thoughts. He and his companions were cut free from the pole and roughly pulled into sitting positions. The guards withdrew behind the captives just as the newcomer strode through the doorway.

Bermegi was not a big man, though he made the others seem small in his presence. One eyelid hung half-closed, as if the right side of his face were sleepy. But the other eye was merciless in its probing. His cheeks were hollow, his nose thin as a knifeblade. And his bushy brows, dark and brooding, gave his face the look of a thundercloud.

"Where my men go to?" he demanded, pulling his long curved sword and planting it in the sand between his feet. "Tell me quick or tell me slow, but you tell me all the same."

Silence. Iskiir did not dare look sideways at his companions.

"Menjians! Your soldiers take my people. Where they go?"

Again silence. There was an obvious answer, and if Dajnen would not speak ... "It must be Hethi," Iskiir blurted out. "Blue-turbaned mages. They took your men to be their cattle."

"Hethi? You pluck your brains from thorn bush?"

Iskiir felt his tongue dry up in his mouth. Yet at Amonib's Tower he had noticed a Karbayra in the blue-turban's group. "I've ... I've seen ..."

The raider shouted something that Iskiir did not comprehend, then held up his hand for silence while he conferred with the tribesmen who stood nervously behind him. After a brief exchange, he turned back to Iskiir. "You want die a small piece at a time. That your choice."

Dajnen cleared his throat. "The *bolu* is less donkey than he seems."

"And what are you, with chain in nose to make gods laugh?"

"Hethi need power," the old one continued, undaunted. "They're tryin' to crush Tajmengus, so there must be others missin' besides your men. Maybe whole tribes vanished."

"Do we lose tribes like hawk drops feathers?" Again, Bermegi spoke with the nomads from the camp. Their gray-haired leader frowned and waved his arms, but the raider pressed his point until the other seemed to concede. As the gray one spoke with his head bowed, Bermegi's eyes widened, he crossed his arms and raised his chin.

The raider put his hand on the hilt of his weapon as he returned his attention to the captives. "Two caravans gone. You tell who does this."

"Hethi!" said Dajnen.

Bermegi lifted his blade and pointed its tip at the Appeaser's throat. "Straw-eater! If Hethi to blame, then why they have business with *you?*"

Dajnen blinked once and did not answer.

"I meet Hethi on road," the gaunt one continued, his voice betraying a hint of uneasiness. "He gives me his stare, and he asks for news of three Menjians. One fat, one old, one bald. I say nothing; I know nothing. But *now* I find them. You tell me his business and then I feed you to jackals."

Dazzled by the long weapon, Iskiir managed to rouse himself from stupor. "Was he on camel or donkey back?" he whispered.

The steel tip swung from Dajnen's throat to his own. "Do I slice you up first," Bermegi growled, "for having business with that camel-beater?"

"He trapped me at Jalween . . ."

"Then you confess?"

"He . . . tried to make me one of his cattle. Suck my life out—the way he's draining your men. I stopped him for a little while. Stopped him with magic." Iskiir felt dizzy. He closed his eyes and thought he was losing his balance. He must not fall on Bermegi's sword.

Then he heard a swish as the weapon was again sheathed

in sand. He looked up at the nomad's expression which some-how combined curiosity and rage. The half-closed eye seemed to have taken on new life. "What you know of magic? Acurlat *mine*. All its power, *mine*."

"We need no water f'r our magic," said Dajnen.

"No? And what spells of yours can stop Hethi?"

Iskiir doubted that Acurlat's guards had told anyone of the crawlers' attack. What proof could he offer other than another risky experiment? "I . . . can show you," he offered in desper-ation.

The raider frowned, then suddenly began grinning slyly. "So," he said, tapping the side of his head with his long finger. "Now I have plan. You give me fun and *then* I skin you. You show tricks and I show true Karbayra magic. Then I know your lies."

Yeni cleared his throat. The talk of conjuring, Iskiir thought, had reminded him of his profession. "What if . . ." said his cousin. "What if our magic is more powerful . . . than yours."

Bermegi showed his teeth, and Iskiir counted three gaps. "If yours more powerful? Ha, ha. Then we go find your Hethi friend. *He* know how to take care of you."

Chapter 10

Not long after sunrise, Adeh approached the spire at the northern end of the city. She had promised to look for Iskiir every day from the top of a fire-temple, but as a wearer of the amulet she now felt reluctant to climb the sacred steps. Fortunately, there was an alternative. With her companions in the Binding handling many official functions, she could gain entrance to the city's watchtowers. The Bey's guards had fled their posts; the Binding's makeshift corps had replaced them.

The streets were busy despite the early hour—women hurrying to queue up for water or bread before the lines grew hopelessly long, merchants opening their shops to sell what little they could offer. As she walked, Adeh clutched the covered cage tightly by its small handle, lifting it over her head when the crowds grew thick. From time to time she glanced at her parcel, recalling the silvery wings within and wondering how such a delicate creature could survive the rigors of the desert. Yet Salparin had assured her that the *buri* could fly as far as Permengord. Certainly Iskiir was much closer than that.

Whether the small messenger could *find* Iskiir was a different matter. At Salparin's advice, she had held the cage on her lap and shared everything she knew of her friend—how he walked, his musky scent, the feel of his strong hands. "Open your secret thoughts so the *buri* can catch his spirit," the mage told her. In the end, perhaps she revealed too much. In addition to love, she spoke of her service to the temple and her growing feelings of duty. The ceremonies before the great bowl did not attract her. But she was learning that one might serve the Fire in many ways.

Now she stood at the base of the slender limestone spire. She was acquainted with the guards who stood yawning at the stairway's entrance; they waved her past with barely a glance at what she carried. Quickly she spiraled around the outside of the tower with but an occasional grasp of a handhold for reassurance. At the top, leaning on the flat roof's balcony, she found two men of the Binding. The first was Haraj, who had helped her in the wheat field; the second was a shorter man she had also seen there. And below, in the near distance, stood the demon stones. She tried not to think how close they were.

"Adeh, you seem recovered," said Haraj, who had become the north quadrant's leader. "I hear you've business with the mages now." He glanced at the covered cage, but did not frame a direct question.

"There's more trickery afoot," she answered. "Tonight we may catch someone at it."

"If you catch the one who did *this* to us, he won't see another dawn." He pointed toward the jagged boulders, and she was reluctant to follow his finger.

"How . . . how much more time?"

"They're playing with us," Haraj said darkly. "They're drawing out our suffering."

"Even so," she said, "this tower will not stand three more evenings."

He lowered his voice. "Two is my guess. After that, who can say what'll happen? People are losing their wits already." He pointed toward the northwest. "Over there. Look. Last night some donkey-brains tried climbing out with a ladder. When the rock jumped, the ladder tipped them off. One climber fell underneath and was crushed. Today we'll see more of that."

Adeh shook her head, trying not to believe what she knew to be true.

"And the bakers say they've no flour," Haraj continued. "Though we know the temples give out enough every evening." He clucked in anger, then turned back to lean over the parapet.

"Still, we must do what we can," Adeh said resolutely. "And today, with your permission, I'd like a few moments here alone. At Salparin's request."

The two evidently knew of Myranu's brother, for they nodded respectfully when they heard the name. The men took to the staircase and she heard them step partway down.

Unobserved now, she lifted the dark cloth from the cage. Use of the *buri* lay outside official Guild magic and Salparin had insisted on secrecy. But Adeh could see no harm in the delicate creature. She looked into the cage to admire one last time the beauty of the flyer, its head covered with golden fur, its wings the color of moonlight. As she opened the catch to the wire door, the creature crawled forward on insect legs, opening its woman's mouth in a sudden burst of song.

"Free . . . let me free . . . let me free . . ."

The voice was quiet but intense; Adeh did not think the others heard it. The *buri* paused for a moment on the balcony as if getting its bearings, then lifted its wings and flew lazily around the tower. It dipped once, hovering just out of Adeh's reach and sang again. "I am free . . . I am free . . . I am free . . ." Then it playfully brushed her face with its wing. As it did so she felt a sensation of Iskiir's presence, so strong that she was briefly certain he stood by her on the tower. Here was proof that the *buri* had absorbed her thoughts.

"Go to him," she shouted, pointing north.

"I can go where I please," sang the *buri*.

"You can become a moth again, too," she retorted. Salparin had warned that *buris* often became intractable when first released. This one laughed at her threat, rose and flew toward the south.

Adeh could no longer see the flyer; she glanced despondently at the empty cage. The creature had been docile when imprisoned, promising a speedy flight. Now she had only Salparin's word that it would fulfill her request. She was about to abandon the roof in favor of the sentries when silvery wings again swooped out of the sky and touched her cheek. Once more she felt Iskiir's presence; and with that came another awareness, one so familiar that it brought a smile. Herself! For a moment, it seemed that she possessed a twin who stood beside her. This was how the flyer would carry her message to Iskiir. *If* it chose to obey...

"I am free! I am free!" sang the *buri*. Then it rose, headed north toward the mountains, and was gone.

The captives were left sitting in the tent to await Bermegi's test. As soon as the guards stepped outside, Yeni raised his double chin as if to regain an air of dignity. "These nomads..." he whispered. "They have Acurlat water, and they think that makes them sorcerers. Ha! Let them give me my bag so I can show them Guild magic."

"They want to see somethin' that can work against Hethi," replied Dajnen. "*Bolu* says your Guild tricksters couldn't even *slow* the demon stones."

"I've been practicing a certain effect..." Yeni insisted.

"Enough from you!" Dajnen turned his attention to Iskiir. "*Bolu*, you've got to *change* somethin' for these camel-growers. Even if you can't look first, you've got to do it."

"The old magic means trouble," Yeni grumbled. "The Guild had good reasons for banning it."

"May buzzards relish your fat lips!" The Appeaser glared at Yeniski until he fell silent. "Now, *bolu*," he continued, turning back to Iskiir. "Remember what you did at Jalween. Even with a crowd watchin', you were able to focus."

"What if I convince them that I have magic?" the young

man protested. "Tell me what I do afterward when they take me to find the Hethi."

Dajnen smiled. "I thought we had no chance against blue-turbans. But that was before I saw what you did at the well."

"Then..."

"Listen to me, *bolu*. The Hethi are full of tricks. They know shopkeepers' magic and plenty more. But they can't *see* the way you can. That's where you have an edge. They can bring things across, but they have to find 'em first."

"Even if they have followers?"

"They need 'em. You don't." Dajnen closed his eyes as if pondering an explanation. "Suppose..." he said, raising a finger. "Suppose a blind man wants to catch a one-horned goat on a hillside. He goes this way, he goes that way, up and down, feelin' around everywhere till he finds it. Tires himself out. Uses up his strength... or draws on someone else's. But you, *bolu,* you see that goat right off and grab him by his beard."

"But..."

"The followers give Hethi the energy they need. Your magic works different. Believe me, *bolu,* you've got a talent that can make those blue-turbans shiver..."

"Then tell me one thing more." Iskiir heard footsteps and voices approaching; in a moment his lesson would be over. "What makes the *other* side of something stay here for a time? Like the thorny garden at Jalween..."

The Appeaser frowned. "When the trance breaks, the thing usually goes back," he said. "But if you put enough of yourself into it, you can make the change last." He scratched at his beard and stared at the low roof of the tent. "Yes... and another thing I heard once. If you bring something *living* across, it may have a will of its own... It may not *want* to go back."

At that moment the guards returned and Iskiir's thoughts of magic were interrupted. The tribesmen freed his legs, but left his wrists bound; they hustled him out of the tent. The full sunlight made him blink, and he wished he could shade his eyes. Behind him he heard the guards muttering as they brought his companions out as well.

To the side, in a clearing between the shelters, Iskiir saw Odeema hammering a knife blade on his anvil. Waiting by a pile of coals in the sand, Ergar held a small pair of bellows while his eyes followed the strangers. A moment later, the Menjians were pushed forward along the line of tents.

The air smelled first of charcoal smoke, then of freshly tanned leather. Iskiir passed two men building a camel saddle, cursing as they stretched skins over the frame. He looked about in surprise at the crafts practiced by the tribe; he had never heard of such skills among nomads. Karbayra raised goats, sheep and camels, he knew, or carried goods from one city to the next for profit from trading. He hadn't heard that some tribes served as artisans for the others.

The variety of objects in the camp made his thoughts spin. Though each thing in this world had but one magical side, he might well find something suitable here. But suitable for what? If he could choose his magical feat, what would it be?

The young man walked as slowly as the guards would allow, scrutinizing each tool, each length of rope. The women of the camp were busy also, he saw, some weaving reeds into baskets, others working simple looms. Beside them, children polished brass plates that jangled against each other, or strung clay beads on tethers. So many possibilities . . .

As the captives passed, the nomads glanced up only briefly from their tasks. This test was not to be a spectacle for the camp's entertainment, Iskiir surmised. Yet whatever happened would surely attract notice.

The Menjians reached a large open area before the biggest tent. Shielded from the sun by a canopy of scarlet cloth, Bermegi sat cross-legged on a thick golden carpet. Beside him sat the bulbous-nosed leader of the tribe and several others with long beards. Bermegi beckoned the captives to approach.

"First we show magic of Acurlat," he said with a smile that split his narrow face. He turned to the graybeard beside him, a wiry man garbed in the tight-fitting robe of a raider. His head was covered by a cap of black wool that was topped by a long red tassel. The mage, if that's what he called himself, held a small clay jar by its neck. In his lap lay a patchwork of furs from many animals, one piece speckled, another striped, one with bristly hairs and another like wool.

"*Oss!*" said Bermegi's mage, lifting the jar. He began an incantation that started with single short sounds chanted monotonously. Gradually his speech quickened, the words growing longer until his lips seemed to blur. He threw back his head, exposing his wrinkled throat as he flung high-pitched syllables at the sky. Then, without watching his hands, he tilted the jar and sprinkled a few drops of water onto the furs.

Iskiir was thrown back by a blast of cold air. Suddenly the sky had darkened; around him swirled white puffs that stung when they hit his face. *Snow!* In the high pastures he'd several times been caught in brief flurries. But never had he heard of snow in the desert. He looked up to see heavy clouds covering the sun. Huge flakes were falling all about him; already the carpet's red canopy showed a white coating. And Bermegi sat beneath it, his wide smile displaying all the gaps in his teeth.

"A simple trick," declared Yeniski to the raider. "Give me the jar and that rag of skins, and I'll do the same without the chanting."

"You say you need no water," Bermegi reminded him.

Iskiir realized that the illusion was already fading. Suddenly the sun returned. He twitched his cheek, where he had just felt snowflakes melting. Now his skin felt dry. And the canopy bore no signs of moisture. The snow had not simply melted; it had never been there at all.

"A decent conjurer could keep that going for half a day," Yeni muttered.

The mage evidently understood the remark, for his face darkened and his eyebrows raised in fury. Suddenly, he upended the jar and poured its entire contents onto the furs. The icy wind knocked Iskiir to his knees, and with his hands still tied he could not keep his balance. He sprawled under the onslaught of the storm, snow whipping about his face and feet.

The young Menjian tried to rise, got up on knees and elbows, and saw only whiteness around him. In this wind, he could not stand. Slowly he crawled forward, hoping he was moving away from the storm's center.

His head hit something soft. He swung his arms to brush off the body that lay in his path, and winced as icy powder filled his sleeves. "Yeni!" he cried when he saw his cousin stretched out and motionless. "Yeni, you grandson of a hyena. I'd like to see your tongue freeze and fall out of your mouth."

But Iskiir could not leave his cousin. He used his bound arms as a wedge under the plump one's shoulder, managed to roll him over once, twice, three times. The exertion left him panting, but so far as he could tell they were no closer to escaping the storm. Seeking an easier approach, he turned and tried to shove Yeni with his back, but his feet slipped when he tried to dig in his heels. Again he wedged his bound hands beneath the conjurer's shoulders.

Could a man die in such an illusion, Iskiir wondered. He had heard of someone drowning in an illusory well. Convinced he was under water, the victim had coughed and sputtered and then stopped breathing. If Yeni believed himself frozen, might his blood not stop flowing? Iskiir's hands were coated with slush and his fingers had lost all sensation. Every breath filled his lungs with icy air. But once more he turned the heavy body. Ahead, the storm appeared to be thinning. A few streaks of sunlight spurred him on; the border of the illusion was just ahead. Applying his knees and elbows, he worked until he rolled his cousin out onto dry sand. Then he dropped, exhausted, and tried to catch his breath.

Yeni groaned. Iskiir looked up wearily to see that the storm still raged just two paces from where he had fallen. The illusion, he realized, was as confined as it was intense. The chief's tent was obscured, but Bermegi and the others had moved to snow-free accommodations on the opposite side of the clearing. The nomads had taken their carpet with them. Now they were crowded together beneath the shade of a small black tentflap.

The leader of the artisans' tribe showed a worried look, as if the demonstration had been more startling than he'd expected. Bermegi and his conjurer, however, bore grins of jack-

als who have just spotted a dying camel. "So, Menjians," said
the raider chief. "You see what my Acurlat can do. Now *you*
show magic."

Iskiir slowly raised himself, first on one knee, then on his
wobbly legs. Yeni still lay trembling on the ground. And what
of the Appeaser? The young man turned just as Dajnen emerged,
squirming on his belly, from the maelstrom. Though his face
was red and his breathing heavy, he managed to sit up and
glower at his captors.

"Which one is mage?" demanded Bermegi, striding forward
to confront the captives.

Yeni groaned again. "The *bolu*," rasped Dajnen. "The other
one's . . . got only a mouth."

"You?" The chieftain turned and poked his dark finger at
Iskiir's chest. "Then show what you do."

"I . . . I'll need some things. A skein of wool . . . an awl . . .
a handful of beads . . ."

The raider began to laugh. "We give nothing. You do magic
now."

"But . . ."

Bermegi twitched his cheek and suddenly a pair of nomads
drew their knives. "I tire of game," he said, his smile suddenly
gone. He returned to his shady place on the rug, sat down and
crossed his arms.

Iskiir opened his mouth to protest again, but quickly shut
it as the armed men stepped closer. Still dazed from his struggle
with the storm, he hastily tried to gather his thoughts. Earlier
he had selected targets in the camp that seemed promising, but
now he must choose instead from the few items at hand.

There were the exposed weapons, of course. The knives
might become vipers. If they turned and bit their bearers, how
would that be received? The Menjian watched nervously as
the closest tribesman advanced. The sun shone on the blade,
and Iskiir could think of nothing else. He knew that Dajnen
should be next to him to break his trance if needed, but there
was no time for caution. If the nomads suffered from his magic,
then they must blame themselves for forcing his haste.

His thoughts were filled with the knife, the sharpness of the steel and the feel of the gnarled handle. It had drawn blood recently, he was certain, and then its edge had been honed. He thought he could picture the face of its last victim...

The tingling started, yet the change did not quite come. The bright reflection on the blade faded, turning to something insubstantial he did not recognize. Almost there, he thought, as he reached with his mind for the shadowy *other*. What beast, Iskiir wondered, was now taking shape before the nomads' eyes? He caught a hint of green and guessed that a huge snake was forthcoming. With a last effort he grasped the *other* and made it solid. Now he heard the droning wind, and now the weapon was gone. In its stead, the tribesman held...a long palm frond that waved in the light breeze. The nomad shouted with surprise and turned to show his leaders.

Was that all he'd achieved? Iskiir stared open-mouthed at the absurd result of his magic. With a scowl, Bermegi stood up and tore the greenery from the tribesman's hands, then ripped the frond to pieces. Iskiir's trance ended, the prickling and the windy sound gone in an instant.

"You think this joke?" said the raider. But then he glanced down at the shards of blade, the torn bits of steel that his man was collecting from the sand. His lips tightened and one eyebrow twitched. Iskiir noticed a troubled look also on the face of his conjurer. "You show magic to stop Hethi," said Bermegi. "I give one chance more."

Iskiir saw more weapons being drawn. He dared make no excuses, yet he seethed over the outcome of his test. His first try had made real magic, had it not? Otherwise the knifeblade would still be intact. But the result had been laughable. What if his next feat turned out no more impressive?

He needed another object, something larger, perhaps. His gaze fell on the nomads' carpet with its red patterns against the rich gold. Iskiir eyed it cautiously, studying the tasseled edges. How could he know what the rug's *other* side would be? Yet it drew his attention. He felt its softness; in his mind, his fingers traced the red swirls. As he imagined himself sprawled out and asleep in its comfort, the prickling began.

The whining came, and Iskiir saw the threads of the carpet glimmer and grow. Now he knew what was coming. For a moment he thought he might turn away and halt the transformation. But Bermegi had run out of patience. There was no choice but to finish the task, regardless of the harm it caused. He reached for the glowing fibers and the change was done.

Suddenly, shouting nomads were leaping from the pit of fire that erupted beneath them. The men beat at their flaming robes or rolled in the sand to quench the burning. A thick smoke rose above the blaze and soon the overhanging tent flap began to smolder. The tribe's leader brushed himself off after his hasty escape, then began shouting for aid. Already his men were arriving with buckets, but the flames had spread to the rest of the tent. The sand they threw arrived too late; Iskiir was nearly overcome by the smell of burning hair cloth, which dropped in charred sheets to the ground. He heard camels screaming in fear as the smoke spread.

The flames raced along the cloth and leaped to a second tent. From the shouts and cries, Iskiir thought the whole camp had converged on the fire. Tent pegs were yanked and shelters hurriedly collapsed to keep the blaze from spreading. Recalling Ergar's language lesson, Iskiir understood a few words of the shouting. *"Sand, more sand,"* they were saying. The burning tentpoles collapsed and the embers smoked on the ground.

Now the air was so filled with flying grit that a sandstorm might have been raging. Still, Iskiir's attention remained with what had once been the carpet. All about him the firefighters worked with frenzy, yet he held his focus and the blaze on the ground did not go out. The tent fires, however, were soon contained; now the nomads turned their efforts to quenching the transformed rug. Again they swung buckets, but sand only seemed to feed these flames, the grit bursting into sparks as it reached the heat. Men shouted in dismay and bent to try again. Iskiir's eyes streamed, yet he would not move away.

"Enough!" said Bermegi, shaking Iskiir roughly. "Menjian

tricks. Children's magic." He pushed the young man to the ground. Would nothing convince this raider? Silently Iskiir cursed himself and Dajnen, and then every mage who had ever muttered an incantation.

The raider gave no orders regarding the Menjian. Instead, he turned toward his mage, who stood nearby scrutinizing the results of the demonstration. At the black-cap's feet, the carpet had now returned to its original form. Soiled and sooty though it was, Iskiir could still make out some of the original red patterns. But two tents were destroyed, and the singed robes remained singed. The Karbayra mage was studying a piece of burnt cloth, sniffing it cautiously and then holding it to the light. For a time he ignored his chief.

Then Iskiir heard the Appeaser's rough voice. "A fire *illusion* leaves no ash," he whispered. "And it can't burn anything. Let 'im think that over awhile."

Iskiir opened his mouth in puzzlement. "The other side of the carpet . . ."

"It's *demon* fire. Burns everything, and nothin' can put out the source of it. He wants to fight Hethi for his men? Let him cut up the rug and throw the pieces into their camp. Then you can work your change." Dajnen licked his lips as if contemplating roasting a brace of pigeons.

Iskiir could only shake his head in confusion, but he saw that the mage had begun to share his opinions with Bermegi. Evidently the graybeard was taking Iskiir's second attempt more seriously, for his brow was furrowed and he continued to stare at his scrap of burnt cloth. As they spoke, the chieftain became increasingly agitated until he began to beat his chest with his fist. Iskiir could not understand the argument, but he heard the word "Acurlat" repeated several times. When Bermegi kicked sand, the mage merely shrugged.

Meanwhile, the nomads who had fought the fire remained crowded around the site. The signs of magic were now all but gone, yet the onlookers peered about in curiosity. The snowstorm had vanished, leaving not even a trace of dampness. Of Iskiir's blaze, only dark smudges and charred tentpoles remained. The tribe's leader paced up and down, trying to send his people back to their tasks. Each man or woman he faced would appear to obey his orders, yet the crowd did not seem to shrink.

Bermegi was still arguing with his mage, but the black-cap held up for his inspection first a torn piece of the knife and then the darkened hem of his robe. They exchanged a few more words; at last the chieftain turned to stomp angrily toward Iskiir. "You want see your Hethi friend?" he asked, pulling the Menjian to his feet. "We find out if he hiding my men." He pulled a knife from his belt and cut Iskiir's wrists free with a careless snap. Then he put his arm on the young man's shoulder and pushed him roughly forward. "You ever ride camel?"

Chapter 11

Behind the tents, a half dozen of Bermegi's men were lounging by their couched camels. When the men saw their chief approaching, they leaped to their feet and stood stiffly. These nomads bore signs of battle; one lacked an ear, another, three fingers, a third, one side of his broad nose. Each wore a simple russet robe, with a knife at the waist and a sword hanging from the shoulder. Only their mounts showed signs of the raiders' reputed wealth, bits of silver and painted leather decorating saddles that rested between hump and neck.

Bermegi paused to shout orders to two men, who hurried back into the camp. The other raiders began to mount their beasts. Having no experience with these animals, Iskiir watched the process with attention. Each man stepped with ease from neck into saddle, then sat back casually while the creature raised first its hind legs part way, then its front legs, then its hind legs fully. Iskiir studied also the differences between these camels and those of the caravan, noting how much sleeker were the raiders' beasts, with legs well-muscled down to the knee and lean from knee to foot.

Shortly, one of Bermegi's men arrived with another mount, this one bearing the simple saddle of the artisans' tribe. With a slow hiss between his teeth, the raider yanked the headrope down to couch the animal. The Menjian climbed into the saddle, and all went well until the camel began to rise. First Iskiir was thrown forward, and only a quick grab for the pommel kept him from plunging headlong into sand. Then he was snapped against the low backrest, and then he pitched forward again.

Once the beast was upright, Iskiir tried to arrange himself in the manner of the other riders, hooking one leg about the saddle horn and swinging the other down over the first. This offered a precarious grip as the camel began to pace, for the beast lurched from side to side at every step. Iskiir was not used to riding so high above the ground. While the view was fine, the thought of the long drop if he should fall took away any possible enjoyment.

The young man glanced back once at the receding tents of the craftsmen. What would happen to Yeni and Dajnen he couldn't say, but he assumed they would be safe—at least until the success or failure of Bermegi's mission was known.

To Iskiir the situation seemed clear, and not without hope. The Hethi needed bodies to fuel their attack on Tajmengus; in all likelihood, the vanished nomads were filling that need. If this could be proved, then the Karbayra and the Menjians would have a common enemy.

He had no time to ponder the matter further; the pace quickened, and he reached for the pommel with one hand. The other riders were beginning to leave him behind, for his stouter beast was seemingly unable to keep up with them. He watched helplessly as the raiders continued to pull away.

It was not long before one of them, shouting and cursing, rode back to deal with the problem. The two animals gave a bubbling roar as the nomad forced them to kneel so that the riders could trade mounts. The Karbayra quickly moved off

on the stouter beast, swatting its neck with a long stick and
shouting in its ear.

Iskiir was certain that his new camel would keep pace with
the others, but wondered how long he could stay on it. The
creature's speed startled him. Its neck stretched forward as it
plunged through the hollows and up the small crests. The thin
blanket over the saddle offered no protection against the bouncing.

The ride continued southward, through an area where small
mounds of sand lay piled against clumps of coarse grass. When
the party halted at an outcropping of crumbling dark lava, Iskiir
was relieved that his mount stopped with the others. He had
no notion of how to control the beast.

Fresh camel droppings, shiny and black, dotted the ground
about a water hole at the base of a boulder. Bermegi and another
man dismounted and knelt to the ground to study tracks. The
men pointed to one mark, and then another, peered out over
the rocky landscape, and seemed to come to an agreement.

Travel resumed at a slower pace, and with occasional stops
to study signs. All afternoon they rode, with no pause for rest
or water. Iskiir's thighs and buttocks grew more tender with
every lurch of the camel. He tried to vary his position, leaning
one way or another to take the pressure off sore spots. Only
by tucking up his legs and resting on his knees could he find
relief, and that position left him vulnerable to falling. Despite
all he knew of Hethi, he found himself hoping that the mage
would soon be found.

Toward sunset, they climbed a low ridge where dry bushes
clung to crevices in the rock. Bermegi raised his hand. Beasts
and men halted, and there was only the sound of breathing.
On the far side lay a gravel-strewn plain, its ruddy stones
gleaming under the sun's last rays. And in the distance three
figures were following a dry streambed, their shadows raking
the gully.

"Hethi," the men whispered, and Iskiir saw several pull
tarnished copper amulets from their necks and press them to
their foreheads. How were they certain they had found their

quarry? He squinted again and saw that two riders swayed limply in their saddles; the third rode ahead of them, his head up, his body erect.

Bermegi hissed an order and all camels turned. Beasts who moaned or coughed received swats from their riders' sticks. Shortly all the animals lay quietly on the ground at the base of the hill, while their masters stood up to stretch their legs. Iskiir climbed gingerly from the saddle, tried to stand, and collapsed against his mount's flank. His legs wobbled as if they didn't belong to him, as if someone else ought to be directing them. The raiders grinned and traded banter with each other while he tried another time to right himself.

At last he could walk again. He glanced up at the crest of the ridge and spotted the robes of the two lookouts who were crouching behind a wind-worn boulder. Night was coming, and the Hethi would soon be out of sight. Iskiir pondered what Bermegi's plan might be.

"You. Menj." The raider's chief approached, with his black-capped mage by his side. The graybeard carried a small tasseled saddlebag that Iskiir had noticed earlier hanging on the first camel he'd ridden. "When time is right, we catch up with Hethi and I talk with captives," said Bermegi. "*I* talk. Your job is keep him busy."

Iskiir frowned in puzzlement. The nomad raised two fingers.

"Two men with him. Karbayra. Camel breeders." Bermegi shrugged. "No matter which tribe. Two Karbayra. I find what they know about missing others. Your job..." He tapped his mage's arm and the sour-faced one opened the woven bag.

Iskiir felt his eyebrows raise as he glimpsed an assortment of tools and supplies from the artisans' camp—a small hammer, a strip of leather, a carved peg of acacia wood... What might he do with these? He glanced up nervously to meet the mage's stare. The old man's intent was clear, but had he any idea what would result?

Iskiir thought he knew how to proceed. He would focus on each object in turn, and try to learn its magical nature. With his hands free, he hoped to stop himself before each transformation actually took place. Perhaps that also was the mage's expectation. The graybeard motioned for him to follow, then led him toward a flat piece of ground that was well away from the camels.

Something to keep a Hethi occupied. Iskiir wondered, uneasily, just what sort of magic that might be.

Adeh listened to the slow breathing of Gla beside her and wished that she too could sleep. She opened her eyes and stared up at the cross-beamed ceiling of the acolytes' room. A lamp burned at each end of the long hall, but above her she could see only shadows. The room was nearly unoccupied, of course. It was too early to sleep; the evening meal had just ended. But she and Gla were to spend the late hours on watch. If they could doze now, they would be less likely to fall asleep at their duties.

She turned to lie belly-down on the rug. At other times of sleeplessness she had made imaginary journeys, long walks about the city or even treks across the wastes. Now her thoughts turned to the *buri*. Which way would she travel, she wondered, if she were the flyer. First she imagined herself swooping from one watchtower to the next, skimming the low rooftops of houses, or rising to flit through the temple's cupola. Then, as her imagined flight became more vivid, she found the Street of Potters and the Demilu shop, finally coming down to land on one of her father's jars. He was haggling with a customer, the pretty wife of a saddlemaker, and Adeh was able to listen unobserved. She noticed that he agreed to sell a tureen for a price that was foolishly low.

"Look," said the customer, turning toward the *buri* who was Adeh. "What a lovely moth! The Karbayra ask five *menos* for such a creature and today I can have one for the trouble of catching it."

"Be careful of my jar," warned Adeh's father.

"Give me a cloth to throw over it," said the woman. "I have an empty cage at home that's just the right size."

Adeh laughed, for she was not planning to become someone's pet. She had a task ahead of her, to deliver a message to Iskiir. Only briefly had she stopped to play; now she must fly to the desert.

Hurriedly, she flexed her wings to depart. But her smile vanished when she did not rise. No matter how hard she beat the air, she remained in place. At last she tried to leap aside, to dodge the woman's attack, but discovered that her feet had become fixed to the jar! Frantically she tried to break loose, even if it meant leaving her legs behind. *Too late*. Adeh cried angry tears as the cloth dropped over her . . .

"Get up," said Gla. "Hurry."

"Uh?" Adeh sat up suddenly and looked around. "We didn't oversleep?"

"It's time for our watch."

Barely awake, the potter's daughter recalled the last moments of the dream. Did it deal, she wondered, with the *buri*'s plight or her own? "I'm coming," she said without enthusiasm. The meaning of the dream continued to trouble her as she followed Gla from the room.

"We're to meet the guards," her friend reminded her as they wound through the corridors of the temple. Adeh tried to shake off her drowsiness and review what she knew of her assignment. Both outer and inner doors to the storeroom were under constant protection, she recalled. And inside the room, watchers stayed on duty at all hours. When a sack was taken out for the miller, she had seen how its number was marked off against the list. No other sacks had gotten past the doors, yet many were unaccountably missing.

"You two ready for a long night?" The first guard grinned as Adeh and Gla came toward him. The door from corridor to storeroom was secured by a pair of bars that evidently had been installed recently. The heavy wooden poles and added framework seemed out of place in the placid simplicity of the hallway. The second guard slid out the bars and swung the door open; a thick dusty smell from within made Adeh sneeze.

"Change watch!" the guard shouted into the interior. Shortly, two sleepy-looking young men stumbled out. Each handed over his lamp and then the two women hurried inside.

"See anything?" asked the first guard of the watchers as he swung the door shut. Adeh did not hear the reply.

The two women climbed the stairway of sacks leading up to the observation point. From the top, Adeh could see lamps set on the floor, burning at regular intervals along the aisles. The shadowy sacks stood high around the lights, each reflecting only a little of the orange glow.

The seating was lumpy and coarse. "We won't fall asleep sitting here," Gla joked.

Adeh smiled as she felt the sack's contents shifting under her. There seemed no way to make herself comfortable, so she returned to scanning the room. "Nothing can move without one of us seeing it," she said. "I'll watch this half and you watch that half. That way we can sit back to back."

They tried the position, each with her legs stretched out before her. "This is fine," said Gla. "If one of us nods off, the other will wake. Now all we need is a way to pass the time."

Adeh knew what was coming—another tale of Gla's flirtations with Haraj. How the two met so often in the midst of the crisis, Adeh could not explain. She was beginning to think that Gla's imagination had supplied most of the incidents. Nonetheless, she resigned herself to listening . . .

There was no way to measure time except by the burning down of the lamps. When their flames began to flicker, Adeh made a round with the oil pitcher to refill them, then returned to her perch. Gla seemed talked out at last, and Adeh was glad of the silence. For whenever her friend spoke of Haraj, Adeh's thoughts flew to Iskiir. At least Haraj remained in the city. Adeh could not know whether she would ever see Iskiir again.

Gla's silence continued. Adeh felt she must stretch her legs one more time. She descended to the floor to make a tour of the aisles and found everything still. If trickery was at work stealing the grain, she thought it must lie beyond her powers of detection.

Then she sensed, as she passed an empty corner, an odd

sweet smell in the air. She had noticed the odor earlier, taking it to be a fragrance that Gla used. But why should it be stronger down here? She stopped. The room was silent.

Looking at the bare wall in the corner, she had a suspicion that all was not right. She picked up the closest lamp. The oil flame provided little light, yet Adeh thought she saw something odd about the plastered surface. Though she could not say what was wrong, it lacked the substantial appearance of other walls.

Salparin had taught her to look for edges in an illusion, but here the edges blended in with the reality of the rest. She stepped closer, scrutinizing the place where wall and floor met, and then she saw a gap, a thin line that reflected less light than the surrounding surfaces. By studying that place, her ability to see through the trickery began to increase. Before her stood a piece of the wall that was surely different from the rest!

But before she could examine it further, the sweet smell intensified. A feeling of drowsiness came on so quickly that she felt she must close her eyes at once. *The fragrance!* She fought her drooping lids, and turned back to Gla. Leaving the lamp behind, she hurried as if she were being pursued, but now the odor seemed everywhere. Halfway up the staircase, she saw her friend slumped over.

Before she could think why she was doing it, Adeh's hands were tearing threads from unraveling ends of sack cloth. She began to stuff her nostrils with the fibrous cords, all the while feeling her head grow heavier. At last she gave in to languor; dully, she felt herself pitch forward onto lumpy sacks. For some time she lay in a state midway between wakefulness and dreaming, seeing in her mind movements of faint shadows and lights. Slowly her thoughts began to clear. Her precaution had worked; the harsh smell of sacking seemed to cover the other fragrance and cancel its effect. Adeh opened her eyes and sat up.

At once she turned her attention to Gla, shook her friend roughly, but could not rouse her from stupor. Should she call for aid? If the guards came in, they, too, might succumb. Gla was breathing evenly and appeared to be in no danger.

And surely the culprits were about to reveal themselves. Any disturbance now would warn them off, ruining her chance to identify them. Hurriedly Adeh moved Gla, stretching her out in what she hoped was a comfortable position. Then, slumping as if she, too, were asleep, she turned to watch the peculiar patch of wall. It was thin, perhaps a mere illusion. Already she saw hints of movement behind the partition.

Then she saw the wall breached, and knew her suspicions had been correct. But what creatures was she watching? At first she thought she saw sacks walking. More trickery? When they stepped closer to the light, she realized that the figures coming through the opening possessed human arms and legs. The sacks that covered their bodies had holes cut for eyes—childrens' costumes! But the sleep-inducing smell and the false wall were not child's play.

Adeh tried to still her breathing, as if that sound might betray her. The intruders glanced only once in her direction. They began to walk confidently along the aisles, pulling down a bag here and another there to rest on the floor. She dared not move as they passed out of her line of sight. Now she could follow their actions only by the muffled scrapes of sacking on stone.

The thieves showed no haste. They lugged their burdens to the wall's opening, and she saw hands on the other side reaching to receive them. Adeh counted more than a dozen bags vanishing through the hole. Then the intruders followed and the room was still again.

At once she crept down to the floor, then scurried to the corner and pressed her hand against the false surface. She had seen the thieves walk through freely, but to Adeh a barrier remained. The feel was like that of her father's soft clay; with a little effort, she could push her fingers through. But what about the rest of her? Could she push her body through as well?

The resistance she felt was part of her response to the illusion—Salparin had explained this at length. Though she had detected the effect, she had yet to overcome its influence. Only by fully convincing herself that nothing was there, could she pass with ease. But if she lost her wits to trickery, she might trap herself halfway through, might even suffocate with her face imbedded in the wall.

No time! she thought. In a moment, the thieves would be gone. She looked at the illusion and tried to clear it, studying the thinnest part until the surface melted into the darkness behind it. Then she knelt and put her hand through what felt like soft cheese. Quickly she pressed her head against the weak place, took a deep breath and plunged in.

For a moment her face felt unbearably slimy. She pulled her legs after her, and then dared to breathe again. Feeling about in the blackness, she touched a wall running parallel to the other, the space between them scarcely wider than her body. Perhaps she had entered a hidden passageway, one of many the fire-priests had tucked away in the building. And what of the thieves? Up ahead she heard scuffling.

Feeling her way, she stood up and followed the sounds to a sharp bend in the passage. When she rounded the corner, she saw lights bobbing in the distance and faint shadows sweeping the walls. Which way were they headed? She was familiar with only a few of the temple's corridors and rooms; from the orientation of their path, she believed that the thieves were moving away from the great hall. If they were to escape, she knew of no exit here. But she had heard of secret doorways . . .

Cautiously she followed, remaining well out of range of the lamps. At first she thought there must be another turning, for the lights began to wink out. She crept closer still, and discerned what must be another false wall. The sacks and marauders were slipping through one by one, and Adeh realized that she was about to find herself in total darkness. Quickly she tallied in her mind how many paces she must take to reach this new opening. When the last lamp was gone, she began to count her steps.

As she went, she ran her fingertips along the wall. Slowing down as she neared the target, she spread both hands on the rough surface. Everywhere the wall felt like stone, yet now she was past her count! What if she were trapped in the corridor, unable to follow, and equally unable to return to the storeroom? She was not sure that her resistance to illusion worked in complete blackness.

Her hands flew over the wall, pressing here and there frantically. Surely she had gone many steps past the opening. The problem must be in her thoughts, in her willingness to accept first impressions. Salparin had taught her to focus on what she knew to be real, until the false disappeared. But first she must calm herself.

Adeh recalled for a moment the acolytes at the temple and her friends in the Binding. Everyone was engaged in one task or another to preserve the people of the city. For most of her life she had been concerned only with the welfare of the Demilus. But in only a few days, she had begun to feel part of a new, larger family. She could not quit when she was so close to explaining the mystery of the stolen grain.

Slowly and deliberately, she pressed her hands to the wall. The opening she had observed remained clear in her mind. The surface was not solid; she had seen men walk through it without pausing.

Step by step she backed up the corridor, all the while picturing the opening she knew to be there. Five paces, ten. Her hands pressed firmly against the surface that soon must yield. Five paces more; suddenly her fingers sank in.

Now that she had found the place, her breathing quickened again. The wall was deep here; with her wrist buried, her fingers had not broken free. And the consistency was heavier than that of the first opening. She dropped to her knees and forced another hand partway through. It took all her strength, yet she could not get her other wrist into the wall.

Once more she tried to control her thoughts. Evidently, she had not convinced herself that the gap was open air. Perhaps, with a lesser goal, she might still make an exit. It would suffice to *soften* its apparent texture.

The wall was not clay, she told herself, but the stiff dough that bakers kneaded into flat loaves. She imagined her hands immersed in watery flour, and felt the wall loosen. More water! Her mother often made a thin batter for special treats, adding goat's milk and butter that made her fingers smooth and slick as she worked. Here was the texture she wanted: a wall of oily batter! With that thought, her hands plunged through, and Adeh pressed her forehead and nose to the surface.

Imagining a last dowsing of milk, she closed her eyes and pushed her whole body in. Cold liquid smeared her lips, swirled through her hair and around her ears. How thick was the barrier she must cross? She recalled the huge limestone blocks that made up the outermost temple walls. There was nothing to grab onto here, nothing to use to pull herself through. She was off-balance, falling forward while her arms thrashed for support she could not find. Gasping for breath, she tumbled out onto hard-packed dirt.

Then she realized that she was outside the temple, in a narrow alley that she did not recognize in the gloom. The thieves had had time to get well ahead of her, for she saw lights only in the distance. Breathing heavily through her mouth, she raced down the narrow path between houses, trying all the while to keep her sandals from slapping against the ground. As she ran, she realized that the sacking still plugged her nostrils. She pulled out the threads and flung them behind her. But she was still panting as she drew closer to the lights.

A laden donkey cart blocked her way. Piled high with straw, the cart was moving painfully slowly, a lantern dangling above the driver. There was no way past it.

Adeh hung back and studied the load in the cart. With a coating of straw for concealment, the bulk it carried was about equal to that of the stolen grain sacks. And why would anyone be driving such a heap of straw down this street at this hour? She had not lost her thieves after all.

The cart moved out into a wider street and the driver was able to pick up the pace. Adeh darted from shadow to shadow, wary of backward glances from the driver or the man who sat next to him. They moved toward the southeastern districts, where one house seemed larger than the next. This was where merchants and traders lived, Adeh knew, and soon they would enter the luxurious section of walled compounds.

The cart stopped. She hid herself and watched the driver and his passenger descend to the street. They stood aside while another figure emerged from beside a house, mounted the bench and clucked to the donkey. The cart continued on its way, leaving the two thieves in the road.

Now what? The taller man shouted an order to the other, and they both turned their heads away from the departing load of grain. There would be no witness to its route but the new driver, Adeh thought, unless she could follow him. But the two marauders were staring in her direction. If she turned back, she might find a way around them, but by then the cart would be gone.

She took the opposite approach and began to run toward the grain thieves. "My Heshee! Did you see my white cat?" she cried.

The tall man shrugged; the other spat against a building. They seemed as unhappy to see Adeh as she was to encounter them.

"Heshee!" Adeh raced past the guilty pair. "Is that you, you naughty queen?" Then she was hurrying around the bend the cart had taken, and then she saw the driver pausing to smother his light.

There remained moonlight over the city, and here and there lamplight flickered from a niche above the street. Adeh followed the wagon by sound more than sight, as the character of the buildings suddenly changed. The row of houses gave way to a series of high walls behind which she could see the outlines of palm trees. Here were the enclosures of the wealthiest families, whose fine dwellings sat in the midst of gardens.

On occasion, Adeh had walked through this district on breezy afternoons, inhaling the rich scents of lemon or orange that wafted over the walls. But the gates had always been shut, and she had never glimpsed what lay within. After such walks, she would sometimes imagine that someone had invited her inside, and she would picture the houses and their rich furnishings.

The possibility that such dwellings harbored outlaws and des-
ecrators had never occurred to her. Yet why else would the
wagon be here?

The driver gave her no rest, pressing onward toward the
outermost reach of the city. At last he halted and Adeh thought
she might catch her breath. But at once, she heard a gate's
hinges squealing. The cart began to turn. No lamps burned
here, and she wondered if she dared follow the wagon through
the entrance. She looked down at her jubbah, cursing its bright
weave that seemed to shine in the moonlight.

Perhaps she already had learned enough. She could wait
outside until dawn so that she would be sure to recognize this
place again. Then the guards would deal with the culprits. But
what if more trickery was at work inside? What if the marauders
used illusions to hide their spoils?

For a moment, she saw Iskiir's face, and heard him calling
her his "mountain girl." With a quick lunge, she grabbed onto
the rear of the cart, ducked her head low and pulled her legs
up to dangle between the wheels. Only her small hands would
be visible, she thought, if someone should glance in her direction. She heard the gate clank shut and the bars drop. Hushed
voices gave orders, and the wagon rolled deeper into the enclosure.

As soon as movement ceased, she fell to hands and knees
in the dirt and crept forward to the dark space beneath the
load. The donkey snorted; voices spoke in anxious whispers.
The wagon began to creak as sacks were shifted to the rear
and then dragged off.

Men came and went, but Adeh could see only the hems of
their robes. Next to the wagon there seemed to be an opening
to a cellar. She watched the sacks vanishing into the ground,
and wondered whether there would be any trace of a doorway
if she came back to the spot. She must be certain of the location,
but how could she get her bearings?

She tried to recall how far they had come from the gate,
and whether they had turned. Absorbed in recollection, Adeh
barely noticed the shuffling sound behind her. Then her mouth

was clamped by a hand that tasted of dust. As she strained to free herself, other hands gripped her ankles to drag her from shelter.

"What's that?" whispered someone.

"Caught her under the wagon. Temple spy, I'll wager."

"Fouling jenny! Tie her mouth shut. We'll give her to the mage."

Chapter 12

Though night had fallen, the blue-turbaned mage and his followers had not stopped to rest. Iskiir's aches were now a general soreness that spread upward from buttocks and thighs. He had not thought he could endure such pain, yet the ride continued and he did not fall from the saddle.

One raider scout traveled ahead, watching the Hethi's progress, while the remainder of Bermegi's party trailed at a safe distance. Stealth was the main concern; the nomads had even tied shut the camels' mouths so that no sounds would betray them.

The gibbous moon shed a pale light on the pebbled plain. From time to time, Iskiir noticed cairns of small stones, signals from the tracker, lying in the midst of the path. The Menjian had deduced the raider's plan—to confront the Hethi when he was weary, his stomach full, his eyes ready for sleep. But when would that time come?

Iskiir's mount followed Bermegi's closely, so the Menjian was among the first to glimpse the pebble messages. Though he couldn't interpret their meaning, he noticed an immediate reaction from the chieftain when the cairn took on an elongated shape. Bermegi raised his hand for a halt; all beasts and riders remained in place until the scout came running back.

Bermegi and the man on foot exchanged a few words and then the chieftain grabbed the headrope of Iskiir's camel. The two rode on, and Iskiir realized that they were going into the Hethi camp alone. For protection they had only the raider's sword and Iskiir's uncertain abilities.

The young man felt for the pouch inside his sash, which held a nomad woman's coil of black thread. This alone he had selected from the contents of the mage's sack. What sensible person, he wondered, would trust his fate to such a weapon. Perhaps only because his mind was dazed with weariness and pain did he have any hope for Bermegi's ruse.

A small cookfire flickered in the distance. Not until they were almost upon it, however, did Iskiir smell smoke. The camel evidently sensed the odor also, yet it turned its head slightly away from the fire as it sniffed. Iskiir also thought briefly that the smell came from the side, but assumed that a slight breeze had confused him.

The Hethi sat cross-legged before the fire, his profile to the visitors, while his two followers lay sprawled on sleep mats in the open air. Iskiir knew the power of the sorcerer's eyes and voice. Nervously, he held the coil of thread ready. But the turbaned one did not glance up from the flames. The riders approached unchallenged and halted just behind him. Bermegi reached for the headrope of Iskiir's mount.

"So you come back to me, *bolu*," said the seated one abruptly without turning. "We could have joined together at Jalween and spared you the trouble of finding me again. I would have enjoyed my travel better with your company."

"I find Menjian," said Bermegi. "This husband to hyenas steals my water, but we catch. You want him?"

"I already *have* him," said the mage drily. "Did you think I would pay you for your trouble?"

"Not pay. But look at sick boy who sleeps on far side of

fire," replied the raider, evidently referring to the shabbier of the two followers. "A fair swap for my healthy water-thief."

Iskiir's hands were trembling. This was not quite the scenario that Bermegi had described to him. He couldn't tell if the raider was serious about trading him for the Karbayra or merely making talk. There was no time to ponder the raider's intent. Iskiir let the coil slip down along the front leg of his camel; it fell into a pool of shadow behind the mage. In response to Iskiir's reaction, Bermegi tugged the headrope and backed both mounts away slowly.

"So you plan to keep him if I won't trade?" To Iskiir's relief the Hethi made no attempt to look at the visitors, but reached to his side for a few more roots to poke into the fire. The camels continued to retreat until they stood ten long strides upwind of the sorcerer.

Iskiir immediately began to focus on the thread. Though he could scarcely discern the skein's outline, he had studied the piece carefully and could picture its every twist and loose strand. As he slipped into trance, he shut out the bantering that continued between Bermegi and the Hethi.

This was going suspiciously well, protested one voice in Iskiir's mind. The mage seemingly had known who was coming without using his eyes. If he had some other way of seeing, then surely he would have noticed the black coil. Why then did he continue to chat idly while Iskiir worked the change?

Perhaps the mage was overconfident, playing with his victims until he was ready to dispatch them. Iskiir must do what he set out to do, before the Hethi realized the folly of his carelessness. Deeper he immersed himself in the feel of coarse threads and the odor of goathair. The tingling began.

And then, as the familiar windy sound grew, he saw a dark funnel rise from the sand. He had watched this once before. At the black-cap's testing place, by stopping his ears, he had sent back the dust devil to its other world; now he did nothing to halt the change. The camel shook its head, tried to turn away from the threatening vortex, but Bermegi was holding its rope firmly and somehow controlling his own mount as

well. The narrow whirlwind grew, lifting not only the finer
grit but small stones and bits of litter. This was no illusion;
the wind would quickly shred the Hethi's clothing. It would
toss the coals of the fire and scour the flesh from his bones.

The whirlwind roared, but Iskiir barely heard it for the
hissing of spirit winds. The camel moaned through its tied
jaws, bucked and fought, but Bermegi held it in place so that
Iskiir would keep his trance. Everything at the base of the
funnel was being sucked up, twirled or torn. At a distance of
ten paces, however, the air was calm. Only the Hethi and his
immediate surroundings were at risk.

Yet Iskiir thought he still saw traces of the Hethi's fire
peeking through the maelstrom. And then he watched an arm
poke from the dark swirl. Another arm. A robe. The mage
stepped calmly out. How could that be?

Bermegi shouted with surprise as the turbaned one cracked
a cold smile. Standing five paces from Iskiir, the mage raised
his hands. At that moment Iskiir felt his robe tugging him
sideways, pulling him from the saddle. He reached for the
pommel too late; already he had lost his balance. When he hit
the ground, he felt a sharp pain on one shin as if he had fallen
on a large rock. Then a burning sensation on his foot made
him jerk his leg to the side. Yet the ground where he had landed
appeared bare.

Then he understood how the blue-turban had tricked him.
Bermegi and Iskiir had been conversing with a displaced image!
The mage and his followers and his fires were not where they
appeared to be, but safely by the *side* of the path where Iskiir
now lay. And the whirlwind had woefully missed its target.

The Menjian began to crawl away from the heat of the real
fire, but a moment later found himself rigid, unable even to
blink. He remained in place, his head tilted upward, his legs
askew, waiting for the blue-turban to finish with him.

"Now, nomad," said the mage to Bermegi. "Now let us
come to an agreement. You have eight fighting men crouching
in the darkness. I can kill them all, but that will cost me

something. Why waste my energies on such a useless battle when we've had such a long understanding with your tribes?"

Understanding? Iskiir's mind spun in disbelief. If Hethi and nomads were truly allies, then there could be no future for Menjians.

"I come for one purpose," said Bermegi. "I speak freely with men by the fire. Then I am gone."

"You have no business with my companions."

"They are Karbayra."

"You are a gnat who tries my patience. Do you leave now, in peace?"

Iskiir was unable to turn his head, and his view was nearly blocked by his camel. But in the glow from the false fire he could see Bermegi's form atop his mount. Suddenly the raider stiffened as if something had struck him. He took a moment to recover; then, as if dazed, he began to back up his beast.

The young man tried to cry out, but his tongue would not obey. Bermegi was abandoning him, and the other raiders were following his retreat. Was this their bargain? What dealings could they possibly have with the Hethi?

Iskiir had lost control of his limbs, but his thoughts were free to run. Perhaps, he considered, Karbayra gave up a youth now and then to the blue-turbans, so long as the other nomads were left alone. For years they might have had such an arrangement. But now the Hethi's ambitions had grown; to carry out their plans they were swallowing whole tribes.

He stared helplessly at his camel; he could see nothing else. For the entire day the beast had tormented him with its lurching gait. Now all he had to look at were its firm flanks, its well-muscled legs, its broad feet...

A whisper at the back of his neck caught Iskiir by surprise. *What might he do with the camel?* Though Dajnen had encouraged him to practice on Yeni's scorpion, he had never actually changed an animal.

"I sought you for good reason," said the mage's voice. "These desert boys drain quickly. But you... ahh. You are special. I sense strengths I've never imagined. You will replace

the one who is nearly used up. Yes. And a dozen like him."
Iskiir could not see his captor, but was aware that the Hethi's
sorcery had begun. The Menjian's toes felt numb, and the lack
of sensation was slowly spreading upwards. The blue-turban
had started to take possession.

The raiders were gone. Iskiir's own uncertain magic offered
his only hope of escape. Hastily, he immersed himself in thoughts
of his camel, imagining that he stood by the beast's side. After
a day's riding, he was intimate with every straggly hair patch
on its shoulders. In his thoughts, his nostrils filled with the
scent of its urine and his fingers rubbed its rough hide.

But the distractions were too much for him. The Hethi's
voice continued, and as the sorcerer talked, the numbness crept
to Iskiir's knees. He was being made over, he thought, into a
servant who could not disobey. And when the numbness covered him, his conversion would be complete.

Sweat ran down the young man's face as he strained to find
the *other* side of his mount. This was not at all like changing
a stick or even a goatskin. It was as much work, he thought,
as trying to *lift* a camel. The focus must be stronger, his trance
deeper.

More was required than to know the appearance of the beast.
He put his thoughts *inside* the camel's body, feeling the an-
noying weight of the saddle on his back. Iskiir had noticed the
animal favoring its right front foot; now he felt a soreness in
the pad, a dull ache that was starting to throb. He recalled a
clump of salt grass he had seen earlier, and imagined the cool
and refreshing taste it might have had. A tingling spread over
the back of his long neck.

And then Iskiir was outside the creature, looking with his
own eyes at his mount's *other* side. The new beast loomed
twice as tall as a camel, yet its appearance was far less substantial. Enveloped in a blue-green glow of sunlit pools, it
turned its great head slowly. Iskiir saw the image flickering,
and noticed also that the usual whining sound had not come.
He was merely *seeing*, he thought, leaving the last step incomplete. Though he was not sure how, he had slowed the

process enough to leave time for making a decision. But in this case he had only one choice; whether this transformed creature would aid or harm him, he could not guess, but he was determined to bring its substance across.

As he continued to focus, he heard the spirit wind rise. The sound droned in his ear, and the beast solidified. Two huge nostrils flared at the end of an ox-like head. A fluted crest shimmered from the base of its neck to the start of its bushy tail. For a moment two eyes of cool fire stared at Iskiir. Then the beast lowered its head to point the twisted horns, one sprouting from its forehead, the other from its upper jaw, in his direction. Hooves struck green sparks as the beast pawed the ground.

It bellowed once, a cry of a hundred angry bulls, and then it charged. Iskiir felt the mage's control loosen. He fell forward, tried to rise, but stumbled as the beast sprang toward him. A chill passed overhead. Somewhere behind him, the mage screamed a curse.

Iskiir was not gored! Looking up, he saw that the creature had leaped over him to attack the Hethi instead. But the beast had overshot and was turning for another attack. And where was the mage? Perhaps the horned beast could sense his true location. Iskiir could not see him at all.

Then the young man realized that his trance had been broken, yet his mount retained its magical form. Whether the creature still clung to this world through Iskiir's will or its own, he could not say. But he marveled at the fighter his camel had become. It lowered its head again, and then Iskiir caught sight of its target, an ungainly two-legged creature crouching on the sand. A jinn! Here was the Hethi's response. The mage had changed himself into the two-headed thing that Iskiir had glimpsed at the tower.

The Hethi-jinn opened its mouth, pulling its jaws so wide that they bent backward. It gave one long snarl, as if that would frighten the crested beast away.

But the changed camel was not easily intimidated. It charged once more. The jinn merely stepped aside. The two-horned one was fast, Iskiir saw, but with its great bulk, it could not change course quickly. The jinn evidently realized this also. It waited calmly for the next lunge, and this time raked the other with its talons as it passed. Glowing drops of the two-horn's blood hit the ground and burst into sparks.

The crested one shook its great head and wailed like a chorus of hounds. Green flames streamed from its massive shoulders and its tail. Its crest stiffened. Yet once more it charged, allowing the jinn another swipe of the talons.

Now Iskiir's hopes for his demon fighter began to wane. It was powerful, he saw, but pitifully stupid. Continuing its poor tactics, its hide would be raked to ribbons. "No!" shouted Iskiir to the blue-green creature as its snorting grew more frenzied.

But all the beast would do was lope back and turn for another wild charge. The jinn had only to watch how its course began, then dance awkwardly to the right or the left and inflict further wounds. The former camel was bleeding badly, the sand around it aglow with patches of its blood.

The crested one was doomed, the young man knew. But it was holding the jinn's attention, and for that alone he gave thanks. The mage's grip on him was gone now. For the moment, he might escape. He scrambled to his feet and hurriedly searched the ground for the raiders' tracks. He could follow them on foot, at least for a short way.

Shrieks from the jinn alternated with the bellowing of the other as Iskiir began to follow the trail. Had his creation gotten in a lucky blow, Iskiir wondered. He dared not stop to look back. He ached in more places than a bush had thorns, and the ground would not stay still for him. Trying to hurry, he stumbled, sprawled headlong in the sand. The beast behind him roared, and he feared that he was hearing a death scream. He stood up wearily and looked again for the raiders' tracks.

Then he heard another sound, the pattering of camel feet. Suddenly a stout arm encircled his waist; he was lifted against a camel's flank and held, his feet just clearing the ground. The animal continued to trot across the plain, and Iskiir was squeezed so tightly that he could scarcely draw breath. Only when the night air was silent of battle did Bermegi set him down.

"Now you ride Hethi mount," said the raider. Iskiir glanced around and saw one slumping figure in the saddle of another camel. *The mage's follower*. Another, evidently the second follower, lay tied with his head dangling from a second mount. Iskiir believed that the blue-turban had consumed that man's last breath. And the third camel's saddle, he saw, was empty. "You ride," said Bermegi. "Hethi walk home," he added with a twisted grin.

At sunup they paused at a stand of ruddy stone columns, thinner at their bases where the sand had worn them away. Iskiir glanced briefly at the dead man as they pulled him from his mount. Though his hair was white as desert salt, his face still appeared youthful. Where had Iskiir seen that face before? *Jalween!* This was the tall lad who had demanded money at the well. Evidently, the unfortunate had fallen under the Hethi's spell after Iskiir's escape. It was his life that had been swallowed to make the mage into a jinn.

Bermegi held up a goatskin and poured a dribble of water onto the dead one's forehead. The nomads mumbled a quick incantation, then two riders stood on their saddles to climb atop a high rock. The men reached down for the vanquished one, lifted him, then stretched him out in a posture of repose. Without further words, they left him to the elements.

There were no backward glances. But Iskiir could not help turning to stare at the follower who still lived. Here was a rare person indeed—one who had been freed from a Hethi and still could tell of the experience. Iskiir burned to know what this sickly man had to say. He wondered if Bermegi had already questioned him.

The riding continued, and Iskiir wondered if he had begun to grow used to his camel. His aches had not lessened, but now seemed easier to bear. Perhaps this was only because of his new knowledge: a Hethi might seriously be challenged.

Where was Bermegi heading now? The direction seemed

southward toward Tajmengus, yet nothing along the route looked
familiar. There were hills and plains of gravel and sandy hollows, with little to distinguish one from another. Then the party
jogged eastward for a short while and suddenly reached the
edge of a round depression. Below lay a dense cluster of date
palms, with smaller trees growing in their shadows. Iskiir blinked
with surprise, but the long, rush-lined pool in the center did
not vanish. Here was an oasis that was probably known only
to Karbayra.

Bermegi rode down toward a cluster of camels who stood
drinking at the pool's edge. He shouted to their riders, gestured,
threw stones and sand in the air. Before he had spoken long,
the tribesmen were pulling their animals back from the water.
Bermegi watched as the men mounted and headed out, some
north, some west. Then he waved to his own men and they
brought their animals down to drink.

Iskiir tumbled from the saddle and dropped onto a shady
spot where orange and lemon trees grew beneath the palms.
He wanted to hear what the freed follower had to say, but his
limbs would not obey him. His head sank onto his hands. For
a moment he imagined Adeh watching for him from the high
steps of a temple, scanning an empty landscape. *She must
believe by now that I've failed,* he thought miserably. When
he opened his eyes again it was mid-afternoon.

"Menj." Bermegi was nudging him with his foot. "Up,
Menj."

"What?" Iskiir could scarcely open his eyes.

"Nomad friend talks. Now we know all. The Hethi hold
two tribes—two Karbayra tribes. And my men, too. Enough.
They eat too many us."

"Then how?"

"Men come. Fighters. All tribes. Magic-makers, too. Now
we fight."

"Fight Hethi?"

"Or they eat us all." Bermegi pulled Iskiir to his feet. "You
help and then . . . maybe we let you free."

Chapter 13

The gag burned Adeh's cheeks and tore at the corners of her mouth. She bit fiercely at the cloth, but could not clear her tongue. One man held her bound ankles; another clamped her about the shoulders to carry her across the yard. She fought as well as she could, tossing her head, thrashing her legs, twisting her wrists against the chords that held them behind her. But the men merely tightened their grips. Then she heard scraping as wide stable doors swung open.

"In here?" said one voice. Another grunted assent. A second set of hinges creaked and she was taken into a small side room. The men tossed her roughly onto cold bricks. She saw only the shadowy backs of her captors as they left her in darkness. The narrow door they shut did not fit perfectly, and a ribbon of dim light showed beneath the lintel. From the other side came muffled voices.

"Where's the conjurer?"

"I thought he was upstairs. We shouldn't have long to wait."

Adeh jerked her body around until she lay on her side.

Hoping to find a sharp edge to use against the cords, she stretched her bound arms until her fingers touched the floor. But she felt only bits of straw and grit. With a soft cry, she hitched herself forward to try again.

"I rode out to have a look today," said the first voice. "I tell you if Wunal's behind this, he's carrying it further than anyone expected."

Another voice laughed coldly. "If not Wunal, then who?"

"I don't know. But you still can't show me what profit he's making from it. So far as I know, *we're* the only ones who benefit."

"We'll do better than anyone thought. Prices doubled again this afternoon. The fools are hoarding whatever grain they can buy, no matter what the price. And I understand Wunal. He doesn't want money. That's not his game. If he can make the priests bray like donkeys and the mages kiss his hands, he'll be satisfied."

"Then explain this to me. The stones should've stopped by now. What's the point? Wunal doesn't gain anything if they come closer. Why doesn't he wave his hand and stop them so he can be the hero you say he set out to be?"

"I don't know what you're getting at."

"That maybe it's not Wunal at all. Maybe it's some old-time . . ."

Another laugh, this one more nervous. "You've been hearing childrens' tales. Be careful; the mage is coming. Don't let him catch you making such talk."

Adeh heard other voices approaching. Her searching grew more frenzied, but struggling did nothing to speed her progress. She could no longer remember which parts of the floor she had covered, and her arms already ached from the strain of her awkward position.

"I'll need to prepare something," said a high-pitched voice. "Open the door when I raise my finger."

A silence followed. Adeh abandoned her explorations and began to rub the cords against the rough surface of the bricks. She heard a hiss. A bitter odor of burning drifted in from the

direction of the doorway. Then the heavy portal swung open
and she saw the outline of a squat man whose arms seemed
oddly long in proportion to his body. His head bore a white
turban and his robe, decorated with golden discs, glowed faintly.
The staff in his right hand gleamed in the light of a lamp he
carried in his other, but his face remained in shadow.

"Be careful you don't fall yet," he said in his irritatingly
sharp voice. "I have some questions to ask you first." He held
out the lamp and Adeh gasped. She lay on a narrow brick
platform just broad enough to hold her. Were she to move
forward the length of an arm, she would fall into the surrounding depths.

Illusion! she cried to herself. Of course there would be no
pit like this in somebody's stable. She'd been thrown into an
ordinary storeroom and then a first-rank mage had worked some
trickery. But if this was an illusion, where were the thin edges?
She peered down and saw glowing red creatures that scuttled,
far below, about the pit's bottom. For lack of a better victim,
they were attacking each other. Three surrounded a fourth,
leaped onto its back and began to tear its flesh with their jaws.
And several creatures glanced upward, as if anticipating a new
treat.

Adeh tried to find comfort in reason. She had already ex-
plored a good distance in each direction. Surely, in the darkness, she had pulled herself over parts of the floor that her
eyes now told her did not exist. Cautiously, she hitched forward
until she could lean her head over the smooth side of the
excavation that sliced neatly through bricks. She bobbed her
head down through the empty air; the creatures responded by
leaping toward her, their hairy tails waving as they jumped.

An illusion can kill, Salparin had said, if mind and body
are thoroughly convinced. In this case, Adeh could find no
room for doubt. She began to wonder whether in fact she had
moved very far. The thought that she had narrowly missed
falling over the rim made her face flush and her heart hammer.

"And now for my questions," said the mage. He lifted his
arm, poking the tip of his staff at her gag. She tried to dodge

the long rod, but it smacked the side of her head. The gag-cloth fell away. "Now you can speak." Adeh had meant to cry out as soon as her mouth was clear, but now she did not. Something was happening to her thoughts, as if someone were squeezing her mind, limiting her freedom. "Tell me who sent you," he insisted.

Her lips were no longer fully her own; she felt them parting without her consent. Yet she held back, biting the corner of her mouth where the cloth had cut. The pain helped keep the mage's will at bay.

"Who sent you?" he demanded again.

When she did not answer, he squeezed tighter, until Adeh's own will was numb. Her bite loosened; her jaw fell open. Her tongue began to move of its own accord. "Kyr . . . Karkilik!" she spat, the sound distorted from fighting the urge to say "Myranu."

"No doubt," said the mage. "But name me His earthly servant."

She filled her thoughts with the image of the temple mosaic: the Fire-breather triumphant over His enemies. "It was Karkilik Himself," she shouted again, this time with better mastery. "No other."

The mage shook his head. "A strong-willed jenny. But I know how to break you."

"You'll break, too," she answered back. "When the stones march over you. You think they're somebody's grand prank . . . a trick to be undone when the fancy strikes him . . ."

"Enough chatter. If you know something about it, you'll tell me soon enough." He lifted his staff with one hand, and tossed a pinch of powder into the air with the other. The creatures below suddenly ceased their haphazard battling and began to congregate along the inner wall. A dozen squeezed together and another dozen crawled onto the backs of the first. A tower of bodies began to grow.

Adeh's shoulders shook as she watched the heap of red vermin rise, and tried to guess how much time remained. Their heads were sharply pointed and full of teeth. A hairless fleshy ridge encircled each of their necks. As they reached higher she discerned tiny bulbous sacs studding their collars.

She shook her head, refusing to accept what she saw. An ordinary brick floor was all that surrounded her. Surely the illusion had a weak point, a place where she must focus her attention. She leaned over again to examine the edge of the cut more carefully, but found nothing awry. The cross-section showed a single layer of brick on a thin bed of gravel; below that the pit was sunk deep into hard dry earth.

What of the far side, where the digging met the unsurfaced brick wall of the storeroom? From her viewpoint, the match there, too, seemed flawless. She glanced down and saw that the creatures were halfway to their goal. The pile swayed as the vermin streamed upward, the snapping of their jaws growing louder moment by moment.

"What does it matter who sent me?" she shouted at the mage. "Everyone knows conjurers are stealing grain. It started in the fields and continues every night in the granaries. Do you think they won't find you out?"

"You can still save yourself," he replied calmly. "But you'll have to speak quickly. Even so, I might not have time to send them back." He pointed his staff at the pulsing mass of bodies.

Adeh could not sit still. Pushing with her feet, she swiveled away from the side where the attack would come. But she had no room to move in the opposite direction. Then the first red limb reached over the top, and she saw the creature head-on. Its sacs oozed sticky fluid that matted its bristly coat, and its teeth were illuminated by their own steely glow.

The thing lunged, and she kicked it aside with a backward jerk of her heels. The slimy fluid that sprayed her ankles had a fiery sting, but her blow pushed the beast back into the trench. Then another creature scuttled over the top. This one dug tiny claws into the floor and did not go over the brink when she kicked it. Then there were three more on the platform, and then there were six.

Now she was butting the creatures with her head as well, but she could not fight them all. Their secretions scorched wherever she touched them. She kicked again, but could not dislodge the pair that clung to her ankles. Their teeth pierced her skin. She thrashed hopelessly. Other paws scrabbled at her calf. Could she at least deprive the mage of hearing her screams? She clamped her lips together as she squirmed, fearing what she might reveal if she should cry out. The bristly creatures were all over her face.

But they had no smell! Surely such beasts, were they authentic, would carry the odor of their filth. Without a stench they couldn't be real. But they were blistering her fingers and her thighs. She was dizzy with pain.

Adeh forced herself to look carefully at one of the assailants. Was this thing really a living creature, a beast that ate flesh? The others were gnawing at her hands; she twisted her body and arms until she could see her fingers. Fighting the searing fluid, she grasped a creature from behind and pried its jaws open at the corners. She could see no tongue! She dared poke her thumb inside to feel around. No gullet either! How could it eat? She laughed bitterly as she flipped the body into the depths. Here was the edge of the illusion.

Absurd creatures! At once the pain lessened, the burning eased. The more she thought about the impossibility of the beasts, the less she noticed their presence. The glimmering vermin continued to swarm over her, but the feel of each bite was reduced to a mere pinch. And their secretions now seemed only mildly warm. She drew up her legs, and resolved to wait out the assault. Did the mage understand that she had overcome his trickery?

She stole a peek at him just as he was turning away from her. Did he think she had fainted from pain, she wondered. Or was he going after the wherewithal for a more terrifying illusion? The door shut behind him, and the room was dark again. The last remnants of the vermin vanished with the light.

Now there might be a chance for escape. She had heard no barring of the door. Indeed, if this room was used merely to hold straw, then it might lack a means to secure it. But cords still held her, and then there was the illusory pit.

She tried turning her wrists, and realized that she had gained some freedom of movement. The struggle had loosened the bonds, and her skin was slick with perspiration. She squeezed her fingers together, felt the cord slip, and pulled one hand free.

Holding back her cry of triumph, she immediately reached for her ankle bonds. But the captors had done a more thorough job there. The knots were still tight and there was no prying them loose. Perhaps she might still find a tool.

Wary of the pit's edge, she began to slide her fingers across the floor. Surely the brink had been closer than this . . . Suddenly she struck something sharp, and jumped back with fright. No. Not the rim of the trench. Again she ran her fingers over the floor, until she rediscovered the hard lump. By touch, she judged it to be a piece of broken brick with a long, harsh edge. This was what she needed, but before she used it she must learn something else.

Clutching the piece in one hand, she advanced again, this time with more confidence. Perhaps she had destroyed the one illusion along with the other. Possibly the mage's presence was needed for either to operate. If the pit were gone, she could be free . . . Once more, she dragged herself forward, keeping her attention on the thin line of light above the door. With a cry, she fell forward, hitting her face on the floor as her hand pushed through empty air.

The pit was still there! Frantically she felt about for the rim, almost losing her cutting tool in the process. A few moments of scrabbling convinced her that she was cut off from escape. When she dangled her hand over the side, she could not touch bottom.

"Mother of maggots!" she swore softly as she turned to work on her ankle bonds. She sawed at the tough cord with the piece of brick, scraping her flesh raw. With her fingertips, she could feel the fibers fraying. Fragments of the brick crumbled away, and she applied the new edge again. She strained, felt a snap, and her ankles broke free.

But now, what of the trench? If she could first judge its

depth, she might also overcome that trick. By her side lay all
she needed. Hurriedly, she fumbled for the discarded cording,
tied an end about the remainder of the brick, and lowered it
over the side. When all had been played out, she leaned down
and let her arm hang over the edge. Still the brick did not
touch bottom.

Adeh swore again. Now she understood why the mage had
left her unattended. The illusion, he expected, would keep her
safe for him. But she recalled what had happened in the temple
storeroom, and tried to still her anger. The mage had not reckoned on her peculiar resistance to magic. She had reason to
believe that there was no pit here at all. If she could find fully
convincing proof, then she could escape. But certainty, in all
things, was elusive. Perhaps, as with the false wall in the
passageway, a compromise might serve.

Intermediate between stone and air was water. If liquid
rather than air filled the trench, she wondered if she might
cross it. She had heard that a skilled person could propel herself
through water, but in Adeh's lifetime she had never *seen*, much
less entered, a pool or lake. Water in the trench might not be
enough, but it would serve as a start.

How could she modify the illusion? She lowered her arm
over the brink and waved her hand. If nothing else, she felt a
hint of moisture, a dampness that rose from the chilly depths.
That dampness must have a source. In her thoughts, the laden
air became a mist that hovered above a wet surface. And the
level was rising. She stretched her arm and waggled her fingers,
all the time telling herself that the water was there. *The pit
was not empty.* If the trickster could make her believe one
thing, why could she not convince herself of another?

Again, she saw in her mind the trench filling with water.
She leaned over until she was about to fall headlong into the
depths. She stretched until her tendons burned . . . And then
she dipped through the surface! Excitedly, she splashed, and
felt droplets on her arm. Now her wrist was immersed, and
now the level rose above her elbow.

But what would be the result of so much water? She thought

of soggy fields at the end of the rainy season, and then she pictured the trench brimming with mud. In fact, there was no trench at all, she decided. Someone had merely taken up the bricks and soaked the underlying ground. Already she felt a thickening. She pulled free her hands.

More mud! Drier! she told herself. Pressing in a thumb, she found that the surface still yielded, but now only slightly. Should she try for a firmer floor? Without waiting, she stood up and plunged in a foot. If her conviction failed, she would be stuck, imprisoned in place for the mage's amusement. She took a step. The mud sucked at her feet, making the next step even more difficult. She felt heavy cakes adhering to her feet. Then one leg would not come free at all.

She strained, thinking she would be happy to leave her sandal behind. Hoping to find a handhold on the other side, she leaned forward and touched her fingertips to rough boards. Then, with a loud smack, the suction broke, and she fell against the door.

Another step forward. Now she could straighten up. She clawed at splintery timbers and found she could widen the crack at the jamb. The door was not secured!

She peered through the narrow opening but saw no one outside. Again she seemed to be sinking; now was no time to linger. She wrenched her feet free one last time, slipped out into the larger room, and ran toward the wide stable door. Someone was standing guard, slumped before his lamp. Her noise would wake him, but he would need a moment to come to his senses.

Then she was out in the cool dawn air, her imagined impediments gone. She raced across the garden, trampling flowers and vines, dodging trees whose branches bowed with fruit, until she spotted a small ladder leaning against the limestone outer wall. Behind her, shouts echoed as the guard tried to rouse the others. She was up the ladder while footsteps beat across the ground. Then she placed her hands gingerly on the flints set into the top of the wall. She could not help but press her weight on the sharpened stones as she swung her legs up and leapt over.

For a moment the breath was knocked out of her and she lay helpless at the foot of the wall. She heard the bars drawn back. In a moment the gate would swing open. Adeh stood up, saw the blood welling on one cut palm, and hastily pressed her hand to the porous stone. *Let that mark the place*, she thought, as she hurried across the road into an alley, and then began to run. They might send a dozen men to chase her. She must leave them two dozen turnings. She darted left, then right, then right again, losing herself in unfamiliar streets. People were already coming from their houses. She dodged the early risers, who stared at her as if she were a thief.

At last she stumbled, by chance, into a street that ran past the high dome of a fire-temple. Remembering Myranu's amulet, she used the last of her strength to climb the broad stone steps.

As evening approached, the nomad fighters continued to arrive at the oasis in increasing numbers. The moans of thirsty camels being led to drink sounded above the harsh laughter of the men about the pool. Iskiir, under constant watch by one of Bermegi's riders, wandered from one knot of Karbayra to another. So far as he could tell, these men were armed only with knives and curved swords. What chance could such weapons have, he wondered, against the power of the Hethi? Yet the Karbayra were determined to free their kin. And if the blue-turbans were to lose their followers, whose lives they were draining for power, then the attack on the Menjians would falter. In that possibility lay Iskiir's hope.

More interesting to the young man than the fighters were the Karbayra mages. He watched them sitting cross-legged, each with his head covered by a tasseled cap of black wool. Some muttered incantations, while others studied the markings on small clay jars that they pulled from their woven bags. Here and there a mage bent over a copper amulet, inscribing with a narrow tool of flint what Iskiir took to be spells. To him, their letters were like the footprints of lizards in soft soil.

Now and then a mage would look up at him with raised eyebrows, as if recalling a questionable tale. Iskiir wished he could find one who spoke his language. He had not the slightest notion of what powers they might bring to bear.

Meanwhile, as he wandered, he noticed the crowd becoming increasingly boisterous. Men dropped their swords to clamber up the trunks of date palms, plucking unripe fruit and pelting their friends below. Others gathered about small fires to brew coffee in dented, sooty pots. A single porcelain cup was passed from hand to hand, each imbiber taking but a drop on his tongue. The stories that passed about the circles became louder and the laughter more raucous.

The Menjian felt isolated in the midst of the huge gathering, confused by differences in language and customs. How, he wondered, could these men put aside concerns over the upcoming battle. Iskiir could think of nothing else. Even when he tried to remember Adeh, he found difficulty in holding her image. Perhaps it was already too late. Perhaps the demon stones had done their work and the city was no more. He could not allow himself such despair . . .

Suddenly, in the crowd of so many strangers, Iskiir encountered a familiar face. *Odeema*. This man had been his captor but a day earlier, yet Iskiir greeted him like a long-standing friend.

"So, pigeon," said the smith, his thick lips showing an affable grin. "You are clever enough to keep your head together with your body."

"Bermegi . . ." Iskiir glanced uncomfortably at the raider bodyguard beside him. Though the man showed no signs of speaking the Menjian language, Iskiir was careful in phrasing his thoughts. "Bermegi thinks I can be of some use to him."

Odeema pulled his huge sword from its scabbard and held its edge close to Iskiir's face. "This is what he needs. The best I ever forge." His voice dropped and his face darkened. "I quench in viper venom," he confided. "We spend two years collecting it."

Iskiir had to hold back from asking how well it would do against a jinn. He studied the bone hilt with its carved pattern of interlinked rings. Perhaps some magic lay in its design. "May it serve well," he said simply. He glanced again at the swordsman's round face and wondered if he might now inquire about his companions.

"Your friends," began Odeema, saving Iskiir the trouble of broaching the ticklish subject. "The fat one is put to work. Helping the women with their weaving. I hear he does good." The nomad threw back his head and bellowed with mirth. "The old one . . . he comes with me." Odeema turned and peered at the crowd, then shouted to a wiry man of his tribe. A moment later Dajnen shuffled forward, his nose chain dangling, his face in its usual scowl.

"*Bolu!*" His lips barely showed a smile of greeting. "These camel farts think I know sorcery. I told 'em I can't help. My oaths to the gods. Do they care?"

"You can help *me*," said Iskiir. "By teaching me everything you know about Hethi."

The Appeaser sighed. "I've told you most of it already. They know illusions . . . and a few bits of real magic. And after they use up all their tricks, they'll turn themselves into jinns." He glanced at Odeema's scabbard and dared to utter what Iskiir had kept to himself. "Easier to cut rocks than jinns," he said, evidently unimpressed by the hilt. Then he turned around and studied the undisciplined crowd.

As he watched, he shook his head and clucked despondently. "These men against Hethi? I'd rather send rabbits against jackals. No, *bolu*. What we need are some magical fighters. You hear me? Better practice changing a few *people* if you're goin' to make yourself useful."

"People?" Iskiir had never considered attempting such a feat. Yet the transformed camel had been too stupid to best a jinn. How much better, he wondered, might one of Bermegi's raiders fare?

Following Dajnen's gaze, Iskiir, too, stared with curiosity

at the armed Karbayra. Might he truly make a man over into someone or *something* capable of destroying a Hethi? And if so, he wondered, who would be willing to submit to such a change?

Chapter 14

Demon warriors! The thought made Iskiir's head spin. Despite his misgivings, he sought Bermegi in the crowd. The hollow-cheeked raider was easy to locate; he stood at the center of the greatest commotion, arguing while he beat his fists first on his own chest and then on those of his companions. Iskiir pushed his way through the throng and managed to attract the chief's attention by waving his headcloth in the air.

"Show us this trick," Bermegi demanded when he had heard the plan. "How many men you need? Here... take him... and this fox, too." He slapped the arms of several tribesmen, shouted an order to each, then led the group out to a quiet place far from the pool. There, Dajnen caught up with them.

"Try this one first," said Bermegi, pushing forward a short man whose face was hidden in shadow. "No good to us as he is, so why not?"

The former goat-boy glanced at Dajnen with renewed uncertainty. The old one had forced this test on him. If he failed at it, the nomads might lose all faith in Iskiir's abilities. Yet, without magical warriors, he did not know how the battle might be won. "I–I need light," he said nervously.

Bermegi barked and someone came running with an oil lamp. "What else you want?" the chief demanded. "Tongue of buzzard? Eye of scorpion? We have none."

"N-nothing else." Iskiir held out the lamp and glimpsed the flat nose and sneering face of the man he was to change. *Man?* This youngster was scarcely older than Ergar, his chin beardless, his cheeks smeared with dust. His breathing was heavy, and a film of sweat covered his brow. *What if I succeed and then can't change him back?* The question was on Iskiir's lips, but he dared not ask it in Bermegi's hearing.

"I wait," said the raider.

Iskiir knew he could delay no longer. He had asked for a subject and now he had one. He could only hope that Dajnen's advice would prove sound. At once he focused on the youth, studying first the smooth lines of his face, and then the rumpled dark robe with the ragged hem. He had found the camel-changing task difficult; this one would surely be harder.

As with the camel, he strove to bring his own thoughts into the nomad's body. He tried to feel the cool sand beneath the youngster's bare, calloused feet, and the headcloth that brushed against his cheeks. At once there came a sensation of struggle, of pushing a bulky load up a hill. The camel had seemed heavy; this weight was immense.

In his mind he moved step by step, tugging the youth's body upward to meet its new form. Iskiir felt a whisper at his nape, and then caught a glimmer of a golden figure in the distance. But the *other* was still far away; he must labor to reach it.

Iskiir's face and arms ran with sweat as he wrestled with the image of the nomad. What was this resistance, he wondered, that made him feel he was dragging a balking donkey up a mountain path? Yet before him, growing nearer as he climbed, stood a giant with a scaly, golden head.

The Menjian waited for the wind to rise, but he heard nothing. And where was the tingling? He had felt it moments before and now it was gone. He was losing his concentration. The sounds of nomad laughter were breaking through. His vision of the giant vanished and the boy's face leered up at him.

"*Bolu*, you almost had it," said Dajnen with disgust. "Try again. Do that ugly fellow next to you. He might be easier to work on."

But Iskiir hung his head in exhaustion and closed his eyes. He was not ready for another try.

In the safety of the temple, Adeh's hand still throbbed. She glanced down at the bloodstains that darkened the white stripes of her jubbah, then at the cloth wrap that bandaged her palm. She wished that both could be unmarred again. But even if the signs were to vanish, she could not forget what she had seen.

"More broth?" asked the acolyte, a girl a year younger than Adeh, who sat beside her holding a porcelain bowl. The two were alone in a narrow chamber, seated on a thick sky-blue carpet that ran the length of the room. Sunlight spilled through high grillwork windows to spread diffuse light across the floor. On one wall hung a woven depiction of the Fire in its bowl, on the other a tapestry showed gazelles of pale gold drinking at a water hole.

"If you please . . ." A male voice interrupted. Seeing a fire-priest at the door, the acolyte rose. She turned to give Adeh a shy parting smile, then hurried out carrying her bowl in two hands. The priest, wearing his tall, tapered hat and white vestments, entered with Salparin at his elbow. "You'll want privacy," said the priest. He turned stiffly and closed the door behind him.

"Adeh, I am sorry." Salparin, whose face bore fresh lines of worry about the eyes, took in her condition and pursed his lips with concern. "But I'm glad we found you quickly. When you vanished from the storeroom, the guards were blamed for dozing at their posts."

"I didn't leave through their doors."

The magician raised his eyebrows. Hastily she recounted the events of the evening, starting with the sleep-inducing scent

in the granary. As she spoke she watched Salparin's expression
turn from thoughtfulness to curiosity to dismay. He asked her
to repeat several times the conversation she had heard through
the stable door. But his expression brightened as she described
her escape from the illusions.

"You've proved your abilities twice over," he said with an
approving nod. "And you've found our grain thieves as well.
The mark you left will stand out to trained eyes—even if the
scoundrels try to clean it off."

"That turbaned mage should suffer for what he did to me,"
she said bitterly.

"We'll have him in custody by noon today," Salparin assured
her. "We won't lose him the way we did the other. He'll tell
us what he knows. And then the Guild will see to his punish-
ment."

"But the stones . . ."

Myranu's brother shook his head sadly. "I believe these
thieves know as little as we do about the stones."

"But what of this Wunal the men blamed?"

"I should tell you about him. He's a dabbler in magic, a
man of great means who has no need for the Guild. Such a
person would naturally fall under suspicion, and so we've been
watching him. But there's little chance that he's our culprit.
For one thing, he's been busy preparing his escape."

"Oh?"

Salparin crossed his arms and glanced up at the high windows. "He's building a wheeled scaffolding just outside the
city wall, a high ladder mounted on oxcarts. I don't know how
he's getting the wood. Wunal has such wealth that he can
probably have trees grown to his order."

Adeh tried to picture the construction. "He's going to *climb*
out?" She knew how others had tried that and failed.

"His design is clever. With wheels, the structure will roll
instead of toppling if the stones push against it. But the climbing itself is still a problem. He's an agile fellow for his age,
yet I wonder how he expects the rest of his family to do it."

Adeh shook her head at the thought of the task, yet she was

forced to admire this Wunal's ingenuity. And surely if he could halt the attack on the city, then he would have no use for his construction. "Then my work is finished?" Her voice trailed off, and she stared down at her hand again.

The mage sighed. "Yes, this part of it. And we have accomplished something. With your help, we've caught up with the last of our suspects. Yet none, so far as we can tell, have ties with this evil sorcery. Until we examine your first-rank scoundrel, we won't be certain, but I'm nearly ready to send in my report."

"To..."

"To the Permengord Council of Mages. Now that we've eliminated the other possibilities, they'll realize that outsiders are to blame. And they'll have time to prepare for the next attack—wherever it may come. For that warning, many will thank you."

"But what can the Permengord mages do for Tajmengus?"

"Adeh, there is no way they can help us. It would take half a month for them just to get here."

"Then *we* must do something." She felt her eyes stinging, and quickly rubbed her sleeve against her face.

"Our only hope lies in following Wunal's lead," he said quietly. "I wish someone had thought of it sooner. But we've begun the construction. And if we can convince people to flee, then we may save a few of them—though the old and infirm won't have a chance."

"Even so, we must try." She turned her thoughts from herself. Her wounded hand and the bloodied jubbah no longer had any significance. What mattered now was finding a way over the stones before they crushed all life from the city. But if escape became possible, she wondered how many would go. Even as the monoliths neared the high wall, her father and uncle continued to scoff at the danger. And their views were echoed, she believed, in nearly every household.

"Come," the mage said wearily. "We still have work for you, though it makes poor use of your talents."

*   *   *

Iskiir was wakened harshly, then pulled to a sitting position. Before he could open his eyes, he felt a crusted cup being pushed against his lips, and smelled the sharp, rich odor of the nomads' coffee. "Drink!" said Bermegi. "We ride now."

"Now?" Fighting sleep, Iskiir raised his heavy lids to glance at the dark sky. There was no sign of morning. He took one swallow of the bitter brew before the cup was pulled away. Groggily he pieced together what had happened.

One by one, he had focused on the nomads, failing twice before he managed to work a change. With a better understanding of the process, he had gone back to his first two subjects and finished their transformations as well. But the effort had so exhausted him that he had soon collapsed in sleep.

And what had he accomplished? His mind refused, for a moment, to return to those recent events. Meanwhile Bermegi was hurrying him to his camel, pushing the young man through the throng of nomads and beasts. As they approached the rim of the oasis, Iskiir caught sight of a tall silhouette well beyond the edge of the crowd. *That's one of them!* The enormous two-legged thing tilted its oblong head, and Iskiir remembered its golden skin and knobby hands. Formerly the sulky youth, this creature still retained its magical form. What of the others?

The first, he now recalled, had become a squat and hairy creature, large-bellied and wolf-jawed, which also walked on two legs. The thought of its horned feet made him shiver. And the third—that had been the least successful of the lot. Instead of a potential fighter, the plump-faced Karbayra had been turned into an ordinary sheep. Frightened, or embarrassed by jeers, it had run off into the night.

"Mount," ordered Bermegi. Quickly the chieftain gathered the rest of his small party. While the bulk of his force still milled about the oasis, he signaled for Olkar, the freed captive to ride ahead. Here was the one man who could lead them to the main Hethi camp. Three of Bermegi's raiders and his black-capped mage filled out the group. And as they advanced across the sand, Iskiir realized that there was one more member. The shimmering giant was following, keeping himself downwind of the camels. With his huge, slow strides he seemed to have no difficulty keeping pace.

The silence was almost complete, broken only by the soft footfalls of the mounts. Iskiir had no estimate of the distance his party was to cover. He knew only that they must be heading toward Tajmengus, for somewhere in that vicinity the Hethi had encamped. Despite the prospect of battle, the ride began to make him drowsy again. His eyelids drooped and his chin fell . . .

His thoughts drifted back toward Adeh. At the oasis he had not been able to picture her clearly. Now he saw her as if she stood before him, her brow wrinkled in thought, her cheeks aglow. Startled by the clarity of the image, his eyes opened wide. He saw an unexpected flutter before his face. Blinking he realized that he was looking at a huge moth with a faintly glowing head. The insect flew closer, and Iskiir made out the tiny features of a woman.

The young man wondered if he was dreaming after all. But he recalled a similar creature at the caravans' market, where he had blamed the vendor for trickery. Were Hethi illusions already beginning? He looked around and saw the caravan proceeding as before. Nothing had changed, except for the surprising appearance of the flyer.

The moth came closer and he heard its voice, just as he had heard the other sing. "Adeh sent me, but I couldn't find you. You weren't in the mountains. You weren't in Lact. Adeh sent me, but I didn't have to come." The creature then flew closer to brush Iskiir's ear with its wings. In an instant he was overwhelmed by a sense of Adeh's presence—her mouth, the subtle scent of her hair.

Sorcery! he muttered. Yet he did not take this as a Hethi sending. The moth touched him again, and he felt suffused with Adeh's thoughts. Her troubles in the days following his escape flashed before him. Without hearing words, he knew what had happened to her in the wheat field, and about her training with the priestess's brother. And he knew also that the city's mages remained helpless before the onslaught of the stones.

"I can fly back to her," said the moth. "I can if I want to. But I'm free. I'm free." Suddenly the creature landed in the middle of his forehead. Iskiir was again so filled with Adeh's presence that he could not bring himself to brush the flyer away. "Tell me what you've learned," it said. "She wants to know all you can tell her."

Iskiir wondered briefly if this could be another Hethi trick, a subtle truth spell far crueler than the original. But he was unable to keep his thoughts from Adeh. He barely noticed the progress of the camels as he whispered his experiences of recent days. From time to time he glanced nervously at the nomad mage's back, fearing the old one's disapproval, but the vinegar-face did not turn. The sky was growing light when the flyer lifted its wings.

"Now I'll go to the mountain," said the hovering moth. "Now I'll do as I please."

Iskiir felt as if a trance had been dissolved. The air was chilly again, the camel's gait was lurching and the saddle made his bones ache.

"I'm free," taunted the creature. "I can go where I choose."

"May a cliff owl digest you slowly if you fail her," Iskiir replied. Then he watched the wings rise into the pale sky.

For some time Iskiir could not turn his attention from Adeh's difficulties to his own. He wondered how long ago the moth had left her, and whether the city still stood. Now that dawn had come, he peered across the dry landscape for a sight of Tajmengus. If only he could glimpse a watchtower...

About him he saw only Bermegi's riders and occasional clumps of salt grass. In the near distance, the tall figure of the giant still strode with them. But there was no sign of a city and no hint either of the vast body of tribesmen that had assembled. Presumably they lagged far behind, their disposition to be settled by the fate of the frontrunners.

Would the others charge the Hethi camp, he wondered. Or was their strategy to surround it to spread thin the defense

Recalling Dajnen's guess that the nomads outnumbered the Hethi, the young man shook his head. He did not think numbers alone would serve. A hyena pack had been known to harry a lion, but then a lion possessed only claws and teeth for protection.

Olkar waved for a halt as they neared a clump of tamarisk. The frail rider looked about with a frown and then Bermegi began to interrogate him in a low whisper. Iskiir was puzzled at the confusion, for the former captive had told of making several trips to the blue-turbans' camp. After another exchange, the chieftain muttered to his mage and then spoke a few words to Iskiir. "Hethi trickery," he said. "They change look of land. They hide from us. But we find."

Iskiir watched the black-cap extract a slender stick from his baggage, a rod banded by scaly patterns. The mage spoke a short incantation, then opened a leather pouch and dipped the end of the staff into its contents. Iskiir caught a harsh, smoky smell. The wand emerged with a dark smudge at its tip, and the mage held the piece at arm's length. Suddenly the rod seemed to bend sideways in his hand. Bermegi barked an order, and all began to ride cautiously in the direction the wand had pointed.

Soon they sighted a distant string of low hills which glowed red in the early morning light. Perhaps from the top, Iskiir thought, he might finally glimpse what remained of Tajmengus. But as the riders followed the mage's course, they reached a deep and narrow cleft. The appearance was as if a monstrous ax had bit into the earth. Too wide to leap and too steep to descend, the barrier appeared impassable. When Bermegi pointed toward a possible way around, the black-cap clucked and shook his head, then couched his camel. At the chieftain's orders, the other animals were backed away from the chasm while the mage remained to probe the ground with his staff.

Iskiir suspected conjuring, but he was aware how powerful illusions might be. The mage opened a small jar, and poured a drop of liquid into the depths. A puff of steam rose from a point just at ground level. Turning with a look of satisfaction, he reported his findings to Bermegi.

Moments later, the riders were tying cloths about the camels' eyes. Iskiir found a strip of tentcloth in his pouch and did the same. Then the riders turned their mounts' heads toward their tails. Iskiir tried pulling his headrope sideways, and striking his beast's neck as the others were doing. The animal seemed confused, lurching first left and then right. At last, the Menjian discovered the proper signal, for he, too, had his animal walking in circles.

When the camels had surely lost all sense of heading, Bermegi led his own mount directly toward the cleft. Iskiir halted his dizzy spiral to watch the nomad's course. He gasped as the blinded camel advanced, put a front foot down at the edge of the cut and lifted its other foot to step forward. If the rift were mere illusion, then the camel could not know where it was expected to stumble. But if the mage were wrong . . . Suddenly Bermegi and his mount toppled over the edge. The men groaned with despair, but their anguish was short-lived. For camel and rider reappeared at once, calmly continuing their journey on the far side of the chasm.

The mage gave a nod to the others, and by turns each followed the chieftain's route. Iskiir could not bear to watch as his own beast stepped forward fearlessly to plunge into the narrow opening. He felt himself falling; clutching the pommel he bit his tongue to keep from crying out. The earth was rushing toward him. He felt the cold breath of the deep on his face as he tensed for impact. When the blow did not come, he opened his eyes and saw that he was riding safely on the other side. He loosened his grip and began to smile.

The riders were all across, but what of the giant? Iskiir glanced back to see the huge warrior approaching the chasm. He wore only a loincloth, and his skin was slick and golden. From knee to ankle a thick membrane sprouted from the back of each leg. His feet were like long donkey hooves. His head was covered with yellow scales. Without breaking stride, the giant leaped the gap and continued to run toward the ridge, all the while clutching his fearsome lance.

The heights lay before them; with no further obstructions, the party began to climb a rocky path. They had surely reached their goal. Iskiir could think only of the view they would have at the crest. But Bermegi signaled for caution. Still blindfolded, the camels picked their way slowly, and the young man wondered if he would ever reach the top.

Then suddenly, in the distance, he saw Tajmengus, tightly ringed by demon stones yet still standing. The tips of watchtowers and temples rose above the dark rocks. Alive! But his joy was brief. "She is finished," came a voice in his head, a voice all too similar to the one he had heard at Jalween. Seated calmly on a ledge, a blue-turbaned mage stared up at him. "Turn around. Save yourselves many deaths," said the voice. Behind the Hethi stood two Karbayra who leaned on walking sticks and stared dully at the ground.

"So," Adeh's father said to her. "It's your advice that I abandon my shop to vandals. It's you who urge me to leave my house unguarded. What have you learned in nineteen years? Not even how to clean the coffeepot..." Seated before the last crumbs of the morning meal he added peevishly, "But fortunately for you, these days, it needs no cleaning."

"Demid, you can't blame her for that." Passela glanced at her daughter as if she had much to say. Surely, Adeh thought, her mother was more sensible than the men. If it were up to Passela, the Demilus would grasp eagerly at the chance to flee.

"The traders are behind this," said her father. "I've known it all along. Nothing but a trick to push up their prices."

"We'll be so glad when they come back," her uncle added. "We'll pay anything they ask. A sack of *menos* for a sack of coffee beans. Anything." He slapped a fist into the palm of his hand. "Let me have one of those thieves alone, and he'll answer for this."

Adeh tried to speak calmly, but her voice rose in fury. "When the stones came, I saw traders running from the market. Did they fear their own magic?"

"And what were you doing in the caravans' market?" asked her father.

His daughter could only glare at him.

"Out!" he said, pointing up at the stairs. "Let's hear no more from you. Go to your temple. See how many priests you can badger into leaving their fires. But now I have work to do."

Adeh glanced helplessly at her mother, who gave a barely perceptible nod of acquiescence. When Demid was this stubborn, both knew, there was nothing more to be done. Adeh held back her tears as she rushed to the doorway. What chance was there now for her family? If the carpenters succeeded in building a scaffold, then some other families might survive. But her father would not believe in the forthcoming doom until bricks rained down on him.

Once outside, she tried to gain courage for the task she had drawn. The construction crews were already at work. But their pains would be for naught if no one was willing to make use of their efforts. Adeh had failed at her first recruiting attempt, and now she must approach strangers. How could she succeed elsewhere when she had failed at home?

She had been assigned to canvass a block of nearby houses. Timidly she climbed the stairway of the first and knocked for entrance, then explained in a loud voice that she had come from the fire-temple. Evidently the householders thought her intent was to beg alms, for they were slow to admit her. She heard a muffled argument. At last the door creaked open, and she was led into a tiny room furnished only with a thin gray rug.

The sole man present was narrow of face with sparse, white chin-whiskers. "Talk to my brother," he kept saying, though the other did not appear. The two women, one elderly with a puffy face, and one Passela's age with rich, dark eyes, said nothing. Adeh repeated her offer of a means to escape, but could elicit no response. That all three were frightened she had no doubt. They looked unhappily down at their clasped hands and would not meet her eyes. This she understood. Without the consent of the head of the family, they dared not speak a word of encouragement. When Adeh would not relent, they sent her to the Street of Lampmakers to find the one who might decide.

Entering the street, Adeh saw that most of the shops were still open, though their usual heaps of merchandise had dwindled to small piles. The lampmaker she wanted sat tapping at a circular sheet of brass, working it around and around his small anvil as he shaped it into a bowl. His rounded hammerhead made a steady rhythm and he paid her no heed. Beside him, an apprentice was applying greasy polish, poking a small cloth around the loop handle of a finished lamp.

She contrived to bump against a basket of brass scraps, making a rattle that set her teeth on edge. The proprietor threw down his hammer and shouted at the apprentice. "Can't you see we've a customer?" He looked back at the half-finished work in his hand as if trying to recall where he'd left off.

"I . . . come from the temple," Adeh said in a quiet voice. "I need to speak to you . . . about your family."

The craftsman, whose sparse chin-whiskers made him a near double of his brother, glowered at her from close-set eyes. "What do they want of me? I gave 'em the same offering as always. Didn't hear any complaints." He picked up his tool again.

"Not that. It's about the demon stones. They haven't stopped, and now . . ."

The lampmaker lifted the hammer over the basket and smashed at the pile of small scraps, setting up a racket that the whole street must have heard. Again and again he set the pieces jangling, all the while staring furiously up at Adeh. "Not you, too," he said. "I have to hear this at home and now here?"

She could not get out of the shop quickly enough. But she paused at the modest collection of lamps heaped by the doorway and kicked the bottom one away. The clatter almost equaled that from the basket, with lamps rolling in every direction.

"That's how your shop will fall," she shouted before she ran into the street. Myranu would not be proud of her for that show of temper, she knew, but the tyrant deserved far worse.

How could she continue? Wiping her wet cheeks, she resolved to ask for another assignment. Someone with more patience was needed to face the obstinate old men and convince them of the seriousness of the matter. But what more could she do for Tajmengus? Even if all the grain in the city were stolen now, it would not matter.

She blundered through the streets, colliding here and there with people she did not see. They were doomed, all of them. Why should she care about corpses? All day, they wandered the streets out of habit, continuing to believe that all would be better in a day or two. *What does it matter to you if the shelves are empty?* she wanted to shout. *The dead don't eat. The dead don't drink.*

Something, maybe a movement half seen, or a hazy face, made her think of Iskiir. He was a corpse, too, by now. What was that to her? She had heard of people throwing themselves from the tops of watchtowers. That would be quicker than waiting for the stones.

Again, she saw him. This time his presence was so strong that she stopped her aimless running and leaned against a wall to catch her breath. Something was fluttering about her head. Silvery wings glinted as the *buri* made another try to touch her cheek.

"I found him," said the creature. "I was free, but I came back."

"He's gone," said Adeh.

"I saw him," said the flyer.

"May cats shred your wings! May you learn what it is to be earthbound like the rest of us!"

Then the *buri* landed on her forehead and her bitter thoughts dissolved, briefly, into joy.

Chapter 15

The Hethi sat calmly on his rock. No one else moved. His two followers, leaning awkwardly against their walking sticks, barely seemed to draw breath. And Iskiir could not even blink his eyes. "Retreat now, fleas," the mage said to the intruders, "before you begin to annoy me." He rolled his eyes back. "Let this be my parting lesson." His pupils vanished completely and his followers sighed in unison.

Iskiir could not scream, which made his terror all the greater. Someone was slitting him open, packing his heart with ice and setting frost into his veins. Cold clutched his chest, spreading its chilling ache along his arms to his fingertips, along his belly to his groin. Still the blade cut deeper, freezing even the marrow of his bones. There was nothing in the world besides Iskiir and his pain.

Yet suddenly the attack ended as if it had never been. "Another lesson, my itchy pests?" asked the mage. "One usually suffices." Iskiir felt the grip on his tongue loosen and knew that the mage was permitting him to confess defeat. Were the

others also being granted that privilege? He could not turn to
see their faces, nor could he hear them drawing breath. He
clamped his teeth together to keep from crying out in despair,
then braced himself for what was to come. But the frigid blade
did not return at once.

Then he saw something at the corner of his vision. A huge
golden arm swung and a lance hissed through the air at the
blue-turban. The shaft of the weapon vibrated where it had
pierced his robe, yet the Hethi merely frowned. Iskiir could
see no damage to mage or clothing. Surely the Hethi sat, not
before them, but in a safe spot nearby. *Another displaced image!*

The golden fighter strode forward, still free to challenge the
blue-turban. The mage had not been able to restrain the giant
as he had the others. A knobby hand retrieved the weapon and
struck again, this time to the side of the blue-turban's apparent
place. The changed nomad had caught on to the Hethi's trick,
Iskiir realized with sudden hope. The mage's frown deepened,
and again his eyes began to roll. The weapon plunged toward
another spot. The mage sprang from his seat and started to
alter.

Both followers let out deep groans. One fell to his knees.
The other turned pale as the Hethi became a jinn. The new
opponent drew back its lips. The pale hairs about its chin were
stained yellow by its slavering. Its dark teeth were the length
of chisels, its mouth big enough to bite off a camel's head.
But the jinn was already wounded, Iskiir saw, for rust-brown
juices oozed from a rent in its side.

The giant poised his long weapon to fend off the other,
keeping the talons away from his rippling body. Iskiir marveled
at the sight of the creature he had brought across—the golden
muscles, the graceful control. Here, as Dajnen had predicted,
stood a warrior who might defeat a jinn. And Iskiir believed
that the changed Hethi already was faltering, for its magical
grip continued to weaken—the young man found that he could
turn his head. Beneath him, despite the blindfold it still wore,
his camel was straining to flee.

The jinn sidestepped first left and then right, but the rocks and low bushes hindered its footing. The fighting seemed to disrupt the displacement spell, for now the giant could directly address his opponent. The warrior was too quick for the jinn, jabbing and feinting, opening one small gash after another on the hairy one's arms and chest. The changed Hethi slashed with its talons, snapped its enormous jaws, and tried to close with the giant, but each time the golden one's footwork proved too deft. The taloned one was slowing down, while the other dodged and danced without seeming to tire.

Finally the warrior had a moment's respite from the jinn's attacks. He pulled back his arm. The great lance whistled through the air and struck center, the shaft piercing cleanly, the head emerging to lodge in a cleft behind the jinn. The taloned one screamed a curse, writhed like a skewered rabbit, and spewed brown blood. The talons drooped, and suddenly the jinn was a mage again, his robes torn and blood-soaked, his turban knocked askew, his hands clutching in a death grip the shaft that impaled him.

Iskiir's camel, free now of all magical restraint, shook its head in frenzy. *It smells the foul blood,* Iskiir thought. Fearing the animal would plunge to its death on the rocky slope, the Menjian dropped to the ground and leaned all his weight on its headrope. The other riders, too, were fighting their camels, but they managed to remain mounted. Bermegi held his sword in the air, twisting it to catch the sun. A signal? Iskiir was too busy with his mount to see the result.

At last his animal calmed. For the first time, Iskiir was able to scan the landscape immediately below him. Here, on the outskirts of Tajmengus, lay remains of an ancient city he had seen previously only from afar. Piles of stone blocks lay scattered over the plain. In the larger ruins, pillars remained upright, supporting slabs whose immensity made him gasp. These were the old temples that Olkar had spoken of, buildings in which the Hethi now hid themselves and their Karbayra prisoners. But so far only one blue-turban had been destroyed, one out of hundreds. The others were somewhere below, concealed in the rubble. By what means, Iskiir wondered, could the captives be freed?

As his gaze swept the far side of the hill, he suddenly saw tribesmen, far to his right, descending on foot with their mounts in tow. The other fighters had already arrived! Surely, they had traveled not behind him, but on a parallel course. He looked to his left, and saw another contingent heading toward the ruins.

And at that moment, a crowd of blue-turbaned figures swarmed out from the central temple. Behind them straggled Karbayra with shuffling gaits. It was from these unfortunates, Iskiir knew, that the Hethi would draw power for their defense.

Meanwhile, atop the hill, Bermegi's mage paused briefly to tend the followers of the dead sorcerer. The hapless pair now lay on the ground, their limbs twitching and jerking in a demon's dance. The black-cap brought a jar to one man's lips. At the same time, Bermegi barked an order, and his party began to descend the jagged path.

Looking back, Iskiir could not tell if the fallen ones improved under the mage's treatment. But he did notice, with puzzlement, that one of Bermegi's fighters had no camel. Then he recognized the short youth who walked alone, the flat nose familiar though he had glimpsed it only in lamplight. The boy had returned to his human shape, perhaps jolted out of his magical form by the battle with the jinn. The reverted giant appeared dazed, and he walked seemingly without watching his steps. The Menjian feared that his wits had not returned intact.

Iskiir knew nothing of the risks of his transformations. What happened to the ordinary side of a thing, he wondered, while its magical side moved to this world? Or were both sides somehow part of a whole, each always present but only one apparent? There were too many questions he had never had time to ask, and Dajnen had volunteered few answers.

Now there would be no time to fret over consequences. Below, he saw the Hethi rousting more followers from the old buildings. The bareheaded victims, too dazed to understand their danger, trailed after their captors as the sorcerers spread out to meet the oncoming force.

Bermegi's party was halfway down the hill when the ground began to shake. In the mountains, Iskiir often had felt the earth tremble. *Demon-belching,* they called the tremors, which were always over as soon as they were noticed. Now the path shook from side to side without ceasing, and Iskiir began to stumble.

The camels moaned softly and spread their legs wider apart. Did they feel the illusion as strongly as he did, Iskiir wondered. Perhaps the blindfolds protected them from the full brunt of the trickery. But they were balking at every step despite the rapping of sticks against their flanks. And Iskiir could barely convince himself that the hillside was not about to fall on him.

The quaking grew more violent. The young man understood why the mage had called the tribesmen fleas. The hill was a cur now and the men its pests. The ridge heaved, but it could not shake the insects from its back.

The nomads began a singsong chant to keep the animals moving. This helped calm most of the animals. They made headway at a slow but methodical pace. Iskiir took a quick glance to his right and saw that several camels had broken free from their masters. One beast blundered into a jagged rock pile, fell to its knees and began to thrash. But the other mounts remained under control. The right flank of Bermegi's force had nearly reached level ground.

Abruptly, the Hethi changed tactics. The quaking ceased, then eerie howls filled the air. The baying of wolves had kept Iskiir awake on far too many nights. The camels clearly knew the sound. With a frenzy that the tremors had failed to evoke, they began to buck and snarl. As if the howling was not enough, the Hethi filled the air with the pungent, bitter scent of wolf spoor. And for the benefit of the men, who could see ahead, a high barrier of thorn bushes sprouted at the base of the hill.

The men could not get past the illusory bushes without riding the blindfolded camels. But the camels could not be managed for the fear of wolves. Iskiir had only those two thoughts in mind as he fought his plunging animal. The howling made him shiver, and his hands burned from the rubbing of the headrope. To his left he saw more beasts breaking free, some falling victim at once to the rough slope, others finding their way safely down to plunge through false thorns they did not see.

He wondered how much longer he could check his hissing, thrashing animal. Then, from the distant ranks he heard a ram's horn wailing, and in answer other horns began to blast. Iskiir marveled that someone could restrain his camel and handle the instrument as well, but even among his own party a high note sounded. He caught sight of Bermegi with a horn at his lips, and then he knew its purpose. *Noise to drown out the wolf calls!* And the mage was tossing a dark red powder in the air, its suffocating perfume disguising the wolf scent.

Iskiir grinned in appreciation of the nomads' quick thinking. Seemingly, they had beaten the first set of Hethi tricks; the animals now settled into a nervous walk. As the men of the right flank neared bottom, they hastily mounted. Then, without pausing, they rode the blindfolded beasts through the illusory thorns.

Moments later, the tribesmen of the main force were plunging toward the line of blue-turbans. Still descending, Iskiir watched with horror as riders were stricken in midflight, their faces filled with agony. He remembered how the Hethi had sliced at him on the ridge. His fears ran in cold rivers down his sides and chest.

But the sorcerers could not attack everyone at once. While some tribesmen dropped to the ground, others remained mounted and flashed their curved swords. They swung wildly, so that even illusions could not protect their tormentors. Turbaned heads tumbled from necks, and arms raised in gesture were sliced through at the elbow. The Hethi could bleed and die like ordinary men, Iskiir saw.

Before such an onslaught, the enemy mages did not remain long as men. The survivors of the first advance began to change, and within moments a line of jinns stood to face the nomad warriors. A few brave riders tried to hack their way through the transformed Hethi, but their swords bounced from jinn bodies as if they had struck steel. The demon talons, as they passed, tore the riders' legs and gashed the flanks of the camels. Those who could, turned their beasts and fled to the safety of the hill.

Iskiir was dazzled by the noise and rush of battle. He forgot what he had learned the previous evening. All he could think of was keeping his grip on the pommel. Bermegi halted his party at the base of the hill and turned an anguished face to the Menjian. "We need new demon fighters," he called. In response, a heavyset raider jumped to the ground and stood at Iskiir's feet.

The volunteer's nostrils flared and he held himself as if ready for battle, with one hand on his sword grip, and his feet firmly planted. He looked expectantly at the Menjian. A slight quiver at the edge of the tribesman's mouth was the only indication of his wariness.

At the oasis, Iskiir had learned by painful trial how the change could be done. Now he must apply his knowledge. Hurriedly, he threw his thoughts into the raider's body, imagining himself broad of chest and heavy of arm, confident in his raw strength. He felt the ridges of the grip in his palm, and the assurance that came from years of practice in the weapon's use. The tingling at his nape came almost at once, and Iskiir glimpsed a shadowy image of something else. The *other* seemed to exaggerate every feature of the nomad: its arms were so long that its immense hands nearly reached the ground; it had scaly, lizard feet the length of a man's forearm; and the new fighter was as broad as three Yeniskis together.

Now the real work began. *Seeing,* in itself, Iskiir had found to come easily. And dead things he could change with modest effort. But the difficulties had increased as he'd tried to change first animals and then men.

Iskiir sweated as if he were back digging holes for his cousin. He focused on the long-armed demon fighter, slipping deeper into trance as he wrestled with the forces that held the tribesman to this world. Upward he trudged on the spirit-path,

jerking and straining until the wind droned in his ears and he
knew that he had succeeded once again.

The other nomads sent up a cheer when they saw their
brawny new companion. The creature's bulbous, earless head
was totally covered by tight, yellow scales. His mouth was
beaked like a vulture's. The rest of his body was lightly feathered in green, and he wore not even a loincloth. His weapon
was a spiked ball the size of a man's head, chained to a heavy
staff.

With a raucous call, the demon fighter turned to face the
jinns. He charged across the field, swinging the morningstar
in a great orbit until the air thundered with its sound. A scream
erupted as the weapon hit its first mark. Iskiir saw teeth and
rust-colored blood flying from a smashed jinn skull.

Screeching from his beaked mouth, the new fighter advanced, his wild swings connecting again and again as the
jinns scattered before him. He raced forward and back, and
those taloned ones agile enough to dodge his weapon scrambled
for shelter. The captive nomads cowered, and meekly followed
their masters to safety behind the fallen blocks.

Before the enemy could regroup, another demon fighter,
the wolf-jawed thing with horns on its feet, emerged from the
nomad ranks. Iskiir had nearly forgotten this first of his altered
tribesmen, yet here he stood with a gigantic ax on his shoulder.
As soon as he neared the jinns who remained in the open, the
hairy fighter made arcs with the bright weapon. He hewed
jinns the way a forester cuts trees, splitting bodies to expose
splintered bones the color of charcoal. More of the enemy
retreated, leaving a clear path toward the temples.

At once, Bermegi gave a signal to advance. With his party
in the lead, a column of riders converged on a ruin that Olkar
had pointed out. The camels raced across the clearing, Iskiir's
among them, his beast incited by the frenzy of the others. The
young man's pulse throbbed as he rode past the high pillars
and into the old building. Within, a pitiful sight greeted him—
a mass of grimy Karbayra, men and women oblivious to each
other, lay stupefied on the broken limestone floor.

So many to be rescued . . . But Iskiir had not reckoned the full number of nomad mages. Suddenly the black-capped ones were down among the captives, hastily pouring doses of their medicines into every slack mouth. The treated victims rubbed their eyes as if rousing themselves from a lengthy sleep. The first to recover stood and made for the openings between the pillars. Then others rose, and soon the entire crowd was streaming from the enclosure.

Bermegi rode past Iskiir and shouted, "More captives. Many more." He pointed outside, presumably toward additional jumbles of stone. Iskiir emerged from the emptying structure into a milling mass of riders. Now everyone seemed thrown into confusion. While freed Karbayra staggered into the hills, the warrior tribesmen were riding from temple to temple as they searched out the remaining prisoners. At once, Iskiir grasped the difficulty.

Moments before, the site had been uncluttered, holding but a few ruins suited to concealing captives. Suddenly the temples had multiplied. Dozens, perhaps a hundred buildings, all identical in appearance, had sprung up in a dense cluster. How would the fighters find the true location of their kinsmen among so many illusions?

Iskiir had seen dowsing succeed earlier, and was not surprised when the mages began darkening the tips of their staffs. One by one the wands were held out at arm's length, but they merely jerked randomly, unable to provide a direction. At loss for a target, a few riders peered into the nearby temples and emerged with sullen expressions. The mages muttered more incantations, but the staffs would not settle down.

And new troubles began for the nomads. Their demon fighters began to bellow with rage. Iskiir turned to see that the jinns had found a defense. Huge lava chunks, like the ones about Tajmengus, had appeared on the plain and were now hemming in the fighters. As the wolfish one dodged one way, a new stone came up to block his way. As he darted the other way, a tall boulder cut off his path.

The feathered battler was also trapped, walled in by high

rocks. Iskiir could see him screaming with rage, pressing his
great bulk against an opening not big enough to admit one half
his size. The jinns had not closed up the prison, leaving that
small crack for some purpose. Perhaps they were hoping to
have sport with the captured one.

The Menjian beat his fists in anger against the saddle. He
could not idly watch a good warrior destroyed. Nearby, a line
of jinns was lifting a long knobby pole that ended in a flaming
point. Foul black smoke streamed from the end of the weapon.
Iskiir didn't have to guess its purpose.

He had changed the tribesman to the *other*. Why not bring
him back? At once, the young man sent his thoughts into the
form of the battler. The great strength lay on him, but with
that strength came a fury that threatened all rational thought.
He pressed against the harsh rocks that imprisoned him, caring
nothing for the tearing of his flesh. Through him coursed the
blood-lust of the fighter, an urgent need to destroy the horrors
that the Hethi had become. This drive blotted out all else. He
would tear the creatures with his hands if he had the chance . . .

The tingling reached Iskiir's nape and then he was himself
again. The demon fighter began to fade and the raider to reap-
pear. But what would the effort be to complete the change?
To Iskiir's surprise, the undoing was not so difficult as the
doing. To reverse his work was like pushing a donkey back
down a hill—a few grunts and swats and the job was done.
He blinked, and saw that the nomad in his original, far slimmer,
form was already slipping through his prison's opening. Then
he was sprinting across the barren soil.

The jinns dropped their clumsy weapon, for now the fighter
was mortal and thus vulnerable to other forces. The distended
heads swung in unison to focus on the fleeing figure. Iskiir
shouted a curse as he saw the man grimace and stumble. But
then, despite his evident pain, he picked himself up to run
onward. As the nomad widened his distance, the jinns' influence seemed to fade. Seeing him reach high ground, they turned
their attentions to the tribesmen in their midst.

Now the jinns began to take the offensive, for there remained

no fighters who could harm them. Their fellows emerged from
hiding, and the screams of riders were proof of invisible attacks. Men slumped in their saddles, while those not yet stricken
tried to assist them to safety.

What of the wolfish warrior? Iskiir saw no gaps in its stony
prison. And if he could bring forth yet another champion as
replacement, the jinns now knew how to deal with him. Iskiir
shook his head, at last acknowledging his defeat. Some captives
had been freed, but the rest remained where the Hethi had
hidden them. And with those lives for power, the dark stones
would march on.

There was nothing left for Iskiir but retreat, and he found
that he could not even direct his camel. Ignoring his signals,
the beast jerked aimlessly. The Menjian was exposed, alone
in the clearing before the temples. In a moment the jinns would
choose him as an easy target. He screamed at his mount,
swatted its neck, and finally got it moving toward the hillside.
Soon the other riders were all around him, heads down and
shoulders slumped in misery.

Adeh placed the amulet face-up on Myranu's desk, so that
the fire-and-hand symbol of the Order showed plainly. The
priestess pursed her lips but did not speak at once. Her shorn
head was bare, her face even thinner than on the evening when
Adeh had accepted the greenstone piece.

"You do understand," said Adeh. "I'm useless here. If I go
to him, I may be able to help." She had already related what
she knew from the *buri*. Iskiir had been heading for battle when
the flyer left him. If that fight was not over...

"You told me of Hethi tricks," replied the priestess. "If you
can see past them, then I agree you should be of great help to
your friend."

"Then why hesitate to release me?"

"I only ask that you think beyond this moment. Suppose you
defy your father and flee. If you fail in your quest, then
what will it matter? But if the stones are stopped..."

"Then the streets will echo with celebrations."

Myranu leaned forward. Her eyes closed for a moment and the young woman noticed the heavy pouches beneath them. Suddenly the priestess's lids flew open and her gaze locked with Adeh's. "Our men force cruel customs on us, daughter. Have you considered your future then? You'll be called a *numij* in the streets and be taunted at every public well! Unjust as it may be, that is the only reward you'll receive for deserting your family!"

Adeh blinked back her tears. "What does my situation matter? How does one dishonored woman count against the lives of thousands?"

The priestess picked up the amulet and let it dangle by its silver chain. "I cannot allow you to take such a risk when you have an alternative. Here it is. Only the Order can give you the freedom that you crave."

Crave? How could Myranu have sensed her innermost thoughts? "But Iskiir . . . some day . . ."

"Maybe in the mountains you two can find a priest who will marry you. And maybe you can live in a hut where you'll see no one, and no one can call you *numij*. But it will be a pitiful waste of two talents."

Adeh hung her head and would not lift her gaze from the terra-cotta floor. "When it's over I can jump from a tower. I've already come close to that."

"Ah, my little hinny. Don't you see that you can have all that you want?"

"I don't know what I want!" Adeh cried. In her thoughts her needs warred with each other—Iskiir, her family, her city, her talent, her new companions. How could she be true to all these and to herself as well?

"You must take the Oath, daughter. That's the answer that saves you . . . The Fire's Oath, from which only death releases."

"And then I must forget Iskiir." The words caught in her throat.

But a mysterious smile plucked at the corners of Myranu's

mouth. "I said you'll have all that you want. Did you tell me you wanted a house filled with children?"

"N-No."

"Then trust me, daughter. Here. Take this back." She held out the greenstone. Its surface caught the candlelight, and Adeh noticed the beauty of the engraving. The fingers were slender, a woman's hand. The hearth it tended nourished a family far larger than could live under a single roof.

She did not take the amulet at once. Instead, she found herself stroking the long braid of her hair. How many years of careful brushing and plaiting had gone into it? And now, with the stroke of a blade...

The priestess knew her thoughts. "That must come off first," she said in a throaty whisper. "I'll do it myself, and then we'll go to the Fire."

Chapter 16

Ready to leave the city at last, Adeh hurried toward the Eastern Gate. Ahead of her strode the acolyte Gosond, sent by Myranu to travel with her as protector. Adeh followed his steps with her hood drawn forward over her face and her gaze on the hem of his robe. She did not know what she would say if someone recognized her. How could she explain her shorn head and new garb? Yet she belonged to the Order now; her life was pledged to the Fire. The change had gone so quickly, in half a morning, that from time to time she touched the fuzzy scalp above her eyebrows to be certain it was true.

As they neared the gate, she raised her eyes and drew comfort from Gosond's sturdy form. She had thought all men of the Fire to be soft of body and spindly of limb. But the young man Myranu had chosen possessed broad shoulders and powerful hands. Moreover, Adeh knew that he carried a long-bladed knife in a hidden pouch of his robe. This was against city law, but who would dare search an acolyte?

The gate was open, with a nervous guard standing to either

side. Adeh knew one of the men from her work in the Binding.
Now was her test. She held her head up, but he nodded stiffly
and showed no recognition. *He sees only the gray robe and
cowl*, she thought. *I'm no longer a person to be looked in the
face*. The possibility that Iskiir's reaction might be similar was
too painful to consider.

Her other thoughts fled as soon as she saw the demon stones.
"So close!" she cried. No more than fifty paces separated the
monoliths from the city wall. On the previous day she had seen
a comfortable gap, but now it was gone. She did not know if
her chance for escape had already passed.

A commotion of voices and hammering sounded ahead. She
and Gosond followed the noise and quickly reached the site of
the two construction projects. The larger wooden work, evidently Wunal's, was mounted on four joined oxcarts. A ladder
rose in a dizzying arc from the rearmost cart toward the top
of the high rock. Supported from below and from the sides by
lashed poles, the ladder creaked piteously as a lanky boy at-
tempted the climb. With each step, the ladder dipped, striking
its end against the lava face.

So long as the cart held steady, the boy rose without pausing.
But then the great stone pushed forward; the wheels rolled and
the whole framework began to quake. Adeh watched him cling
to the bucking ladder, his legs swinging wildly as he tried to
regain his footing. She felt a twinge of sickness in her belly
as she tried to imagine herself following him. Whether others
had escaped she could not say, but now only a crowd of youngsters stood at the base of the ladder.

The lad who clutched the dipping rungs wore a tattered
robe. He was surely no kin to Wunal. Perhaps the wealthy
family had escaped earlier, though she had difficulty picturing
the feat: A patriarch, his beard immaculately trimmed, reaching
a shaky hand toward that ladder . . . A woman with gold and
silver necklaces that clanked as she ascended . . . Perhaps they
had tried. Now only a few urchins seemed interested in the
contraption.

And what of the other work, the one overseen by the Bind-

ing? Adeh had expected this frame to be finished by now, but
its long ladder lay stretched on the ground beside its base. His
face slack with exhaustion, Haraj stood with a crew of carpenters who were hammering and lashing feverishly. Adeh took
measure of the narrowing gap between the stones and wall.
This scaffold, she knew, would never stand.

And what did it matter? Despite the efforts of the recruiters,
no families stood waiting for a chance to flee. Perhaps the
previous failures had frightened them away. Possibly the stubborn patriarchs had stifled all thoughts of escape.

The wheels on Wunal's oxcarts squealed as the stones jumped
another step closer. Adeh glanced up and saw that the boy had
abandoned his climb. Despite the jeers of his friends, he was
retreating, his feet barely touching the rungs while his thin
arms churned to bring him down. He leaped the last distance
and began to run toward the gate.

The boulders pushed again, their leisurely pace of the previous days clearly over. Perhaps, Adeh thought, the evil ones
had tired of their game and now they would finish it quickly.
There was surely no time left for anyone to climb Wunal's
ladder. With a last lurch, the nearest oxcart smacked up against
the base of the city wall. The crossed supports that connected
the four carts groaned. A moment later the lengthwise beam
splintered as the rocks pressed closer once more. The remaining
urchins ran shouting toward the gate, but Adeh stood watching
the unsupported ladder start to fall.

"Stand back," warned Gosond. He pushed her behind him,
offering his broad body as her shield. Adeh peered past him
to watch the long rope that dangled from the highest rung of
the ladder. Had the climber scaled the stone, he would have
slid down the braid to safety on the other side. Adeh wanted
that rope.

With cracks and squeals, the ladder's side rails gave way
and the whole crashed to the ground in half a dozen pieces.
She heard the carpenters cursing. Some, she thought, had been
hit by flying debris. "Your knife!" Adeh shouted to Gosond.
She reached toward his hidden pouch and he brought out the

long blade with its simple bone hilt. A moment later she was leaping over the wreckage. She reached the rope, cut it free, and ran back with the end of her prize in hand.

The carpenters, some carrying their tools, retreated into the city. Adeh raced after them, the long rope trailing in the dirt behind her. A watchtower stood beside the gate, and no guard blocked her way. She dragged the cording after her as she pumped furiously up the steps.

At the top she found an iron ring set firmly into stone. She threaded the rope through and tried to make a knot, but when she tugged, the end came loose in her hand. Then Gosond stood beside her, his breath wheezing almost as loudly as her own. He took the end and made it fast with a few twitches of his fingers, then gave a firm tug to test its hold. She looked out and saw that the gap between stones and wall had nearly closed. She and Gosond must reach the ground before the tower began to fall. They must step across onto the top of the on-coming boulder and slide down the rope while its end was still secure . . .

Bermegi's nomads retreated in disarray, straggling up narrow paths toward the crest of the hill. Iskiir was among the last to begin climbing. Higher up he glimpsed freed captives struggling on foot to reach safety.

By the time he gained the far side of the hill, the Karbayra had begun to regroup. The former Hethi followers were collecting in one area, where mages dosed them from their stores of potions. Then Iskiir saw riders in the distance. Reinforcements! But he was unable to think how more fighters might help. New magic was what they needed most.

Suddenly the Menjian looked up at the sky in puzzlement. The sun had barely reached noon, yet the light seemed to be fading. An unnatural mist hung overhead. Then he realized that the Hethi would not be content until the nomads had fully dispersed. Some new trickery was surely on its way.

The caravan rode in, and Iskiir saw a stir of attention as its camels were unloaded. Food supplies had come . . . bulky sacks of flour. At once, in every quarter of the camp, men began digging up roots or collecting dried camel dung for the cook-fires. Did they not realize that an attack was gathering over their heads? Iskiir stopped his mount, leaned down to tap a black-cap on the shoulder, then pointed to the sky. The mage merely nodded and hurried off.

And then Iskiir caught sight of Dajnen shouting and waving while an unwieldy burden was taken from another beast. The Appeaser had come to join the siege! In a moment, the young man saw what had arrived with him—the gold carpet from the artisans' camp, the carpet whose *other* side was demon fire. Iskiir managed to steer his mount through the commotion to reach the old one's side.

Dajnen glanced first at Iskiir, then pointed at the dimming sun. "Don't like what I see up there," he said grumpily. "We've got to rework this rug into somethin' useful, but the Hethi won't give us time to do it." The nomads had spread the carpet on the ground, and already a half dozen of them were carefully applying their knives to the weave. A mage rode about the camp, shouting through cupped hands. Soon Dajnen's crew swelled by dozens, each sitting cross-legged on the ground. Painstakingly, each man dismantled his piece of rug, untwisting and retwisting the fibers to make a single cord.

Iskiir knew what would be expected of him later, but could not guess how the dismembered threads would first be taken to the enemy. The jinns would not stand still while nomads wrapped them with golden cords. But the answer arrived soon on the wrists of four new tribesmen. As their camels raced in, the riders held their gauntlets high. On each perched a hooded falcon. Iskiir sucked in his breath at the sight of the fierce birds.

At that moment, thunder clapped overhead and hailstones the color of blood began to fall. At first the men merely pulled their burnouses over their heads and went on working with the threads. The small pellets collected on the ground, but the nomads seemed not to care. Even the camels did little more than hiss at the annoyance. Iskiir felt foolish merely watching the task. At last he slid from his mount and tried to join in. He picked up a scrap of carpet and worked several strands free, but had no success in joining the pieces together. Meanwhile, the hailstones were getting bigger. He felt their irregular patter on his headcloth, and some hit hard enough to sting.

Bermegi strode through the crowd and began to shout orders. The seated ones did not look up, but other Karbayra came running with rolls of tentcloth. Stakes were pounded hastily into the soft ground. Narrow strips of shelter were quickly raised, with open areas left between them to admit the dim pinkish daylight. Iskiir struggled with his unwilling fingers but found no way to link broken threads. Throwing down his work in despair, he glanced at the growing piles of red hailstones and shouted a warning.

The stones were hatching! The pellets were twitching, cracking, opening, and from each crawled an insect that slowly unfolded its long, damp body. A cry rose from the camp, a Karbayra word that Iskiir knew. They were calling for fire.

The Menjian brushed himself off hastily, lest the pests hatch in his clothing. But as soon as he left the shelter he was assaulted again by the sorcerers' pellets. All about him, he saw cookfires being built up into substantial blazes. Nomad mages were busy at the flames, an intoxicating pale smoke rising above their heads.

More fuel was needed. Iskiir saw men climbing the hillside to rip dead stems from the crevices. Here was a task that he could handle. Hurrying to join them, he scrambled up the slope as he had done so often in his youth. The thorny bushes tore his fingers and arms, but he feared far worse if the mages should fail. Already the insects were spreading their scaly wings. At the tip of each crimson abdomen waved a barbed stinger as long as a fingernail.

Iskiir crossed the face of the hill, pulling up handfuls of sticks and dead roots. Now the first insects were airborne, the high-pitched whine of their wings paining his ears. When the pests came near, he used his free hand to slap them away, but moment by moment their numbers grew. The other wood-

gatherers were hurrying back toward the camp, but Iskiir did
not stop until he had collected as much brush as he could carry.
At last he made his way down, juggling the awkward load
while he felt for footing, jerking his head from side to side to
ward off the insects.

No matter how he twisted, he could not keep the winged
ones away. He felt a tickle at the back of his hand, but refused
to drop his load. Turning suddenly, he smashed the pest against
the edge of an outcropping. He scraped another from his face
by rubbing it against one of his sticks. A third he crushed by
striking one sandal against the toe of his other foot. But then
he winced as a stinger dug in above his ankle. The pain grew
with each footstep until his leg ached fully from toe to knee.

There was not much farther to go. Limping, he entered the
thick cloud of the mages' pale smoke. The scent was like
burning cedar mixed with lemon oil, and made his head feel
light. With each breath the pain seemed to slacken, and he no
longer heard insect wings. Nor, with the air fogged, could he
tell if pellets were still falling.

When he reached bottom, the smoke hung thickly in every
direction. He stumbled against camels in the haze, and tried
to remember where he had left Dajnen. All he could make out
were a few bright patches that were fires. He staggered toward
the closest, feeling more light-headed at every step.

One blaze lay but a few paces ahead of him. He thought
he saw figures standing before it, mages continuing their incantations. They would want his pile of brushwood. But why
had the spindly load become so heavy? He felt the sharp twigs
slip from his fingers, and then his shoulder hit the ground with
a painful thump.

Adeh had not yet caught her breath from the climb up the
tower. She let a length of the secured rope slide through her
fingers as she hurried a half dozen steps down again, until her
sandals stood level with the top of the oncoming monolith.
There was no time to reconsider; she grasped the rope and
made her leap across the gap. She fell to one knee, scraping

the skin through the robe. Then she scrambled across the jagged top and looked down at the scoured landscape.

"Jump off!" shouted Gosond, as he landed behind her. "And remember to use your feet."

Adeh recalled how she had overcome her fears the first time Iskiir took her climbing. But to leap from such a height? To dangle with only her hands to hold her?

"Jump or I'll push you," Gosond warned, with a rough shake to her shoulder. From below, the final splintering and cracking of the scaffold lumber rose to set her teeth on edge. In a moment, the tower itself would start to topple. Gosond gave her another shove, and then she was leaning out over the drop. She could almost walk down the rough side of the boulder, she thought, if she used the rope for support.

Suddenly her hands were slipping and her feet, pointing the wrong way, were walking on air. The harsh surface scraped and tore at her back as she fell. "Look up at me," he cried. "Turn and brace your feet on the rock." She tried to grip tighter to slow her fall. Her palms burned, but she managed a brief halt. Then she swung her legs around, kicking at the coarse lava as she began to lower herself hand over hand.

Her fingers grew weaker, then gave way entirely; she felt the rope torn from her grip. She bounced against the stone, then swung out over the onrushing bare earth behind it. Her legs flailed, and she nearly managed to clamp the rope between her knees before she struck ground.

For a moment, she was senseless. Then, beyond her aches, she heard the start of a great rumble. *The wall!* She looked up to see Gosond's robe flying, his arms pumping as he half slid, half bounced his way down. Suddenly the roar became thunderous and the rope jerked Gosond upward. He kicked himself away from the rock and pulled his hands free. She did not hear him hit the ground for the roar of the collapsing tower.

Had she killed him by her delay? She staggered to where he had fallen, his face and belly down, his arms limp. His cowl had dropped back, and his thick nape was beaded with sweat. Trembling, she bent to look at his face. His eyelids twitched, then opened and he stared at her dully. She brushed the dust away. His lips began to move, and she was obliged by the noise to put her ear close to his mouth.

"Next . . ." he rasped. "Next time, *I'll* go first." He groaned and used his fists to push himself upright.

"It is over," said Adeh. For a moment, the sound of the city's destruction made all else impossible. Knowing what would happen by nightfall, how could she continue? Yet the chance remained that Iskiir lived. For that, she must force herself onward.

"Come clear of the wall," she cried, fearing the stones might topple backward and crush them. Hiding her grief beneath the cowl, she tried to tug Gosond to his feet. But the acolyte pushed her away, and did not get up at once. He reached under his robes and felt here and there as if assessing the damage. Then, with a pained frown, he first kneeled and then stood. He rubbed at his face, took a trial step and then another.

What if he could not walk? Adeh was prepared to finish the journey on her own. Southeast of the city lay a valley of ruins, avoided by Menjians as a cursed place. She had seen it from the tower several times, and thought she could find it easily. But the valley was large, and if Iskiir was there, he would be lost among the nomad riders. She had hoped, with Gosond's help, that she might find him.

"I'm coming," called the acolyte. "Let me clear my head and I'll be with you."

Through damp lashes she checked the sun. The day was half gone. Was it possible, she wondered, that only this morning her father had ridiculed her prediction of doom? And that in the same morning she had pledged herself to the Fire? Yet the day was not over. She watched Gosond take several deliberate steps.

An odd sensation overtook her as she studied his stiff gait. Husky, knot-jawed Gosond in no way resembled Iskiir. And his gray robe surely looked nothing like Iskiir's indigo kaftan. Yet she felt her loved one's presence as strongly as she had in the early morning alley. How could that be, she wondered, unless . . . Glancing up, she shaded her eyes against the glare and tried to find a glint of *buri* wings. Then she felt a fluttering against her cowl.

"You're changed," came a high-pitched voice near her ear. She felt a tickle of tiny insect feet on her cheek. "You're changed, but I know you."

Adeh reached up gently and felt soft wings perched beneath her chin. The grinding of the stones, for the moment, had subsided and she thought the creature could hear her even if she spoke in a normal tone. But when she opened her lips, her words exploded in a shout. "Help me find him! Please. We've no more time."

Chapter 17

Iskiir lay in a stupor, neither dreaming nor awake. His eyes were closed, but he heard murmuring and the low moans of camels. Later, footsteps approached; he felt himself being lifted, then carried a short way. A crackle of burning wood sounded close by his ear. Voices muttered and a rough hand touched his face. After a time, his lips were pried open and a bitter drink was dribbled onto his tongue.

His aches began to ease and his eyelids fluttered. Suddenly he sat up to find the black-caps' smoke dispersed, and all signs of the Hethi storm vanished as well. Whoever had helped him was gone; now he sat alone by the embers of the fire. Wherever he looked, the tribesmen were mounting their camels and heading back up the hill. Perhaps only Iskiir, lingering foolishly above the haze, had suffered the full brunt of the Hethi attack.

If the battle was resuming, then the new weapons must be ready, he thought. The nomads had surely been at work while Iskiir lay helpless. Now the sun was just entering the sky's last quarter. Enough time remained for an onslaught before dark.

The Menjian stood up and discovered that his leg felt normal again. The illusory stings had caused him no permanent harm. Recalling the red hail, however, he marveled at the nomads' fortitude under the sorcerous attack. Others would have fled. He could not imagine a Menjian army withstanding such a siege.

"So, pigeon," came a voice that startled him. A hard hand clapped Iskiir on the shoulder. He turned to see Odeema's usual cheerful expression replaced by one of woe. The smith held the headropes of two camels. His empty scabbard swung lightly from his shoulder.

"Your . . . sword . . ." Iskiir's voice trailed off in dismay.

Odeema shrugged, but could not force a smile. "Some things not even venom-quenched blade can cut."

"Then your fighting here is done?"

"Perhaps not, pigeon. But first I do favor for Bermegi. I bring you to hilltop where mages work. Quick now."

Iskiir hurriedly mounted his camel. As Odeema turned to his own beast, the young man noticed the long rent in the side of the smith's robe and the bloodstains that ran its length. Yet the nomad moved as if he had not been touched.

At once they joined the end of the closest winding camel train. All along the hillside, other processions were climbing, riders tapping their sticks against the necks of complaining beasts. Higher up, Iskiir watched the tribesmen fanning out along the ridge.

A knot of troublesome mounts and cursing riders blocked Odeema's way. Impatiently, the smith left the path and headed directly toward a cluster of mages at the crest. Now the nomad and the Menjian had to make their own path over crumbling rock and loose soil. The camels balked and spat. The smith shouted and swatted until they obeyed. Finally, the two neared their goal and Iskiir was able to gaze down at the Hethi preparations.

The blue-turbans had not been idle, he saw. They had been erecting a barrier of great rocks along the base of the hill

When the job was completed, attack from the heights would be impossible.

But the Karbayra were applying a new tactic. Iskiir had heard tales of nomad banquet trays—ovals of gleaming silver for serving a dozen men at a time. Only the chiefs were said to possess such trays, but Iskiir counted five in the hands of the mages. The black-caps were using them to reflect the sun, directing a dazzling light into the faces of the Hethi below.

This trick had certainly disconcerted the blue-turbans, for their efforts at wall-building had ceased. One great stone lay motionless a few paces from the gap it was to fill. Other scattered boulders lay far short of where they might serve. The Hethi were milling about, shielding their eyes with their hands, and Iskiir wondered if Karbayra magic was augmenting the effect of the brightness.

He counted few jinns and even fewer captives in the Hethi camp. Perhaps the blue-turbans were conserving their source of strength, keeping their followers hidden. But without followers close by to draw upon, they would succumb more easily to a nomad attack.

Suddenly, Iskiir understood the mages' strategy—they were forcing the Hethi into a compact cluster. He watched with fascination the subtle manipulations of the mirrors, but his attention was suddenly drawn away by a commotion behind him.

"Menjians!" shouted Odeema. "Look! Two in temple robes come from north." Iskiir glanced to his far right, shaded his eyes, and saw two cowled figures in gray robes climbing the far side of the hill on foot. Tajmengus lay at their backs. Had they, he wondered, found a way out of the city? They seemed to be heading straight for him.

Iskiir noticed that many fighters had turned their attentions from the Hethi to the approaching strangers. Then he saw a familiar glint of wings above the gray robes. His hands began to sweat and his heart to pummel his chest.

"Maybe friends?" said Odeema. "Maybe I go meet them before trouble starts."

Iskiir could say nothing, but he managed a nod that sent the smith riding. Then the young man caught hold of his thoughts. Such a strange delusion had gripped him. For a moment he thought he recognized Adeh's walk, but only a pair of acolytes were climbing the hill. What could these travelers mean to him, he wondered. Might they bear news from the city?

Odeema waved his hand to calm his uneasy comrades. Waiting for battle, Iskiir thought, had made them all edgy. He watched the smith trying to keep the fighters from the path of the newcomers, and wished Odeema still possessed his huge sword. But the brawny one managed to keep his camel between the acolytes and the others, backing up the beast as the two young people approached.

Iskiir rubbed his eyes. There was no doubt that the face under the hood was Adeh's. But he knew the meaning of her garb. The *buri* had given him a hint, telling of her dedication to temple service, but he had paid no heed to the warning. How could he believe that her fervor would go this far?

In truth, he had not expected to see her again. And so the tears that spilled down his face were compounded of joy and despair. She was pledged to the Fire. Alive, yes. And safe, for the moment. But she belonged to the gods now; she could never be his.

He slid to the ground, but could not control his legs enough to run to her. He leaned against his camel, and when she came close he said nothing, but took her in his arms and listened to her ragged breathing. "We're two the same now," she said. She reached up and threw back her hood. She tried to laugh as she stroked his hairless head with one hand, and her own fuzz with the other.

For a moment he was shocked at the sight of her bare scalp. Her hair had been so beautiful. . . . Yet even shorn, she was Adeh, and who was he to complain about baldness? He wiped his face and tried to form his question, but the words would not take shape.

"Don't ask me to explain now," she said. "I saw what a

Hethi can do. I know their trickery; the *buri* showed me. I came because I think I can help."

"But this?" Iskiir fingered the thin fabric of her cowl.

"There was no other way we could be together. Myranu is wiser than ten patriarchs." She pressed her finger to his lips before he could protest again. "Trust in the Fire. The gods have answers we don't dare dream about."

Iskiir could say nothing more. He remained gazing at her in astonishment, Hethi and battle forgotten, until Odeema interrupted his reverie. "Come, pigeon. You have work," said the smith. "Let your friends watch us while we roast sorcerers."

Iskiir noticed Adeh's companion staring defiantly at the nomads. His hand within his robe was surely clutching a weapon. With Odeema also standing by, Iskiir thought she would be safe. He turned to watch the falconers bringing up their birds.

The tiercels were still hooded, each hooked beak protruding from a leather covering that bulged about the eyes. The wings were stark black and the proud breasts white with dark bars. The legs were bound to leashes with slender leather cords. Perched on the gauntlets, the birds stood nearly motionless. Yet Iskiir noticed them shifting their weight from one foot to another. More impatient warriors!

The falconers, arms held high, halted by a mage whose staff was wound with a long coil of golden cord. Iskiir hurried after them to look closely at the finished thread. He knew the fibers well, but he wanted to be familiar with the twists and knots that the nomads had applied. The mage gave him little time. The black-cap pulled the staff upright, and spoke a quick order. The four men lowered their arms, gently twisted the hoods free, then unpinned the leashes. The birds fluttered in anticipation. The first falconer raised a tiny bone flute to his lips.

In response to the note, his tiercel spread its slim wings and snatched the thread's beginning in its beak. The bird swooped down toward the Hethi, the staff spinning between the mage's loose fingers as the cord unwound. A second flute sounded a higher note; then a second bird caught the cord's middle. A third tiercel followed, stretching the thread in a long arc over the valley. The spinning rod hummed until at last the coil was played out. Then the fourth bird caught the trailing end and sailed to join his brothers.

The Hethi had been herded by the mirrors into a tight knot far from the temples. The falconers piped their orders and the birds began to descend. The first three held the points of a triangle while the fourth winged toward the first to close the boundary. The ends met and crossed. Iskiir saw that the sorcerers were encompassed; the work was nearly done. He did not want to destroy the birds, but now he must start the change. He focused all his thoughts on the golden fibers. Possibly because he had changed them before, he felt the prickling on his nape almost at once. Then he saw that the cord had been released and the falcons were soaring.

The spirit-wind whistled in his ears and he saw a triangle of fire fall to earth. Trapped by the flames, the Hethi set up a fearsome howl, and several turned themselves into jinns. A changed one stepped boldly forward to cross the blaze, but it had not considered the great heat of demon fire. The woolly hair began to smoke, and it jumped back with a scream.

Responding to a signal that Iskiir did not see, the Karbayra raised a shout and plunged toward the old temples. There was no keeping to paths; every rocky slope became someone's way down. Reaching the bottom, the riders bypassed the unfinished barrier and began to spread out to search for the remaining captives. And Iskiir wanted to follow, to see for himself the Hethi trickery. Perhaps, with luck, he might find the one genuine temple out of many. But just as he was turning to his camel, Odeema put a hand on his shoulder.

"Pigeon, you are not through here," said the smith. "See. More of them come out of hiding." He pointed to the valley, where scattered Hethi who had not been trapped with the others were scurrying out from their shelters. "We try the falcons again, but if they fail . . ." He left his thought unfinished. Iskiir noticed that the black-cap had not exhausted the remade carpet. Before him lay hoops made of slender twigs, each supporting a thread wound about it, and each just large enough to encircle a man.

The first tiercel had returned to his master. A short blast on the flute sent it back into the fray, this time bearing the threaded loop in its talons. But as the slim, pointed wings sailed toward their target, Iskiir saw that something was amiss. The isolated Hethi all turned their eyes skyward. The mages who held silver trays tried to dazzle the blue-turbans, but the Hethi were scattered too widely for the small number of mirrors. The attacking tiercel gave a piteous shriek, plummeted to the ground and lay still, its hoop fallen far from the mark. When the second bird suffered the same fate, the masters of the remaining two clapped leashes on the survivors. There was no point wasting such fine warriors.

"You see, pigeon," said Odeema in an agitated voice. "I save my request for last. Now we need fighter down there who does not fall to Hethi magic." Iskiir saw how the free blue-turbans were wreaking havoc as they ran among the troops. Disabled by pain, men were falling from their camels to writhe on the ground. Other tribesmen were fleeing the field as their camels panicked. "Change me as you did comrades," said Odeema. "Give me chance to tell grandchildren I was not helpless like baby goat."

"But you saw what they did to the others. They'll wall you in. Crush you with their stones."

"I can run, pigeon. I know their clumsy rocks."

"And what if I can't bring you back again?"

"Then my Ergar have hero for father. Enough for him."

Iskiir glanced back down at the fighting and knew that Odeema, or someone like him, was needed. But he had been careless already, careless of the effects of his magic. It had been easier when he did not know the men he altered. But to transform a friend...

"Quick. Before Hethi break out of fire."

Iskiir nodded grimly, glimpsing in his mind the carnage among the nomads if he did not act at once. Hastily he calmed his thoughts, throwing himself into Odeema's mind and heart.

Having seen the man at his work made the task easier, albeit more painful. He felt the strength in arms that wielded daily the forging hammer and tongs. He knew also the love for the boy Ergar, who would some day master his father's arts. Iskiir poured out his energy, grappling with what bound Odeema's form to this world until he felt the prickling at his shoulders. When he saw the magical form that was to come, he did not dare turn back.

The shape solidified. The creature that stood before him on four legs possessed twin tusks the length of a man's body. Though Odeema had lost his venom-quenched sword, his magical self more than made up the deficiency. His new body was white, with black stripes running across his back and down his powerful flanks. His snub-nosed head had eyes that were green globes the size of fists. His legs were muscled boles.

With a snort of defiance, the altered Odeema charged down the hill, huge legs carrying him easily over bush and crag. Iskiir sagged from his exertions, yet the thrill of the hunt filled him as he watched the creature race through the wall's gap and advance on the nearest blue-turban.

The Hethi was standing over a fallen nomad, and Iskiir feared that the tribesman already had been entranced. Suddenly the Hethi became a jinn. The Karbayra he had drained lay limp at his feet. But the creature Odeema had become showed no fear of jinns, meeting the taloned one at full tilt, and ramming both curved spears through its mid-section. Then he tossed his head until the bleeding body slid off to fall in the dust.

The thought of such animal strength made Iskiir light-headed. He watched with amazement as the tusked one wheeled and pointed his twin weapons at another jinn. Already the nomad search parties were regrouping as the Hethi turned to defend themselves against the new warrior. And, against this demon fighter, their pain spells would no longer serve. Now they had only their teeth and talons, and possibly a few boulders for weapons. Iskiir felt a momentary respite from his concerns. At last he could turn his attention briefly to Adeh.

"They're illusions," she said when he glanced in her direction. She pointed down at the broken temples. "All the ones with three pillars in front and a slab hanging over at the front corner."

"You can tell from here?"

Adeh shook her head. "No. But there couldn't be so many ruins alike. If we go down there, I think I can find the real ones."

Iskiir frowned. "If *somebody* doesn't find the real ones, then we've gained nothing at all. The Hethi will still have their followers, and they can go back to crushing Tajmengus."

"Then teach me how to get up on this camel."

Iskiir spun around. Odeema had left his mount! Surely he could not object to Adeh's borrowing the beast. But Iskiir himself barely knew how to control a camel. How could he teach Adeh in a few instants? "Watch this," he said, as he tugged on his own mount's headrope and hissed between his teeth. Then he quickly explained to her how to steer with the single rein.

She rose in the saddle, and seemed briefly uncertain. When she glanced about nervously, Iskiir repeated his instructions. Suddenly her beast began to move. "I have it!" she shouted. The young man mounted quickly and began to follow her.

Halfway down the hill, Iskiir concluded that Adeh possessed an instinct for riding. "Maybe you're not a mountain girl after all," he said as they neared the plain. "Maybe you're a nomad's daughter, born in a saddle."

"If I am?"

He laughed. "It changes nothing between us." But he caught himself as he realized how he had answered: as if her Oath had never been.

"Faster!" she shouted when they reached bottom. Iskiir glanced about warily, but no Hethi stood in their path. More tractable than he had ever seen them, the camels sped toward the row of ruins. Adeh's hood flew back, and to Iskiir, her cropped head gave her an appearance of bold determination. She was no longer the potter's daughter he had met just days before. What she had become, he could not yet fathom, but she filled him with both love and awe.

Hastily, he put his personal thoughts aside. For now he must have but one goal, and that was locating the captives. In all directions he saw parties of nomads riding in and out through the high portals. Nowhere did he see evidence of the missing Karbayra kinsmen.

The Menjians reached the nearest structure and Adeh paused to study the facade. Iskiir also stared at the tawny limestone blocks, each the length of a man. The surfaces were pocked and weathered, yet over the entranceway a frieze in good condition depicted straight-horned cattle plowing a field. Here, he imagined, the ancients had made offerings to the gods who protected crops.

"Look!" Adeh rode closer until she could reach up and touch the wall. He watched her running her fingers along the gap between two blocks. "It's false!" she called. "There's really no separation at all. Just a thin, dark line. Come and see for yourself."

Iskiir shook his head. "I believe you. But from here, I can't see the difference. If we have to rub our thumbs against each temple, we'll still be searching tomorrow." He turned nervously in the direction of the encircled Hethi and wondered how long the fire could hold them. Odeema was doing well against a few taloned ones, but he could not stand against the whole enemy force. And if jinns came for Adeh, Iskiir would be hard-pressed to aid her. "Is there a faster way?"

She beat her fist against the wall. "I see one fault in their illusion," she shouted in anguish. "That should lead to another." She moved back and scrutinized the entire front of the building. To the young man, the structure looked solid. Even when he approached and touched the dark lines that fooled his eyes, he believed the wall to be real.

"There it is!" she said suddenly, pointing to the corner where a roof stone still lay in place. "See the stains? A buzzard must be roosting on top, but the nest is missing. They left out the nest!"

Iskiir did see whitish stains on the side of the roof block, yet he was not convinced. "Suppose it blew down?"

"Not likely," Adeh answered. Then she sang out in excitement as she pushed her fingers into the wall. *Impossible,* clamored a voice in his head. He warned her to stop, but she leaned over and pushed her other hand in as well, burying it to the elbow. "It's fading! It's nothing but trickery!"

"I see solid limestone," he protested.

Adeh passed her hands in and out of the block as if it were not there at all. Then she glanced over at the identical neighboring buildings. "Now I can see through every one of them," she shouted. "The real ones are over that way."

She coaxed her camel into a trot, and Iskiir could only follow. To his relief, she did not try to ride through any walls. They made their way between the rows of temples, traveling ever farther from the center of fighting, until they reached an area where no nomads had penetrated. And then they were standing in front of the ruin that had surely been the model for the illusions. "The others'll search until nightfall and not find this," Adeh called. The building stood by itself on a small rise. From a distance it appeared identical to the others in all respects but one: a mound of sticks lay atop the stained roof stone!

"Adeh, you're the gold in the Fire's heart," he cried as he followed her charge into the broad portal. Here, certainly, was the hiding place they had sought. But as he passed the high columns, his joy faded. The stench of neglected bodies rose so quickly as to nearly overwhelm him. Everywhere on the floor, sickly people lay senseless. Even Karbayra children had been pressed into this evil service.

Iskiir surveyed the scene and could barely hold back his tears. How many mages, he wondered, would be needed to raise these half-dead? At once, he must ride back for aid.

"Come with me," he called. He was trying to turn his beast when he felt an odd lightness. Suddenly the rein was pulled from his hands. The camel! He looked down and saw that he had left his mount's back and was rising toward the broken ceiling. "Adeh!" he cried, desperately twisting to see if she, too, had been caught. The unseen Hethi hand lifted him higher. He heard sighs from below, from the miserable ones whose lives were being swallowed to fuel the sorcery.

He flew out into open air, and then was falling again. He had but a moment to scan the field of battle, and what he saw demolished the last of his hopes. The Hethi had freed themselves. A great stone had pushed the flaming thread aside. Now blue-turbans were streaming through the gap. And about the escaping sorcerers, a great black shadow was spreading across the sand. As if midnight had fallen just in that place, the pool of darkness grew. Where it touched the nomads, he saw camels thrashing in panic and men tumbling to the ground.

Then Iskiir was plummeting, and he turned from the fate of the tribesmen to his own. He was behind the temple now, falling toward a narrow shaft that resembled an ancient well. The opening seemed to leap up at him like a beast's maw, toothless but deep. Dank air buffeted his face, and he struck bottom with a blow that left him breathless. Dimly he heard another body fall.

Chapter 18

At one moment, Adeh was perched on the camel. The next, she was lifted high, dangled over a field of tumbled stone, then flung into a pit. Her head struck bottom first, and a wave of sickness coursed through her stomach. She could not catch her breath. The high walls seemed to be toppling as she fought for air. Then the dim light vanished altogether.

With racking sobs, she filled her lungs at last. Almost at once she was aware of sounds beyond her own. The other breathing was so loud and fevered that for an instant she did not recognize it. "Iskiir . . . is it you?" When she dared reach out, she brushed her hand against a robe. Hurriedly she ran her fingers up the heaving body, across the bristly cheeks to the smooth scalp. "Iskiir!"

"I . . ." he gasped. "I . . . think nothing's broken. And you?" He groaned and she felt him trying to sit up. Then he put his arms around her quivering shoulders, and for a moment she was not afraid.

"I'm shaken; nothing worse," she said. "They could have

237

finished us in one stroke . . . the way they dropped the falcons. They must have other plans for us."

She turned nervously and discovered that the darkness was not absolute. Something around them was glowing coldly, brightening while she watched. She clutched at Iskiir's arm as she began to discern slender coils of serpents, their bodies covered with spiky scales, their fanged heads turning one way and then another as if seeking a target. Then she looked more closely and realized that the mass was but a single beast. The creature's main body was thick as a man's leg; the heads, sprouting all along its curled length, rose on narrow, writhing necks. Glancing about she determined, with no surprise, that the encirclement was complete.

"Hethi illusion?" Iskiir whispered. "Or some demon beast they've brought across to guard us?"

Adeh had no quick answer. The creature glowed with a light whose color she could not name. But no illumination fell outside the circle of coils. She was unable to see Iskiir or even her own hands.

"If it is an illusion," she replied cautiously, "then I must find its flaw." She crawled forward for a better look. Iskiir pulled her back as three heads turned, their slitted eyes fixed on her.

How, she wondered, could she find the illusion's "edge" with the room about it totally black? There was no reference point, no hold on reality.

"Look over there," Iskiir whispered. Now that Adeh's eyes had grown accustomed to the gloom, she picked out another hint of illumination, this one far beyond the encircling creature. A shaft of daylight! "If we can get past this thing . . ." Perhaps, beyond the coils, lay a chance for escape. She dared not speak her thought aloud.

Adeh closed her eyes and tried to remember Salparin's lessons. Only one phrase came to mind: *Use your wits*. No two deceptions were identical; she must carefully consider each case. And here, she already had a first argument. If the Hethi could readily produce demon beasts, then why were they not using them in battle? The many-headed creature was likely an illusion, deadly nonetheless to anyone it convinced.

She recalled her escape from the mage's plague of red vermin. Until the end, the images had been all too believable. Only when the pests attacked her, permitting a close examination, had she been able to see through the trickery.

And here was work that surpassed even that of a Guild mage. She could find nothing amiss. She stared at the serpents, studying every dance and sway of their necks, but found no direct cause to doubt them. But what flaws might she discover if she could poke and probe? The thought made her flesh crawl, yet she knew that there was no other answer. "Let me go," she said, as she tried to pull free of Iskiir's protective embrace. "I can find the weak point, but I must get close."

He sighed and his grip relaxed. If he knew what she was planning, Adeh thought, he certainly would not agree. Slowly she edged closer to the glowing circles. The heads turned to follow her. She feinted a leap forward and watched the blur of fangs striking, falling short, the heads snapping back from necks that were fully extended. The main body of the thing began to slide sideways.

"No closer!" he shouted. But Adeh had been thinking only of herself, and now she knew how Iskiir might escape. Again she crouched as if to leap; the heads *all* moved toward her. The trunk slithered, and she saw how an unguarded space would soon open on the far side of the circle. If she offered herself as target, she believed that Iskiir could get free. She hurried back and whispered her plan in his ear. "But what about you?" he insisted.

"Remember how I waved my hands through stone?" Before he could think of an argument, she returned to teasing the beast. She snapped her wrist, so that her fingers momentarily flew within range of one pair of jaws. "Get ready!" she told him as the creature continued to rearrange itself. Despite the many heads, it seemed incapable of dividing its attention. Once it had a victim, she was certain it would scarcely notice what Iskiir was doing.

But she must fully distract it. She tried to control her trembling as she prepared for her final plunge. Pulling her loose hood forward, she prepared to stuff the crumpled cloth in her mouth. "Now!" she shouted. This time she swept her free arm along a broad arc of glistening fangs, then tried in earnest to leap the coils. "Go!"

The first strike was a pair of needle stings, sinking deeper than she had imagined possible. She clamped fiercely on the cloth and stifled her scream, knowing that she must not cry out lest Iskiir come to her aid instead of escaping. Other bites followed so quickly that she could not count them. Then fire shot up her arm and exploded behind her eyes. The venom! How could she have known that the poison would work so quickly? She staggered forward, her plans to examine the beast lost in her frenzy to flee. The cold coils were under her, beside her, threatening to swarm over her. The heads were striking again as fast as the fangs pulled free.

Her foot caught on the thick trunk of the creature. She stumbled, then sprawled belly-down on the floor. Fangs pierced her cheeks, her neck, her thighs, each time adding more poison to foam in her blood. Her legs became a mass of agony, yet she kicked and flailed so that the coils could not hold her. Her fingers lost all sense of touch. With dead hands she clawed at the broken stone floor until she pulled herself free. With her last strength she dragged herself out of range of the jaws.

She had not found a flaw in this illusion. The venom shrieked its death song on every nerve. From the side she heard footsteps and hard breathing. "Adeh?" came a voice. She could not answer, nor could she open her eyes. "Adeh, are you hurt?" He must have reached her, for she dimly sensed herself being lifted. Iskiir had escaped the circle; the rest did not matter. "I didn't see what happened," he said.

She was floating then, watching a brightness that grew in the distance, and she thought it must be from the Tower of the Dead. Soon the birds of the gods would descend to pick her bones. Already she heard the temple drums beating their song of mourning. But as she drifted toward the Tower a thought became insistent. *Iskiir saw nothing of my struggle.*

As if from a distance, she heard his voice. "Adeh, are you hurt? You told me the illusion couldn't harm you."

Harm? There was no measure of the damage; how could she tell him that? Yet a single thread of doubt remained unbroken. She forced her lips to move. "Take..." she rasped. "Take me to the light... and tell me what you see."

The brightness grew. The drums beat louder. She saw her mother standing before the Fire while the priestess made the final incantations. But the droning voice was interrupted by another. "You look dusty but no less beautiful," Iskiir answered with a sigh.

Merely dusty? "No... wounds? My face... my hands."

He touched her gently. "None at all."

"Then..." To his eyes she was unmarred. How could that be? His words echoed in her mind, and for a moment she could not grasp their sense. Iskiir had expected no marks and therefore saw none. The beast could not be real.

Now she knew she must lift a hand to check. Did her fingers have the strength? They seemed to move at her order. Slowly she reached up to touch her bloodied cheek. The skin was smooth and dry, the pain completely gone. *Illusion!*

She lay still for a few moments as the last image of the priestess vanished into darkness. "I'll... I'll be all right," she heard herself say. "Of course... I got through. Just as I said I would." She opened her eyes and saw his shadowed face hanging over her.

"My mountain girl!" He hugged her once, then let her try to stand by herself. Her legs were wobbly, and she clutched his arm for support.

The beast had not been there at all! Yet she still recalled the first fangs driving through to the bone. Again she felt the rasping of its coils about her arms. "I'll admit," she said, as she tried to walk on her own. "The image was stronger than

I expected. Stronger than any I'd care to test again." She took a deep breath and then another. Her trembling eased. "I've taken us this far," she added, with a glance up at the daylight that streamed from the wide break in the ceiling. "Now you tell me how we can climb out of here."

Iskiir knew at once that the opening in the ceiling was too high to be reached. And walls hemmed them in on every side. The room stood empty except for broken bits of stone and pottery scattered about the floor. Quickly he paced the entire perimeter, examining the frieze of men and odd beasts that banded the walls, but found no gaps. "Could there be a secret doorway," he asked Adeh. "Hidden by a false wall?" Though exhausted from her bout with the serpent heads, she turned to study the surfaces. But no time remained for a thorough search. In a moment, he was certain, the Hethi would arrive to claim their new prisoners.

Where could he and Adeh find refuge from the sorcerers? There was no returning to the blackness they had fled. Even if willing to face the fangs again, they would be helpless in the dark room. In this chamber, at least, there was some light. Here he might try his magic.

Hastily Iskiir knelt to study the rubble at his feet. A rounded shard caught his interest. If he could transform this fragment of a bowl, he might find a means to reach the ceiling. Or what of this other piece, part of a carving of a bushy tail? Might that not change into a magical rope? The possibilities multiplied, but a quick decision was needed. He reached for a broken pipestem...

And then he heard hoarse laughter as numbness attacked his heels and crawled up his legs. "Too late!" he groaned as he lost his balance and tottered to the floor. He heard Adeh fall also. She lay so still that he could not hear her breathing. He was gripped now as he had been at the Hethi campfire, unable even to move his tongue. From a kneeling position, he had toppled onto his side. All he could see were his rigid fingers as they lay across his robe. The numbness crept higher.

Adeh had said that the sorcerers were keeping them alive for a purpose. Now he foresaw how the Hethi intended his life to end. He and Adeh would grow old together as he once had hoped, but the process would be compressed into a handful of days. They would watch each other sicken and falter. And their lost years of living would fuel the final crushing of Tajmengus.

If only he could tell her something in parting. But his paralysis was complete. So little time remained even for his own thoughts.

The room grew chilly. He felt the cold creeping up his legs. There was nothing here to help him, only the lifeless chamber. Yet his mind continued to explore the room as if he were still free.

Why had the ancients built such a place as this, he wondered. Below ground . . . hidden from the rest. Here one was isolated from all distractions of the world. Was this not a place of contemplation?

He had glanced at the friezes in passing, and a sense of the dual nature of things had come through to him. He recalled a sequence in which a priest turned into a jackal-headed sheep and then back again. Then he remembered the old ruin where he and Yeni had taken refuge, where one figure had overlaid another on the wall. In such ways did the ancients record their wisdom . . . What had Dajnen told him? That every person had a magical self. *Everyone!*

Iskiir felt goosebumps that he did not attribute to the Hethi. In the past he had escaped blue-turbans by transforming a stick or a camel. This time he could see only his own hand. Might he not transform *himself?* If a Hethi could change to a jinn, why couldn't Iskiir change to . . .

His thoughts went racing back to the time of his vision at Wej oasis. Afterward he had boasted of seeing Karkilik's image in the pool, but he had not quite told the truth. He was staring at his own reflection, viewing for the first time the bald head that his illness had left, when a strange tingling touched his nape. Surely that was his first experience of *seeing*. What he glimpsed then was not the god, but a creature resembling the winged lion of the temples. The reflected mane was darker and coarser, the wings far less delicate. No sacred Fire streamed from the creature's mouth . . . But this beast, though not a god, might prove a fearsome warrior.

Iskiir wanted to shout his discovery for Adeh to marvel at, but he could not even blink. The Hethi chill already bound his chest. What could he achieve in his final moments of free will? With desperate effort, he sought the trance that could make his own transformation. In changing others, he had thrown his thought into their bodies. Now he must infuse himself . . . with *himself*.

Here once more was the struggle, the wrestling of unwieldy weight up a slope. Why should it be more difficult to pull himself than someone else? Sweat drenched his face, but there was no crying out from the strain. Something was trying to drag him back.

His eyes shut with his effort and he saw the spirit-path that rose steeply before him. Ahead, at the top of a crag, stood the shaggy beast whose form he sought. But jinns clutched at his legs. With each step he took, they grew heavier.

"In Karkilik's name!" he shouted to the winged one. "Do what you can for me."

"We are one," roared the beast. "There is no other here to aid us."

Iskiir turned to see more jinns linking themselves to those who held him. "Is there no help at all?" he cried. Beyond the lion stood rows of nomad riders. Why couldn't they hear his calls?

"The others," roared the shaggy one, "have already given their blood and their pain."

Iskiir could not advance one step more. The jinns' grip grew even tighter. He looked back to see that the whole valley beneath him was filled with the slavering creatures. Each one's weight, in turn, was being added to his burden. "Adeh!" he shouted, glimpsing her also standing among the high rocks ahead. He held out his hands to her, but she seemed not to see him.

"Only you, Iskiir," said the lion. "Only you can break free."
And then other faces appeared beside the beast—ones he had
not seen since his days herding goats: Reff, who used to wrestle
with him until their robes were tattered from rocks and bram-
bles; Kinur, whose coarse jokes cheered him on the coldest
nights. They stood about a cookfire, eyes focused on a youth
who held the *lailu*.

Iskiir heard a snatch of music, a tune as only a young
herdsman might play it. "Woadar's Journey"! The jagged ra-
vines . . . the crumbling cliffs . . . the wild storms. Here was the
tale as Iskiir himself played it. Long ago he had traveled through
the music with Woadar, and dreamed of having such determination.

"How can one fight against hundreds?" Iskiir asked, but
already he knew the answer.

"How," said the lion, "can one like yourself be defeated by
mere hundreds? Listen again to the song."

The flute played, the tempo climbed, and the music reached
its peak. Woadar entered the lair, and with his gnarled club
began smashing at wolf skulls. As fast as the creatures could
leap at him, the herdsman beat them down. The remaining
pack climbed over their brothers' broken bodies, and yet they
too were slain. Why, Iskiir demanded of himself, was such a
feat possible? Only because Woadar's spirit outmatched the
brute hunger of his enemies.

Suddenly the young man knew that what held him was not
the jinns but his own fears. He had transformed others, sent
them into battle in terrifying new forms, with barely a thought
for the consequences. The nomads had stepped forward willingly for the chance he offered. And now Iskiir himself must
follow their examples. The power was here for his taking, if
he had but the courage to grasp it.

Why did this winged beast make him tremble so? Perhaps
only because it was his own, a part of him that he had never
dared recognize. Yet the proud head, the fierce paws, could
be his if he were willing to accept them.

Suddenly he screamed his contempt for his hobbling fears.

He gave a great kick, and jerked free of one set of jinns. He gave another kick and then he was scrambling up the slope. Behind him, he heard their raucous panting as they strove to catch him again. But now he had reached his *other* self. Now he could make the exchange...

When he felt the first prickles at his nape, he could not be certain if the Hethi spell or his own trance was the cause. But the wind was moaning in his ears, and beyond that sound he could still hear the tune from the *lailu*.

He opened his eyes. The Hethi spell had faded, and sensation was returning to his legs and arms. Arms? "Forelegs," more aptly described them. He shook his head and heard the heavy man scrape against stone.

At once he looked for Adeh, and found her slumped at the base of the frieze. He feared the blue-turbans had taken her over already. Perhaps even now they were consuming her. He glanced up. The break in the ceiling seemed closer than it had been. Standing on his hind legs, he found that his forepaws did not quite reach the top. If he could fly up... Tentatively he stretched muscles he had never known. The feeling of spreading the thick membranes was exhilarating, but at once he felt his wings constricted by walls. To fly in such cramped quarters was impossible.

Hastily he padded toward Adeh. She seemed so small now he feared he might harm her with the least careless movement. Gently he gathered her robes in his mouth and lifted her cautiously. He turned toward the center of the room, gathered himself beneath the opening, and took measure of the distance he must rise. Was he capable of such a leap? His muscles answered without waiting for his mind to decide. Stretching his huge legs, he cleared the gap easily and bounded out onto the courtyard behind the temple. Three Hethi standing there shrieked in astonishment, then instantly made themselves over into jinns.

He could not deal with them now. He had to bring Adeh to safety. With running strides he left the temple behind, speeding toward open ground. Once more he tried the new muscles, and this time met no obstructions. Outward and upward his wings spread, expanding, stretching, until he thought his membranes must burst. The air rushed beneath them, buoying, lifting, holding. Then he was aloft and soaring, his wondrous body free of earth's restraint.

He would take her to the nomad mages atop the hill. They would know how to care for her, how to free her lips so she could tell where the nomad captives lay. And soon he would learn for himself what it was to fight a jinn.

Only as he turned toward the plain of battle, did Iskiir begin to realize the deeper nature of his change. The wings, the mane, the feeling of great strength were startling enough on their own. But the prospect of battle made his blood pulse with an unfamiliar passion. In his life as Iskiir, he had been known for his quick temper, but also for the rapid cooling of his anger. But how could he forget what the Hethi had done? They had sent the demon stones against his kin, and then again to crush his new family and city. Now, with his own strength, he wanted to repay them in kind. His mouth filled with a desire to taste flesh. He felt his claws extending, as his need to tear and batter grew overwhelming.

And what new terror had the blue-turbans brought forth? Earlier he had glimpsed a black shadow on the ground. With his altered eyes, the patch below him appeared to be a layer of dark mist. He swooped closer and saw the plain littered with twitching camels and hapless tribesmen. Sounds of madness rang in his ears and vague hunched figures ran through the half-light. Then he was down in the midst of the confusion, attacked on all sides by shapeless forms.

These dark creatures, with their ceaseless gibbering, could only be illusions. He knocked them aside with his paws, yet he felt them snapping at his legs, climbing atop his back. *Ignore them!* he told himself. *They can only cause pain.* The Hethi were the ones he must fight.

Plunging through the gloom, he found one blue-turban crouching behind his followers. A single snap of the lion's

jaws took care of him. The Hethi's blood was sweet juice to
Iskiir's new tongue. The sound of another mage's cracking
bones was the laughter of a mountain brook. The Hethi were
all about him; he had only to throw back their illusions to find
them. Though dark shapeless beasts hung from every part of
his body, chewing and tearing, he did not halt his attack. Even
so hindered, he could catch Hethi. The sorcerers fled before
his rage, and tried to find strength by draining the downed
warriors. Nomads twitched on the ground, and soon there were
no more blue-turbans, only jinns.

In their new form they came at him from all directions.
Roaring from the depths of his lungs, he turned to meet
them. He raked them with his claws, tore them with his
teeth. They ripped his flanks with their talons, and the pain
was far worse than what the illusions had caused. The jinns
slashed his shoulders and tore his wings, but they could not
pull him down. He snapped their necks, crushed their misshapen skulls...

Each crumpled body made his killing lust greater. Each
wound the demons inflicted merely magnified his rage. He
slashed and snarled until the ground was so slippery with the
ooze of jinn blood that he nearly lost his footing. The taloned
ones screamed and spat and sprawled in pools of ichor as they
died.

The sorcerous mist receded, but now true night was coming
on. When no more jinns would fight him, he limped into
the temples and rousted the others from their hiding places.
His tattered wings would no longer lift him, but he padded
from one ruin to the other, detecting with his broad nose the
vile scent of jinn's breath. The sun was gone, the moon
risen, and still the lion hunted amid the ancient blocks of
stone.

Until there were no more jinns... and no more Hethi.

And then he felt his shaggy bulk tottering, his heavy mane
falling, his battered paws sliding out from under him. He roared
one last time, a weak cry of victory. Weeping, he lay his head
upon the ground.

Chapter 19

Sometimes Iskiir would dream of the high pastures above Dahayart. He would come half-awake, feel gentle hands wrapping
or unwrapping his wounds, and then would slip back to his
flock. But at other times he would see the long talons slashing
at his face, and would wake himself with his screaming. She
was always there beside him, soothing him back into quiet
slumber.

Others came. Though he saw only hazily, he recognized the
black caps of nomad mages. They had brought Adeh out from
under the Hethi sorcery. He could only admire their knowledge.
Whatever evil-smelling salves they administered, he accepted.
Whatever astringent potions they poured into his mouth, he
swallowed. But, try as he might, he could not understand what
they said to him.

At last men came who spoke his language. "Menjian," said
a gaunt-faced tribesman with a laugh, "you more fighter than
you look." He held a large clay jar in his hands. "Here," he
said. "Acurlat water. And more whenever you want. Well is

open to you. As for matter of your stealing . . . I think my men mistaken."

"My . . ." Iskiir could barely move his swollen lips. Bermegi had forgiven his trespassing, but what about that of his companions? When Iskiir spoke, his whole face ached with the effort. "My cousin . . ."

Bermegi grinned as another nomad stepped forward. Iskiir blinked, and for a moment he saw clearly the face of the smith. "I take care of other pigeon," said Odeema. "If he tires of his weaving then I send him home. With his donkeys and few trinkets to remember us. But if he likes his work . . ." The big man shrugged and laughed. "Perhaps we keep him."

Iskiir had never seen a fat man on a camel. No . . . it was not likely his cousin would linger in the desert. He sighed his thanks to Bermegi and closed his eyes.

"As for one who dangles chain," the raider's voice continued. "I take him back to Triangle so he meets his vows. Who am I to say what pleases gods? But enough. Now you sleep." There was a shuffling of feet and the Menjian thought the visitors must be leaving the tent. He had exhausted himself by attempting to speak. He could not open his eyes again.

Yet he felt the presence of a third visitor, and imagined that a wiry form stood over him. Then he heard the faint clinking of a chain and caught a few words before dreams claimed him. "*Bolu*, take care of that talent of yours. And watch what you do around goatskins."

After that came many instants when he could not distinguish waking from dreaming. There were always voices—some questioning, some soothing, some that were nightmare howls. At times he was certain he heard the moaning of camels and the laughter of children. But at other times there was only quiet breathing. Bermegi returned to check on his recovery. Had that visit been a dream? Odeema told him that the "fat pigeon flies home." Again, Iskiir could not be certain later if the smith had really come. Whenever he tried to ask Adeh, she would quiet him with a touch of her finger.

He woke one day to find the tent's front flap open, the air fresh, the sun filtering gently through the palm fronds. He had not known where he was until that moment. Now he looked out and watched camels drinking in the long pool, their necks stretching over the rushes at the water's edge. Dusty-faced boys peered in at him as they went about their chores. Some smiled and waved, then ran out of sight.

"Iskiir!" Adeh turned from where she was sitting at the mouth of the tent.

"I feel . . . better," he said. He lifted his arms and flexed his fingers. There was some stiffness and pain, but no evident damage. Then he wiggled his toes and bent his knees. His limbs all seemed recovered. How long, he wondered, had he lay mending? Now, after the long sleep, he was eager for the open air. Again he flexed each limb, just to convince himself that all were in order. His back was sore, and his muscles balky, but surely he could crawl. On hands and knees he went out into daylight, then turned himself slowly down to sit beside her.

"They told me you would come out today," she said. "I shouldn't have doubted them."

"The Karbayra could teach . . . our healers a few things," he answered. His tongue, too, was stiff with disuse, he realized. He took a drink of water from a small leather bottle at her side, and then his words came more easily. "But without you here, I'm not sure their salves and potions would have brought me back."

She smiled, rested her delicate fingers in his, and they sat quietly for a time, watching the ripples on the pond and the mottled shadows of the palms. He did not care to lift his eyes from the center of the garden, lest he remember the world that lay outside.

In another day he was walking about the oasis, laughing and joking with anyone he passed. No matter that they couldn't understand each other; the feeling of good will came through. He felt stronger in his thoughts also, for he began to consider the time when he must return to Tajmengus. How would his

cousin greet him, he wondered. And would he be welcomed
back into the Yeniskilu household?

But he pushed aside all memories of the recent past. Already,
in his nightmares, he had relived the battle too many times.
Even in daylight, beyond his control, he would see the scuttling
creatures of the mist, or feel the flesh of jinns torn beneath
sodden paws. He would shudder and turn to recollections of
Adeh's soothing touch.

Perhaps sensing his melancholy, the Karbayra did their best
to distract him. As soon as they learned he was eating solid
food again they plied him with trays of delicacies—rare golden
melons, tiny sweet oranges, roasted legs of hares. And in the
evening, perfumed dancers, their slender legs wrapped in gauzy
fabrics, danced before his fire to the sound of drums and flutes.
Then jugglers came, then singers whose long chants made him
think of *lailu* music.

That night when Adeh lay beside him he was fully awake,
all too aware of her rich, musky scent and the quiet sounds of
her presence. Despite the darkness, he could sense the curve
of her robe as it draped over her hips, and the gentle bulge at
her breast. He could not control his quickening breath. Now
he knew that he had fully been restored.

"I think tomorrow we must go home," he said sadly. "I-I'm
not in need of your care any longer. And if your father knew
we shared a tent . . ."

She put a finger to his lips, then brought her warm mouth
close to his ear. "My father? Have you forgotten? He can say
nothing to me now."

"Nothing? But surely . . ."

She took his hand and moved it to her cheek. "I'm the Fire's
daughter now, not his. I don't have to answer to him . . . only
to Myranu. And Myranu has sent me to you! But all these
nights I wondered if you would ever be ready to receive me."
Then she moved his hand lower to press against the exquisite
softness that lay beneath her robe. His pulse drummed as if he
were chasing goats up the crags. He thought he felt her heart-
beat quickening in step.

"Do you know what Salparin told me?" she said huskily. "That we're like opposite poles of the lodestone. Two extremes of talent: one to make real magic, the other to see through illusion. And such poles always seek each other! That's why you found me in a city of thousands." He felt her gently stroking the back of his neck. "To keep us apart, says Myranu, would be as evil as dousing the Fire. You asked me why I joined the Order and now you will know."

His temples were pulsing, his ears burning with her words. He was dizzy with her scent, adrift in her encompassing warmth. He could barely speak, but a whisper came from his throat. "We must . . . must not displease . . . the priestesses . . . or the gods." His words were cut off by the fullness of her lips against his mouth, a finer delicacy than any the Karbayra had brought him, a fruit whose sweetness he had never dared to imagine.

A caravan of nomads brought the Menjians back to the city, halting where the Eastern Gate had once stood. Iskiir saw new walls rising from the rubble. All along the perimeter, men toiled with ropes and pulleys to raise the fallen blocks back into place. And what of the demon stones? Surely they had not returned the way they had come. Yet, though he scanned in one direction and then another, he sighted not a single boulder.

The Karbayra dismounted to bid him farewell, clapping hands on his shoulders in traditional embrace. Each of the four dozen riders insisted on the privilege, and as each man returned to his camel he began a droning chant. The voices multiplied until they drowned out the hammering and shouting of the construction crews. Workers turned in puzzled astonishment at the tribesmens' song. At last the salutation was over and the camels turned toward the north. Iskiir had not realized how his attachment to the nomads had grown. He felt a sting of tears while he watched the Karbayra depart.

The guards at the roadside nodded dully as the Menjians entered the city, Iskiir carrying the jar of Acurlat water, Adeh laden with a sack of Karbayra gifts. Did anyone know who they were, the young man wondered, as they threaded their way through the crowds near the caravans' market. A cart-pusher hooted them aside, the brass pendants on his load of necklaces shimmering in the noon sun. Another man, hurrying from the market with a cartload of caged fowl, nearly ran them down. No one spared the travelers a second glance.

Iskiir suspected that none of them even knew what had happened. The stones had vanished; that was all anyone cared about. Yet bitterness rose in his throat as he glanced at the thankless faces. Perhaps they *will* know someday, he thought, if only through tales passed by nomads in the marketplace. And even then, who will believe that a *bolu* had saved them? He tried to find comfort in being able to walk through the streets unnoticed. The crowds were thick enough as it was. What if his path were further cluttered by admirers and well-wishers?

Salparin Jethlu's house stood not far from the gate. Awkward with their packages, the visitors climbed the steps slowly. Then Iskiir waited with uneasy curiosity for the conjurer to come to the door. Past experiences with the city's magicians had left the young man skeptical, yet Adeh had spoken highly of Salparin. And Iskiir already credited the man for bringing out her remarkable talent.

As soon as the heavy-browed mage emerged, garbed in his robe of red half-moons, Iskiir began to sense what Adeh had discovered. At once, Salparin gave the impression of a man of learning, taste and warmth. He greeted his callers first with a formal bow and then with a double handclasp. "Adeh has kept me informed through the *buri*," he said to Iskiir. "I know, better than anyone, how great is our debt to you. And now, please. My wife has been waiting since morning."

Within the house, Iskiir's eyes widened. The tapestries were finer than any he had seen, with gold and silver threads, and depictions of cities far grander than Tajmengus. The rugs of blue and gold rivaled the carpet of the nomad chief. While the visitors sat on plump cushions, Salparin's wife served sliced oranges from a silver tray, and cool drinks made from crushed tamarinds.

"There's much to be done," said the mage. "The city looks alive again, but don't be fooled. The outermost dwellings must be rebuilt. The farm wells must be dug out and the fields readied for new planting. And there remain those in our ranks who would disgrace themselves for a few *menos*. Adeh will have many tasks to occupy her."

Then he turned and stared at Iskiir with a troubled smile. "And you, with your great talents ... What will become of you?"

Iskiir spread his hands sadly. "I've approached masters of several crafts but ..."

Salparin shook his head. "Crafts? That was before the stones came. Now you know that your career will be in magic."

"Magic?" Iskiir furrowed his brow. He had worked his spells only out of necessity. He had not expected to attempt such feats again. And the change he had performed upon himself he hoped never again would be needed. Powerful as the *other* body had been, he wanted only to remain Iskiir. "Do you mean *Guild* magic?" he asked.

Salparin nodded. "The *buri's* report was thorough. And I am convinced that you could advance up the Guild's ranks so quickly that you would amaze yourself."

"But ..." For a moment the young man remembered his cousin crawling about the weaver's hearth while muttering specious incantations. He tried to imagine himself putting on a similar performance. Suddenly his frown turned to laughter. "I was thinking of Yeniski," Iskiir explained in an apologetic tone.

"I know him." The conjurer's mouth twitched slightly. "Some of our members add ... unnecessary flourishes. And some have grown so old they've forgotten what they once knew. But at the core, there *is* sound magic in the Guild for those with the wit to learn. And more important, for you, is the fact that the Guild must change. In Permengord, the ancient knowledge that you've already touched on survives among a small group of practitioners. The secrets are not truly outlawed, though for years they've been restricted to a gifted few. And now that the Hethi threat is understood, we'll need to spread the ancient teachings again."

"The Hethi? I thought they were . . ."

"Destroyed? So we thought once . . . after Yag Ravine. This time we'll make no such assumption." Salparin stared moodily at his thumbs. "No, I suspect there are a few more of them somewhere. And a few can recruit others. If we're to prepare ourselves for what may come, we'll need talents like yours. Have you thought about increasing your knowledge?"

The young man's mouth fell open as he anticipated, unhappily, where Salparin was leading. The thought that he might one day see another blue-turban made him shiver, but worse was the prospect that he might leave Tajmengus. He could voice no reply.

"In the end," said Salparin, "you must consider Permengord. Only there can you develop your abilities to the fullest."

"Permengord!" Iskiir glanced at Adeh in dismay. How could he undertake studies in that distant capital?

"Not right away," said the mage, with a reassuring pat on Iskiir's shoulder. "If I dared ask you two to part now, a certain priestess would threaten me with the Fire's wrath. And Iskiir, you're not ready for Permengord. First, I suggest this. That you enter the Guild as my apprentice as soon as it can be arranged. I'll teach you what I can, and when you've surpassed me, then we'll talk again about your future."

"An apprentice in the Guild . . ." Not long before, Iskiir had despaired of ever finding a master to take him in. "Only an ignorant goat-boy would turn down such an offer," he declared. But his mind was turning over one thought after another, and he fell briefly silent. True, he had found Yeni's magic laughable. But Adeh and his own observations had convinced him of Salparin's sincerity. There was much the man might teach him. "I may be part goat-boy still," he said at last. "But I am not so stupid as to refuse you." He felt his face flush when he saw Adeh's broad smile.

"Good," said the conjurer. "Then you can move in here at once and we can begin. Though your cousin may regret losing you, I believe he'll make no complaint."

But before Iskiir could rush to Yeniski's house to tell him that he had finally found a position, Salparin insisted on taking them on a tour of the nearby reconstruction sites. "Adeh, you may find something of interest there. And Iskiir also." He led them through quiet alleys that crossed between the bustling thoroughfares. They reached a high section of partly-rebuilt city wall, and strolled through a gap that shortly would be closed. Then the conjurer began to pace slowly along the perimeter, hands clasped behind him, while he scanned the dusty ground.

"Here," he said, reaching for something in the dirt. He handed Iskiir a long, wrinkled date of a variety the young man had never seen.

Iskiir scratched his head as he turned the hard fruit in his hand.

"I could tell you to look for its magical side," said the conjurer, "but why waste your efforts? Keep it as a reminder of our days of trouble."

"You mean . . ." Iskiir had only to glance at the date to sense the potential hugeness of its *other* side. The Hethi, blind as they were to magical views, had somehow, by brute force perhaps, learned the potential of the fruit.

"With no power to bind them, the demon stones changed back," said Salparin with a sigh. "This transformation of Bakah dates is among the most dangerous of all Hethi discoveries. Let's hope they make no others."

Iskiir glanced once more at the wrinkled fruit. Then, with an angry snap of his arm, he tossed it out onto the bare landscape that it had scoured.

Salparin shrugged. "We've talked enough of destruction. Let's look at how we're recovering. And, Adeh, you may take some satisfaction in what I show you." He turned to watch the workmen preparing to hoist another block. One squat man among them seemed particularly unsuited to the task. He was dressed only in a loincloth, but his long, flabby arms suggested a life of leisure rather than of toil. Yet this unfortunate had the arduous task of forcing wedges under the block to lift it for tying. With poorly aimed strokes, he swung his hammer at the tapered stakes, often banging instead his shin or ankle. His legs were covered with dark bruises.

"That man," said Salparin, "wore a white turban not long ago. Thanks to Adeh, he's no longer with the Guild. As for his wealthy friends . . . the ones who paid him to betray his city . . ." The mage gestured at the long rising wall. "They're paying for most of this. Everything they own will go in fines for our rebuilding."

When Iskiir reached the Yeniskilu household, he found the whole family assembling for a meal. When he first glimpsed his cousin, he rubbed his eyes to be sure he was not dreaming. Not only was Yeni's robe clean—it bore the yellow quarter moons of the Guild's third rank!

"You were promoted, cousin," Iskiir said, trying to conceal his surprise. "I didn't think you could have passed the test so quickly."

"Test? I helped get rid of the demon stones," he said smugly. "I was entitled to my promotion."

"Helped . . ."

"Of course, cousin. Don't you remember?" Then Yeni spoke softly and rapidly into Iskiir's ear. "It was my donkey you rode on and my food you ate. Without me, you'd still be wandering the Triangle looking for that old fraud of a sorcerer. And if I hadn't worked from dawn to dusk on those accursed rugs they made me weave, the nomads promised to roast you on the coals and toss the meat to the jinns. I kept you *alive,* cousin, while you were enjoying the rich life of the raiders. Now do you dispute me?"

Iskiir began to laugh. "You kept me safe so I could finish the task . . ." The nomads had deceived poor Yeni, and since he had believed their tale, even a Guild truth grip would have found no fault with it. "Then you deserve your promotion," was all that the young man could add.

"Enough talk," said Rahari, beaming. "Two heroes in one household is almost more than I can bear." She seated Iskiir at the place of an honored guest, and tried throughout the meal to see that he received the finest tidbits. "From now on, this is your place at the table, cousin," she insisted.

Finally Iskiir had to explain his plans. Yeni's eyebrows shot up when he learned his cousin would join the Guild. Was he pleased or dismayed, Iskiir wondered. Yeni himself did not seem to know, his expression alternating rapidly from one of rapture to one of dark brooding. Perhaps he feared the rivalry of a second conjurer in his family.

One of Yeni's young daughters voiced her own opinion. "You'll be mixing up smelly stuff, too," she shouted at Iskiir. She pinched her nostrils and made a sour face.

When the hour grew late, Iskiir gathered his few belongings in a sack and reluctantly said his farewells. This was the only home he had known since the crushing of Dahayart. He had progressed from grimy goatherd to apprentice conjurer in less than a year. Now he could make his own way in Tajmengus, but he would not forget those who had taken him in. He was particularly sad to be leaving Rahari, for she had sheltered him purely out of familial affection. "Come often to dinner," she said as he made for the stairway.

"I will," he promised. "Especially for lamb and *tac* roots!" Then he noticed the jar he had left by the doorway. Of course he had not carried it here merely to lug it back to Salparin's house. He could not even guess at the value of the contents in *menos*, but what did that matter?

"Yeni!" he called. "One last thing. You sent me out once for Acurlat water . . . twenty drops." He lifted the heavy jug and handed it to his astounded cousin. "I couldn't get the exact amount you asked for. Will this do?"

27 million Americans can't read a bedtime story to a child.

It's because 27 million adults in this country simply can't read.

Functional illiteracy has reached one out of five Americans. It robs them of even the simplest of human pleasures, like reading a fairy tale to a child.

You can change all this by joining the fight against illiteracy.

Call the Coalition for Literacy at toll-free **1-800-228-8813** and volunteer.

Volunteer Against Illiteracy. The only degree you need is a degree of caring.

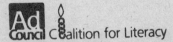